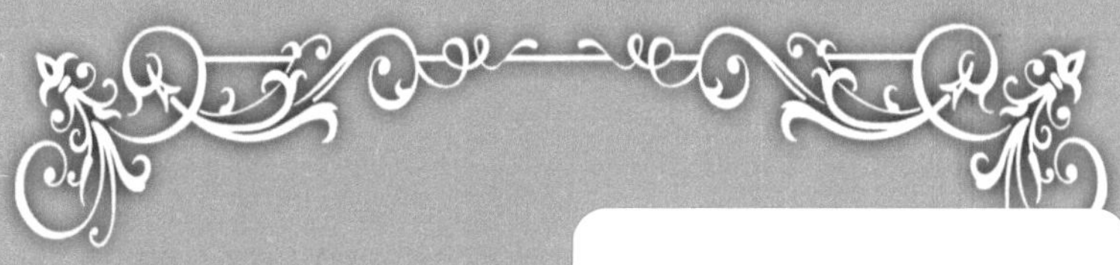

BEYOND THE GOD SEA

BETROTHED

BOOK I

ELORA MORGAN

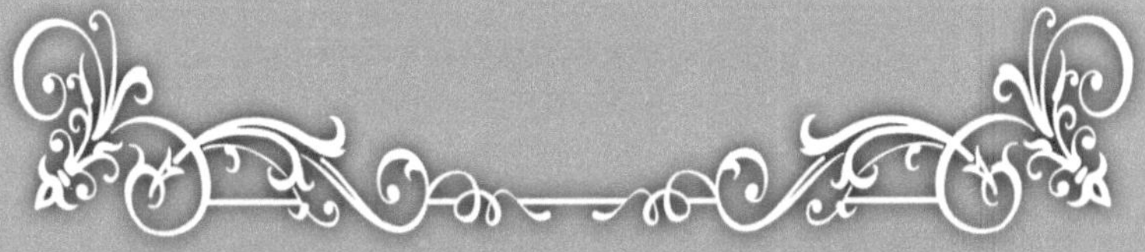

Beyond the God Sea © 2020 Elora Morgan

ISBN: 979-8-9882794-0-2

Published by: Bound & Crowned Press

Content Expectations Including Triggers

The Beyond the God Sea Series matures with the protagonist.

Beyond the God Sea: Betrothed (Book I) is Young Adult.
Bound by Dark Waters: Wed (Book II) is Dark/Mature YA, better suited to older teen readers.
Borne to Salt and Sin: Fated (Book III) is New Adult and includes open-door spice.
Crowned in Shattered Stars (Book IV) is Adult and includes open-door spice.

Potential Triggers: The dystopian world in this book deals with issues such as purity culture, homophobia, and societal/personal control through religious beliefs.

CHAPTER 1

I wasn't sneaking out from a case of betrothal nerves.

Absolutely not.

Maybe not.

Even if I was, did it matter?

I just needed a swim *now* to disperse the unending waterspout of thoughts in my head and to calm the excitement that made me clutch my heart for fear that it would pound right out of my chest.

I shoved aside the mosquito curtain, staring into the darkness.

Co-qui, co-qui, the nocturnal frogs still chirped. I answered with a huff through my nose.

The dark before dawn is the best time to escape. If caught, it's defensible. Because it's not *really* sneaking out. Just getting an earlier-than-usual start for a morning swim in the ocean.

Even at a marriageable age, I was reduced to these behaviors.

For my *protection.*

As if I bore any similarity to the other cuspate girls,

crazed with courting and sneaking out to meet equally silly island boys.

No mere *boy* was in my future and my new life began today.

If today would ever get started.

Narrowing my eyes at the night sky, I ordered the sun to hurry up and rise -- which stubbornly seemed slower than ever in a battle of wills against me.

Co-qui. Co-qui. Nothing but frogs.

I closed my eyes, picturing a mindless glide through cool ocean waters – the remedy for any ailment.

After all, we learn to swim before we learn to walk.

In honor of the Sea God, the Mystics lectured.

A practical decision, in a world with far more ocean than land, village mothers argued.

My only thought on the debate? If the landdammit sun would ever rise, I could be in the sea already.

I considered chancing a jump onto the tree outside my window when my ears picked up the change. The high-pitched "coqui" of the nocturnal frog began to die down, giving way to the first rooster's crow.

Enough.

I shimmied into my seasuit and tossed yesterday's white tunic over my head. I ignored the dirt stain on the hem and vowed I'd clean my teeth with a chewstick when I returned. I didn't run a comb through my hair, either. I'd be sorry later, when my maid brushed out the salty knots, but I couldn't think about that now. My thoughts sailed in one direction, like a boat on a fierce current.

I'd been waiting for this afternoon my whole life.

I tip-toed down the narrow back stair, still clear of servants this early. Flickering torch light cast eerie shadows on walls of Old World concrete. The formula for mixing building paste had vanished with the First Feet, but we retained a residence with a core of the impenetrable substance. Just as the palace retained what few artifacts remained from the early people.

Well, the palace and my cave.

But no one ever needed to know about that.

My sandals made only the slightest shuffle as I pressed myself against the walls, weaving my way to the back parlor. I could almost feel the cool night air on my cheeks when I jumped, halting in my tracks.

Torchlight revealed the fair heads of my mother, my father, my sleepy-eyed brother Gereth, and my baby sister Jona, all sitting down at our table.

"What are you doing awake?" I blurted, heart racing.

A one-sided smile crept over my mother's face. You could see by the swell of her belly that my next sibling would arrive within three moon cycles, and, boy or girl, they'd surely have the same soft-blonde locks.

"Daughter, I think I know you by now," she replied in her easy manner. "Before you're off swimming, I want the family to see you, this morning at least. And maybe get some food in your stomach?"

To anyone else it sounded like a question. It wasn't.

A twinge of rebellion tightened in my gut and my feet tingled with the urge to make a break for the sea.

Dutifully, I plopped down at the wooden breakfast table facing the courtyard.

"I couldn't possibly eat today," I said, but I tore a rough chunk of crusty bread set upon the table, beside earthenware bowls of mangoes and passion fruits.

My father, The Braenar Darius, dwarfing the small stool with his height, nodded at me, then focused on a healthful cup of soursop tea. He rocked Jona, half-asleep in his lap, and her tiny hands curled into the neck of his tunic. A sharp pang shot through me and I concentrated on eating my bread, quickly washing it down with goat milk, still warm from the udder. Not even the Mystics could figure out why so many goats had died abruptly this year, but fresh milk was a benefit of moving the pen closer to the palace, for observation.

"May I go?" I asked, scarcely having swallowed the last bite, resenting still needing permission when I was almost a queen in my own right.

My mother, the Queen, the High Braenese, looked at my barely-touched plate and sighed, "You'll be hungry later." Then, exasperated, as if I had already committed the crime, she added, "Don't be late. You'll need to eat something beforehand and the ceremony will commence promptly at midday."

Her voice caught and my father reached out to squeeze her hand.

Hearing her say it aloud, the familiar flicker of apprehension shot across my stomach like a nervous fish.

What if the High Mystic disapproved of me?

No. I shook my head and lifted my chin. I was *born* for the sea.

And really, the priest's acceptance was more a formality. Never, in all the generations, had the selected braenese been deemed unfit for marriage.

Crack.

I jumped at the sound that broke my thoughts and saw Jona squirming chubby limbs in my direction, having knocked father's teacup onto the floor.

No one paid mind to the broken clay or the kitchen maid who scurried to clean it up. Had an irreplaceable, Old World goblet for night's feast been damaged, my mother would have gotten very quiet, in a way that raised hairs on the necks of anyone nearby.

As Jona continued to squirm for me, I instinctively drew away, afraid she would try to jump into my arms and cause my father to fumble after her.

Queasiness turned my stomach at the fear my father could be put into a position where he might accidentally graze my arm. If that happened, what would they do to *him,* The Braenar?

Thump-thump-thump.

I focused on the rhythm of my leather sandals hitting the dirt, racing against the sun. Dark blue predawn muted the lush shades of green beneath towering palm fronds, but I had been running in these woods since I was a child, and I knew my way blind. No sound disturbed the air other than my footfalls and the first chirping birds -- whether they were plovers or terns or sparrows, I did not know. I could never remember the calls like my cousin, Tomé.

Who cared? I belonged to the sea, not the land.

Well, unlike the stilt-dwelling zealots, I hadn't been born directly *into* the ocean, but I had been born *for* it. Officially, by sunset. As I ran, I smiled so wide it hurt my cheeks.

Today, my betrothal.

And then, *my wedding.*

Exactly one moon cycle away, and the cause of my inability to get a good night's sleep all year.

I could see myself sailing into the Blue Beyond... Keroe, the Sea God, taking my hand to lead me down under the water.

My *hand.*

So long, miserable, ridiculous law! My heart threatened to pound right out of my chest and a laugh escaped my mouth.

I had never been touched by a male before.

Not even by my own father.

It was forbidden. The penalty: death.

THE SOFT *WHOOSH* of the ocean greeted my ears as dirt gave way to sand. Leaning against the rough trunk of a coconut tree, I spotted a grub wiggling by my feet and realized I'd worked up an appetite. Not that my mother was right, but I'd need my strength if I was going to swim the league down to Common Cove.

With a practiced move, I snatched the slick bug and severed its head with the short, rough edge of what passed as my fingernail. I popped the buttery-nut treat into my mouth, absent-mindedly wiping the juice from my fingers onto my tunic.

Sand slushed between my toes as I crossed the beach, still cool in the faint glow of early, orange-gray light. Breathing deeply, my nostrils filled with salty air, and peace. No one would disturb me here, even later in the morning when the guard took post on the cliffs down shore. Only the Braeni and palace staff could cross into the land west of the divide without permission, and royals alone enjoyed the unblemished sand of Queen's Beach.

Matted hair clung to my sweaty back, so I tied it in a knot at the nape of my neck, pulling tight to keep it in place against the ocean current. My hair hung nearly to my waist, a golden blonde like my mother and my siblings. I was not allowed to cut it, though it constantly distracted me on my swims.

I let the waves splash over my feet without bothering to remove my sandals. I could just make out the Blue Beyond stretching to the horizon before me. No one -- not villager, nor guard, nor Mystic -- had ever crossed past half a day's journey by boat. The realm of the Sea God was strictly forbidden, even to the Braeni.

All except me, on my wedding day.

Turning and sweeping my gaze across the beach, the gray sky revealed the outline of something long and thin, shadowed, a few hundred feet down. I squinted. It looked as if a hunk of driftwood, tangled in cloth, washed ashore in the night. The waves lapped gently at its base.

Curious.

I jogged down the sand to have a better look.

No... this wasn't wood. The hairs on the back of my neck stood on end.

This looked like an object from the Old World.

Every once in a long while, something from the First Feet washed ashore -- which would immediately be taken into royal possession. Unable to even imagine such a large prize, gullbumps rose on the skin of my arms and I picked up my pace.

There was something odd about the cloth that nagged at the back of my mind. I frowned and squinted harder. *What was it?*

The breeze picked up, knocking stiff sand vines against each other, making a clicking noise like a swarm of insects beside me. One lone dinbird squawked in the air as it circled back toward the trees.

A few feet from the object, I stopped abruptly in my tracks.

My heart stopped, too.

The whole world around me seemed to stop moving, buzzing, humming. The gullbumps spread throughout my body in the total silence that slowed time, that stretched one second into an inconceivably long moment, long enough for me to have an unbelievable thought crash into me, like a rogue wave on the beach.

No.

It wasn't wood that had washed ashore in the night.

Impossible.

It was a boy.

Yes.

And I could immediately see, he was different.

CHAPTER 2

On the Eastern, common side of the island, there'd surely be a jostle of activity as people headed toward the docks at this hour. The low, loud horn of the conch shell would fill the air, as fisherfolk blew to announce their departures. They'd blow again, to signal their return, after a day's catch.

In the musty Hall of the Mystics, apprentices would be preparing for daily services, lighting the earthy-honey incense that scented our temple. Higher up, on the peak of Mount Flame, the cryptic Fire Maidens who tended the eternal blaze would surely be moving about by now, doing something with their day -- though who could ever say what?

But here, on the Western, royal shores, the air remained quiet. Queen's Beach, empty. My only company the call of the dinbird crying *caa, caa* above me - and this impossible, inanimate body ahead.

Keroe?

I became aware of my heart beating once more, because

I could feel it pounding against my ribcage. Disbelief ebbed and excitement flowed.

Had the Sea God made himself apparent to me before our wedding?

I sprinted the rest of the way to the body, then blinked hard, trying to clear my eyes.

Why did this dark-haired boy look so... odd?

Not only was his skin as pale as a babe's who'd never seen the sun, there was something unusual about his features I couldn't put my finger on. All the parts of a face were in order but they were *different.* He wore black cloth coverings on each leg unlike anything I had seen before, and a funny-looking white shirt, held together with small round objects mid-way up his chest.

I threw myself onto my knees at the pink-and-white creature's side. *Alive or dead?*

Scrutinizing his garments, my mouth dropped and my eyes widened with the recognition.

Old World clothes.

Where did he get those? Despite his coloring, he looked so... human. Could this be some kind of outcast village boy, drowned at sea?

Keeping two feet between us, I slipped off my leather sandal and gently nudged his shoulder with the toe-end.

No response.

I remembered once when the healer was trying to prevent a woman from fainting, she slapped her face and dashed it with cold water. Frantically, I looked to the ocean, but the water would be warm and he'd already been through enough from the look of it.

Poising my sandal beside his face, I snapped it back and gave his cheek a little slap.

Still no movement.

Despairing, I snapped my wrist and this time gave a hard slap to his cheek. The hit echoed on the beach and an angry red print blossomed on the side of his face.

Nothing.

I covered my open mouth in horror as I realized what I had just done. If he *was* Keroe, I just *smacked the Sea God, my future husband, in the face with my shoe?*

Oh God! Or boy. What was he?

Think, Zaria.

The only way to know for sure if he was even alive or dead was to listen for a heartbeat.

It would be impossible for me to place my head on his chest, especially if he was human. Each generation's chosen braenese must, by law, remain untouched. Fit for the Sea God.

A fish flopped in my gut at the memory of what happened to the young boy everyone believed grazed my arm, when I was eleven.

I clenched and unclenched my hands. Could this be a test of my worthiness, like the forthcoming wedding pageants?

Chewing my lip, I looked at the jagged cliff to my right. It sealed off the end of the beach, where the guard kept post. No one yet patrolled the bluff, rising about two stories higher than the palace. The Steel Guard, they were called, because many of them had swords from the Old World.

I gazed back down at the strange creature's face. Whatever he was, he needed immediate help. Anyway, maybe this *was* Keroe's human form. I cocked my head to the side, examining him.

I expected the Sea God to be older.

This boy was about seventeen, my own age. His hair wasn't closely shorn, in the commoner style, but a few inches long, with only the slightest wave, resting by his eyes. His eyes were closed but the rest of his face... there was no denying he was handsome, despite his unusual features.

I leaned down, no more than two inches from his torso, but all I could hear was the *shhhh* of the ocean as waves lapped our feet. So dangerously near his skin, fear shot through my stomach, sick and sour.

But there was something else there, too.

A strange sensation brought on by a forbidden thought... some secret yearning I didn't dare fully acknowledge to myself, or even totally understand.

The ache to touch.

I pursed my lips and glanced at the rocky cliff, brighter as the sun continued to rise.

Still no Steel Guard.

What if...

If I did this, if I touched this boy, there was no going back.

Seventeen years of purity, ruined in a heartbeat. *For* a heartbeat.

Was there any better reason?

No one ever needed to know...

But you'll be ruined.

But... *no one ever needed to know.*

The action felt unreal, as if I were watching it happen to someone else, as if my own spirit hovered outside my body, looking on as it violated sacred law. It wasn't really me. I would never be so reckless, so wicked.

I leaned my torso over his, then lowered my head down toward his skin.

Warm.

It felt as if my spirit jolted back into my body upon

contact. The side of my face touched his chest, right above his heart. I heard the *thump-thump* of his heartbeat: strong, steady. My own heart raced wildly and Solan, the High Mystic, condemned me in my mind.

Sullied.

What had I done?

I squeezed my eyes shut and jerked my head back. The wicked thrill receded and the shock of my callousness washed over me. I wanted to rub at the cheek where we made contact, to rub away the evidence.

At the same time, I wanted to hold my hand to it, to somehow imprint the warmth against my skin forever.

One thought crystalized inside me, without time to sort out why. I wanted to keep this being – deity or boy – to myself.

Quickly, I needed to hide him from the guards who would be patrolling any time now.

He was too heavy to move on my own. I needed gloves. A moment of cheek-contact was one thing, but hands all over... I wasn't prepared to go that far. I also needed something to carry him upon, to haul away from the exposed position we were in now. But where? I scanned the tree line, looking for an answer.

My cave. Yes. Where I hid the Old World artifacts.

Perfect. One part of the puzzle solved. Now, the transport. I looked around, but of course there was nothing in the sand.

Think, I scolded. Something smooth, something that would slide. Various objects shuffled through my brain and then, I had it. *A fish tray.* The kind the fisherfolk used to transport their catch from the boats onto the docks, sliding their haul down the long, polished wood.

I could find one back at the palace, in the servants'

quarters. It was about two miles up and another two back, which I could run in about an hour through the forest.

I gazed up at the still-empty cliff. The sun, which seemed to defy me by *not* rising an hour ago, now eagerly climbed the sky at a remarkable pace. Several more dinbirds joined the one I had seen earlier, as if to call attention to my shameful secret.

Maybe just over an hour to get the tray and clear the beach. By then, would a guard patrol the overlook? I looked up to the cliff again. No one was there. Yet.

I dug my hands into the sand and rubbed coarse grains against my palms, unable to make my feet move into action.

I could confess and suffer my mother's wrath. I'd probably be cleansed by the Mystics.

But then my stomach twisted, remembering that poor, young child when I was eleven.

Bad idea. I had not only sullied myself, but the boy-creature as well. I needed to save him, for it was I who condemned him.

Although maybe I wouldn't need to say anything about the touching, only lead the guards to the body...

No.

There it was — that troubling feeling I had at times. Something that I couldn't name in my gut, something uneasy nudging at the back of my mind.

There was only one way to save this boy.

Run, Zaria. Run.

CHAPTER 3

The mountains no longer held back the sun by the time I reached the beach, throwing the ocean into vibrant shades of teal. Foolishly, I hadn't calculated that trying to run with the large wooden tray would slow me down considerably *and* use a lot of my energy in the process. Which I needed to drag the god-boy into the cave.

If he was still there when I returned.

Go faster, legs. The tray banged against my shins, creating what I was sure would be purple bruises in a few hours.

Just a few more feet.

I burst onto the beach.

There.

The boy-creature lay where I'd left him.

Without stopping, I looked up to see if the Steel Guard had arrived.

Empty cliff.

I half-exhaled, half-squealed at my curious good fortune.

Falling onto my knees next to the boy, I took a deep breath and grabbed his arms, wrapping my gloved fingers around their muscular form and hauling him, fish-like, onto the tray.

Panic that someone had seen me - and seen me at the worst possible moment – tightened the knot in my stomach.

But the cliff remained blessedly clear. I hadn't kept track of the guards' schedules, but it was oddly lucky to have no one yet pass. It must have been coming up on mid-morning.

DRAGGING the god-boy to the cave was a lot harder and took much longer than I thought. Both of us suffered scrapes and bruises in the process. When we finally made it inside, I collapsed beside the stranger on the crimson rug, letting the cool cave air wash over me.

The faded rug was the first Old World item I'd taken from the palace vault, mesmerized by the tightly woven stitches and the patterned swirls of deeply pigmented embroidery, unlike any dye I'd ever seen. Also, I had needed a soft place to sit.

Over the years I'd "borrowed" a few more of my family's artifacts I didn't think would be missed -- including, of course, my prized silver egg. Each item served to decorate the low wooden table along the right side of the cavern. A spurt near the back corner dripped freshwater I used to fill a jug for drinking, making the cave a livable, secret home for me. And the frequent, but harmless, spider.

Barely able to do more than prop my head on my hand, I

scrutinized the strange boy as my eyes adjusted to the dim light.

His ears stuck out a bit, and yet subtly pointed, giving him a look that was at once both goofy and sinister. The contradiction carried over to his lips: their pillowy fullness seemed almost playful, yet their sharply defined outlines hinted at something more intense beneath the surface. The sensuous way his full lip pouted, yet taut manner it pulled back to the corners, intrigued me.

His cheekbones were high-set; his jawline, nicely defined. Though thin, he had good shoulders, strong, like mine - like all who spent their days in the sea.

This odd creature before me might be my future husband, in human form.

I grinned. Despite his strangeness, the form was most pleasing.

I lay my head on the carpet beside him and, without meaning to, fell deeply asleep.

I OPENED my eyes and the realization of where I was hit me like a smack.

No.

I jumped up.

How could I do such a thing?

Landdammit, I'd be late for my own betrothal!

The sleeping creature before me gained a few cuts and bruises from being hauled like the day's catch but remained mostly unchanged from when I found him.

Unlike myself.

Inside, everything had changed.

Would it show on the outside?

Resolving to return that evening, I spun to leave and glimpsed my enigmatic egg on the table, alongside a few everyday objects and the Old World artifacts I'd borrowed.

Just to be safe, I grabbed my prized egg and hid the silver orb behind a large boulder in the recess of the cave. The best part about my prized possession was that it opened – a treat I was saving for my wedding day. I didn't want the stranger to spoil the surprise.

As I ran back to the palace, I sent a silent prayer to Keroe that the boy would be alright until I returned.

Then I prayed even harder that no one would ever know what I had done.

And then, slightly embarrassed and not entirely making sense, I prayed to Keroe that the handsome boy in my cave *was* Keroe.

As I ran, the high arc of the sun told me I was *definitely* going to be late for my own betrothal.

CHAPTER 4

"Mazriah has been waiting for you in your chamber," my mother sighed, meeting me on the patio. "I *did* ask you not to be late."

"I know, I'm sorry," I called over my shoulder. I sprinted up the steps, unsure if it was because I was late or if I was afraid she could see the guilt on my face.

You touched a boy, a hissing voice whispered in my thoughts, and I swatted at it the way one does a fly.

Stop. I can't think about that now. I will think about the stranger after the ceremony.

Mazriah was pacing and wringing her hands when I entered. Those small, veiny hands ushered me toward the cool bathing pool and I hastily washed my hair with a coconut soap and scrubbed with a sea sponge.

As I dried off on my wooden stool, Mazriah stood behind me. She fisted my hair at the base of my neck and began to brush the considerable knots. Then she styled my hair up, allowing room for the first of four crowns I'd receive -- today, a shell crown. I'd earn a coral crown after my first pageant, one of sea glass after the second, and the final tiara of pearls for my third pageant.

Would my husband like the look of me? I wondered as she pulled. *Everyone told me I was beautiful, but didn't they have to?*

I was *built* for the sea, my body "like a tree," as the old women say. Just as trees make the best boats, the best figures follow their form: shoulders spanning wide like branches, back strong like wood, then slim from the waist down, like a trunk.

Mazriah's gnarled hands had just pinned the last lock of hair atop my head when Tomé strode lazily into the room.

I grinned. "Get out! You are not allowed in here!"

His eyes danced, sparkling like the sea kingdom itself. "And miss being the first to see my cousin, the beautiful Braenese Zaria, in her betrothal gown? Not a chance." He flashed his brilliant grin in return. On a less honorable man, it would charm the tunic off of any girl.

I shot to my feet and declared, "Alright, but turn around."

Tomé was only two months younger than me, but we could not remain alone together until six years ago, when he could be trusted not to accidentally touch me. Growing up, I spent most of my time alone. Exploring the forest. Swimming in the sea. What was the point of making friends when I'd have to leave them all anyway?

Except Tomé, of course. As if I could keep him out. I'd have a better chance at blocking out the sun.

Tomé plucked a large fig from the bowl that had been set upon my table and ate it as he reclined on a floor cushion, to wait. He tossed his head back, shaking shoulder-length strands of blonde away from his face.

I paused a moment, studying his bright eyes -- so like his mind. *Sharp, quick.* But also... *genuine, honest.*

Should I tell him about the strange boy from the beach?

Tomé would never betray me.

And yet... I wanted to keep my secret to myself. At least for a little while.

I practically skipped to my betrothal garment. It hung about the same mid-thigh length as my tunic, but was spun from an Old World material I'd never seen before, airy as butterfly wings. The most spectacular part was that it had been dyed purple. My whole life I'd only worn the white cotton tunic of everyday, just like Tomé, just like my mother, just like everyone.

I pulled the dress over my head for the first time. It caressed my skin, smooth and cool, like the ocean. I rubbed my hands down the shiny material.

The dress had an uncommon, plunging neck, cut in a "v." Unlike my loose tunic, the betrothal dress was shaped slimmer, to more closely hug *my* shape. I had to admit a gleeful pride, knowing the *entire* island would see me wearing this garment, fit for the gods.

And why not? Wasn't I nearly one of them?

Unless the High Mystic denies me, came the thought once more, as I smoothed the skirt of the dress.

"Okay. You can look," I said.

"Praise Keroe." Tomé smiled his lazy smile, eyeing me from head to toe. "Glory be *thee,*" he teased, punning on the popular hymn *Glory be the Sea.*

With his gaze locked on me, I could see why the village girls followed him around. The sea-blue of his eyes glittered as if they could form a tidal pool and suck a girl right down to the bottom.

"And you didn't even need the stones," he quipped.

I threw my pillow at him. It missed by several feet.

When I was twelve, Tomé convinced me the old wives tale was true – that if I slept with two large rocks under my bed, I'd awake with equally large breasts. I awoke, feeling foolish, to a very disappointing flat chest. Tomé had hooted when he saw the stony evidence.

"Good thing it's not true!" he gasped between breaths. "Those are huge! You wouldn't have been able to sit up straight."

God, that seemed like a lifetime ago.

"May I?" Tomé asked, stepping forward. Of course he would want to touch the dress. Who wouldn't?

"Sure."

He knelt by me, ready to rub the hem between two fingers, careful not to touch my skin. I caught Mazriah's worried eye and I tried not to roll *my* eyes at her concern. *Seriously.* Tomé would cut off his own hand before he ever grazed mine.

"How did they weave the stitches so closely together?" he marveled, furrowing his brow. He straightened, then asked, "Ready for your betrothal?"

I grinned so wide it threatened to stretch right off my cheeks.

"Only my whole life."

THE SKY WAS a clear blue dream, a canvas upon which my future would be written.

Mother led the family, including Mazriah, outside the palace and down to the Mystic's courtyard on the borderline between the royal and common side of the island. Tomé had dashed ahead of us to watch the ceremony with friends.

How had my Aunt Alette, the last chosen braenese, managed not to scream from the anticipation when it was her turn to marry Keroe?

I bit my lip so hard I thought it would bleed.

I could ask her soon enough.

Crossing the open pathways, the sun beat down relentlessly upon my shoulders and suddenly, instead of thinking about my future husband, I pictured the boy sleeping in my cool, dark cave, and wondered how long the ceremony would take.

Landdammit.

I shouldn't be thinking that.

The pure joy I should have been feeling at that moment was tainted by him washing ashore like some... like some tale from the Mythic Verses. Those strange features...

"You look nervous," my mother remarked, one eyebrow cocked in question as we crossed the Dahlia gardens.

My eyes searched hers. *Did she know?* I smiled. Weak. Crooked.

"Don't be nervous," she soothed, stepping back and squeezing my hand. "Nothing will go wrong. I won't allow it."

I *did* relax a little. Because nothing bad could ever happen to me when my mother was there.

But that something I couldn't name nudged at the back of my mind, making its presence felt.

"I was just wondering," I said, "I mean, I'm still not clear on what happens on our wedding day. Do I grow gills like a fish, or do I just not require the need to breathe any longer? Or is there a sort of underwater city in a bubble where we'll live?"

"These matters are beyond even Mystic knowledge," my mother replied, shaking her head. "It is a matter of faith."

"What about the Fire Maidens?" I asked, thinking the priestesses might know more about the underwater realm. "Will they be there today?"

My mother smiled, teasing me gently. "When did you become so enamored with the keepers of the flame? I'm sure there will be a representative or two in the crowd."

"I just wonder what they do all day up there on the mountain," I shrugged, blushing.

Then, before I even *saw* the people, I heard the first cheers of the crowd, ripping me out of my thoughts.

As we neared the courtyard, I made out pink and white strands of hibiscus streaming down the walls, perfuming the air even with their heady scent. Within, I could see the tops of braided, waxy leaves arched above, creating a canopy.

I caught sight of the throng awaiting me around the stone wall and beamed.

They bowed and rose, exclaiming *"Braenese Zaria,"* as they straightened, trying to catch my attention with waving hands. When I was a baby, our family hadn't social-ized for a time, and the older generation especially rejoiced in our public appearances.

A sea of white tunics parted before me. Weaving around parents' legs to catch a glimpse, children ran barefoot. Few villagers had the luxury to craft shoes for feet that grew so quickly, and the youngest could hardly be bothered to use them anyway.

Boom, boom, boom, boom.

Drums, low and heavy, sounded ahead. The refrain to my heartbeat.

"Braenese Zaria! Braenese Zaria!"

It had begun.

The moment I had waited for my whole life, was finally here.

CHAPTER 5

"Children of Keroe," Solan, the High Mystic, bellowed. "Be welcomed on this day, marking the beginning of the courtship of Braenese Zaria and the mighty King Keroe, God of the Sea!"

The responding cheer hurt my ears, making me want to scream or cry tears of joy in returning delight.

"You may kneel," Solan commanded. The crowd fell to its knees, settling like an ebbing wave.

He raised his arm -- long ceremonial sleeve trailing underneath -- indicating my family should step forward as rehearsed last week. I was dimly aware that the low drums still beat somewhere behind me, but I could barely hear them through my excitement.

I briefly glimpsed Mazriah's face and noticed a troubled frown pulling down the corners of her mouth. Even though she barely spoke to me, would she miss me when I was gone?

I had such little family left on land. When I was just a baby, my mother's sister, Braenese Enith, perished in a boating accident along with her husband. The eldest sister of the trio, Alette, had been chosen for the sacred marriage before me. She ruled by Keroe's side until the next braenese came of age.

Me.

Don't let me fall, I thought, as my mother took my hand. With the other, she pushed a stray hair behind my ear, then cupped one hand under her growing belly for support. My father placed his hand on the small of her back, and we ascended the rise as a family.

Solan, a tall man of fifty or sixty years, stood in front of eleven other Mystics forming a semi-circle behind him. Sunken cheeks and a beak-like nose gave him a harsher appearance than weathering alone. His lips, crooked and slick, looked like two wriggling worms beneath the curved nose, and I couldn't help but picture a bird poised, ready to strike juicy worms below. A necklace of dark seashells circled his torso above layers of white robes.

His grand hand movements gave off an air of self-importance, something I had never liked about him. I suspected he knew I felt this way. The only time I ever found anything to like about Solan was when he spoke out against the sentencing of the young boy the other Mystics believed had touched me.

To his back, eleven other Mystics, all male, ranged in ages from eighteen to eighty. I could see the youngest, a short, olive-skinned boy named Pentyr, concentrating as he followed the movements of the others as they lined up. I'd been surprised someone of his *enthusiasm* had chosen the celibate life of a Mystic, but the coveted position had its advantages.

Solan's eyes bore into me as we neared, causing a fish to flop in my gut and my blood to run cold.

Did he know about the boy?

I lowered my eyes. I lifted them.

His hard gaze seared me.

I lowered my eyes again and gulped.

I am wicked, I thought, heart sinking. *I would devastate my parents. I had thrown it all away, everything I waited for all my life. Why did I touch the boy?*

But then, Solan's lips turned upward in a sudden smile as he addressed the crowd. I exhaled. It was all in my head.

"Each generation, the first-born braenese is selected. She is called upon to become the new bride of Keroe, to live as a goddess in his sea-kingdom. Zaria, first-born daughter of Braenese Pama and Braenar Darius has been chosen. If she is found worthy today, the Betrothal Season will begin. Three wedding pageants will take place over the course of the next moon cycle, culminating in the Holy Wedding during the Hidden Moon."

I wasn't really worried about the pageants, except for the last one. The first - an easy swim across the Wide Cove to show my stamina - would take place two days hence. Pageants were ceremonial, easy demonstrations of my physical, mental, and spiritual being.

Except... for some reason... no one would tell me anything about my final pageant.

Solan's voice darkened. He raised both hands, palms out, as if motioning *stop*. "If she, for any reason, is found to be unworthy of this honor, a replacement in the royal house shall be called upon."

I flinched at his words, fear bubbling up in my stomach once more. It wasn't entirely clear based on *what* the High Mystic made this declaration of worthiness. It had always just been for show.

A young boy, about eight or nine, wearing miniaturized versions of the Mystic robes, carried forth a crystal cup, an artifact from the Old World. Its facets caught the sunlight and sent a thousand sparkles dancing upon the courtyard, like faeries flitting about to bless the day. I felt lightheaded, dizzy with hope.

"Drink of the realm of Keroe," Solan instructed, and I sipped the briny seawater. "Stand, Braenese Zaria," he commanded when I finished.

I wobbled as I rose, smiling a nervous apology.

Booming, Solan declared, "I will look upon the braenese and determine if she is worthy of becoming our Goddess."

I gulped. It was all just ceremonial right? My mother said so.

Then why was Solan looking at me with his lips in such a flat line?

He circled me, slowly. My scalp tingled where I felt his eyes beating into the back of my head.

Please, oh, please, this is my destiny.

Solan settled back in front of me.

There.

There it was -- I saw the flicker in his eye as his face darkened.

He is going to declare me unworthy.

I should have never gone near that boy. Why was I so rebellious? It had all culminated in this. I stole artifacts. I touched the boy. I hid the boy. I was not pure like I was supposed to be, not even close.

Now I had gone much too far. This was the fish that broke the net, and all my misdeeds would spill upon the altar for everyone to inspect, like hundreds of newly-caught tuna gasping for life on the market docks. I closed my eyes, cringing.

Solan coughed.

I snapped my eyes open.

Brow furrowed, he coughed again. And then again.

His hand shot up to his heart, grabbing his chest. Eyes bulged. He swayed left on his feet. Then right.

Like a felled tree, he toppled straight to the ground.

I gasped. It echoed in a thousand gasps behind me. I started forward, to help him, then stopped. Useless. I was nearest. But I couldn't touch him.

"Man fall down!" Gereth exclaimed, pointing.

One of the Mystics, Nasero, rushed forward and lifted Solan's head onto his lap. Nasero was much younger than Solan, probably only a few years older than my father. He laid his hands on Solan's neck and chest, checking his pulse and what I assumed was other vital information. Behind me, the crowd's chatter rose, and I heard pained moans from a few.

Was he... dead?

So focused on the fallen High Mystic, I hadn't even noticed my mother's hand upon my shoulder until that moment. I reached up and clutched it, squeezing.

Nasero gently laid the High Mystic's head upon the ground and stood. He walked back to confer with two other Mystics, heads bowed. I strained to hear what he said, but he was too distant and the crowd, too noisy.

What was happening?

The two Mystics hurried to Solan's side and, with a small grunt, lifted his limp body. *Was he dead?* Without a word, they carried him off the platform and back down the other side, away from the crowd.

Murmurs rose behind me and I turned and searched for Tomé, sure his mind would be racing. I found him standing beside Mazriah. His hand rested on his chin as he scrutinized the whispering Mystics, but I couldn't glean anything from his puzzled expression.

Nasero returned, taking the position where Solan stood only moments before. He nodded gently to my mother. Dismissing her? She looked back at my father and then to me. A wave of Nasero's hand indicated we should proceed.

Was the ceremony continuing? Baffled murmurs rose behind me.

Why wasn't anyone saying if he was alive or dead?

My mother raised her shoulders in a helpless shrug. With one arm she squeezed my torso, as if she could impart onto me her strength, then she stepped back.

Nasero cleared his throat, silencing the crowd. The voices behind me quieted to confused whispers.

I stood alone on the platform. *What was I supposed to do?* My skin tingled with every villager's eyes upon me. I quickly peeked over my shoulder.

My mother and father looked straight up at Nasero, hands clasped, shoulders back, faces blank. Clearly, they would not disturb the ceremony or cause a further scene.

Should I kneel again? Or inquire about the High Mystic? Or rejoin my family? Exposed, conspicuous in my form-fitting purple dress, I longed for my hair loose, to hide my face at least.

"The High Mystic is in need of the healers. They will care for him now," Nasero declared.

A collective sigh of relief sounded behind me, but I frowned. He hadn't really told us anything.

"I will look upon the braenese, and, through me, Keroe will determine if she is worthy of this marriage."

He... *what?*

Nasero stepped forward. The ceremony continued with him replacing the role of the High Mystic. I blinked, hard.

The whispers of the crowd began to die down, but my

own thoughts grew louder. Something was very wrong with this.

Nasero moved closer and smiled kindly, wrinkling his eyes. *I'm sorry,* those warm, brown eyes seemed to say. I searched his face for a verdict – both of Solan's condition and of my fate, but I couldn't scrutinize either answer. I never liked the old priest, but I didn't want him hurt or… dead. Nasero circled me twice before settling back in front.

My lip quivered. *What would he say?* It looked like the former High Mystic would reject me before he… fell.

The unobstructed sun beat upon my shoulders and I wished ceremonies were conducted in the shaded gardens. A ribbon of sweat dripped between my shoulder blades. This Old World material didn't breathe well.

My mind, my heart -- every inch of my body seemed to scream out a prayer, seemed to yearn so deeply it ached.

It is my destiny. I am the chosen braenese. Please don't replace me. I was born to do this. It's me.

Nasero slowly lifted his eyes to the anxious crowd behind me. From within his robes, he withdrew a circlet of pale seashells, appointed with one large, purple clamshell in front. Confusion seized me first – *when did he get that?*

With both hands, he lifted the shell crown high into the air. Relief flooded me so fiercely I thought I would faint.

His strong voice bellowed deep from his gut as he rang out, "Braenese Zaria will be Sea Queen!"

CHAPTER 6

Sitting on the rough stone of my window ledge, I squeezed the ends of my hair to dry. My gaze lingered west, in the direction of the cave.

What if the mysterious boy awoke to find himself alone in there?

Directly following the Nasero's decree, a group of women from the village had hoisted me up in a wicker-cane chair. Many still whispered concerns for Solan, but the consensus was that the Mystics would take care of their own, and anyway, exhilaration infected the very air in a way no one could resist. To breathe was to inhale elation from this grand occasion in history. *A new Sea Queen! Hoorah!*

Even with my thoughts in tumult, it infected me too.

Jostled from side to side, I had gripped the chair with one hand and held the crown to my head with the other, grinning. Following the path over the dunes, strong women, backs hardened from years of hauling fish or chopping wood, led me on my jarring ride to the ocean for the ceremonial submersion. The setting sun, now smoldering a gorgeous orange fire, blazed as if just for this occasion.

Ahead, rickety towers of the stilt-dwellers – zealots who built shacks on tall poles by the shoreline – rose out of the water. As a religious practice, their kind never set foot on land. Children exited the womb directly into the ocean – a practice not even the Braeni held since the days of my great, great, grandmother.

The women carried me into the sea by their ramshackle network of dwellings, connected by rope ladders and planks. Forty, maybe fifty pairs of sharp eyes stared from above. It was told that generations of deep diving had sharpened the stilt-dwellers' eyes beyond the normal human scope, and they could see better than land-dwellers.

Maybe it was true. I shifted uncomfortably and focused on the sea ahead.

Rising higher and higher, the warm ocean first lapped my toes, then my knees. I braced myself. My heart hammered.

Down and up and I'm betrothed.

The women lowered the chair. I inhaled and gripped the crown tighter.

This is it.

Calloused hands pushed me down, holding me against my own buoyancy. I imagined it would be a story they'd tell their children. *I was one of the women who helped dunk the braenese on her betrothal day.*

After a few seconds, I bobbed to the surface freely, adjusting my seashell crown and rubbing the salt water away from my eyes.

I am now a bride!

And yet...

I didn't feel different, like I thought I would. Changed. Into a future goddess.

I looked around for... something.

The gauzy purple dress, now soaked, clung to my curves in a very un-goddess-like way. I kept my arms across my chest as I sloshed back toward the shore, trailing fawning fishwives in my wake. They fought to be heard over one another – *you're a vision, braenese, the most beautiful bride Keroe will ever have.*

But now that it was over, I wasn't thinking about Keroe.

I was thinking about the dark-haired stranger.

Running my fingers through my hair told me it was dry enough to be presentable, and I made my way downstairs and into the rear gardens. Unless the weather turned hostile, we dined outside, beneath a trailing canopy of vines and moonflowers.

The water table. Meant to remind us that our bounty, our lives, came from the sea.

My father pulled back Jona's splashing hands as I entered. Fascinated by the table, a shallow pool on which the dishes floated in the middle, she smacked her palms into the water whenever we sat down. I had done the same at her age, although my father certainly never held me back.

"How are you feeling?" my mother asked.

I couldn't find the right words to reply. Exhausted? Ecstatic? Like I had just ridden an enormous wave onto the land, tumbled three times, and landed on my feet with a bounce. I wanted to do it again. I wanted to sleep.

I wanted to return to the boy from the beach.

My mother didn't push for an answer. Instead, she kissed my forehead and sat down next to my father.

They presented a striking couple, and well-matched, too, because my father almost always let my mother have her way concerning island business. Hereditarily, he also let her have her way - at least with me - because I had my mother's wide eyes set inside her soft face, and not his broader cheekbones and longer nose. Father's doting perhaps made up for the scandal of his untraditional selection as High Braenar- a mate both younger than my mother and outside our extended kin.

My ears picked up on it first -- dinner was unusually quiet. I looked up from my seafood stew and realized Gereth was missing. Had I been so distracted not to notice?

I flicked my eyes from my mother to my father. My father squeezed her hand as they both gazed back at me.

A tug pulled at my stomach, telling me bad news was coming.

"We need to talk to you," my mother said, softly.

Terrible liar that I was, my eyes flicked in the direction of the cave. *Did they know?*

I looked back and forth between my parents, holding my breath.

"It's about Solan..." my mother began.

Was he dead?

No... this was something else. *Oh, Keroe, I was right.* He was going to reject me at the ceremony. And my parents knew why.

My father moved his fingers, stroking my mother's hand.

"He did not survive."

In my head, ten questions fought to be the first spoken. Most were some version of *what happened?*

Instead of getting an answer, I got another question. A bigger one.

"He's going to be landburied."

I gasped, covering my mouth.

The *shame* of it.

We'd not had a landburial in six years, not since The Mystics thought that young boy touched me...

What could Solan have done to warrant such a hideous fate? No grand funeral procession to the ocean? To be denied the return to the sea, to be forever locked upon the land? There was no greater punishment.

"But, why?" I blurted.

My mother shifted in her chair and flicked her eyes toward my father. "We don't know."

She was lying. I knew it. I knew it because she had never lied to me before, and something was different about the way she spoke.

I stared at her, mouth parted, questions on my lips.

A thought occurred to me that seemed to fill my stomach with cold water.

It was my fault the last time this happened.

Maybe it was my fault this time, too.

Maybe the old priest was going to deny my worthiness to marry Keroe, and when he died, The Mystics found out somehow. Now, they'd bury him in disgrace. He would forever walk the land as a tortured spirit, unable to rest at home in the sea.

For a judgment of me that was accurate. I *had* broken the Sacred Law. I *was* unworthy.

I sank into my chair and folded my arms against my body, holding myself.

I was now responsible for the damnation of not one, but two, souls.

I couldn't sneak out tonight. Not after this.

CHAPTER 7

Co-qui. Co-qui.

The frogs' high-pitched mating call kept me company throughout the night. I leapt out of bed and paced to the window, determined to return to the cave at dawn.

I quickly paced back to my bed, sick with the knowledge of what I had done, clutching the sheet around my neck.

Resolving to go once more, I kicked the sheet off and thought about what foods I could sneak to the boy-creature in the morning.

Suddenly changing my mind yet again, I buried my face in the pillow, biting my lip and wondering what to say in confessing to my parents.

What to do with the stranger if he was human?

I squeezed my eyes shut against the thought of causing another landburial.

Then I popped them open, scared I'd see Solan's tortured spirit hovering in my room, pointing at me, accusing.

∾

I awoke to the rooster's crow.

I would go to the cave. I had to know who or what he was.

Sugar apples, ripe plantains, dried strips of goat meat. Whatever was easiest to grab, I tossed in my sack, along with my new shell crown. I'd wear it in case I was able to rouse the boy-creature. So he'd know I was the chosen braenese.

"I'll be out all day," I told Mazriah, too brightly. She was hunched over a wooden table, kneading bread. Hearing me, she straightened, eyes searching mine. But she remained silent.

I headed out the front patios of the palace, both trying to look like I wasn't hiding anything and to avoid the growing stink of the goat pen behind. Maybe we'd move it again soon – it had been weeks since herders woke to find the last group of six bucks, lifeless, on the ground.

Although perhaps the new location was the cure, ending the puzzling illness which raged throughout the pen this past rainy season, threatening our food supply in a way that made even my mother worry.

"Zaria!"

I whipped my head left, hearing Tomé.

Marcin grinned by his side, both boys standing on the path leading down the hill toward the artists' huts. Marcin, two years older, currently trained under his father, the Master Scroller. I held up my finger – *one moment* – and checked to ensure my sack was tightly closed before heading over.

As I walked, Marcin threw his head back and laughed at something Tomé said, displaying rows of perfect white teeth in his wide mouth. He wore his hair to his shoulders, although it was often tied back in a leather cord. No doubt helpful for the tedious hours required to conceive, sketch, and carve the dizzying patterns of scrollwork adorning the palace walls and gates. Although he certainly could afford or craft his own shoes, Marcin currently walked barefoot.

A figure emerged from the opposite side of the path to join the group. I saw wisps of dark hair atop a heart-shaped face, culminating in a pointed chin which poked into view as she made her way up the hill. *Lida.* Marcin's third or fourth cousin. Not exactly a commoner, but not entirely a part of the artist class, either.

Growing up, there was something stuck-up in the way she didn't have an interest in swimming or fishing or hunting or any of the things most kids liked to do. She had quickly dropped her attendance of Sunday services once her schooling was complete, until a few weeks ago when she picked it back up, and now seemed more religious than anyone. She even wormed her way into permission to study the few Old World, fairy tale books that made up our small, but sacred, library.

"Hey," Tomé greeted. "I was just on my way to see you."

Lida looked down, as if interested in the vibrant pink Dahlias by her feet. I ignored the slight. Marcin dipped his head in a small bow.

"Oh, I... wanted to hike in the forest today," I lied. "Do you want to come over for night's feast?"

Tomé gave me a funny look and I shifted my weight.

"Can't. Marcin and I are helping his father install a new carving for the Dahlia garden. There," he pointed, indicating a space in the flowers to our left. "I'll see you at the pageant tomorrow though. Maybe we can come over to celebrate after?"

"Sure." I shifted my weight again, eager to escape his gaze. I wasn't ready to tell him yet. Maybe later.

"I'm sure Mazriah will be supervising a five-course feast for the occasion, probably with Old World wine. I'll tell mother to expect one more for dinner."

Did Lida just roll her eyes? It was hard to tell with her focus on the flowers.

Marcin flashed a white-toothed grin across his handsome face.

"Old World wine, you say?" He raised his eyebrows. "Can you tell her to expect two more?"

"Absolutely," I replied, and hurried down the path.

FINALLY ALONE IN THE WOODS, my sack bobbed against my back as I ran at full speed. I wished I could morph into a wild boar or some faster animal.

Was the boy from the beach alive? Was he a manifestation of the Sea God?

In record time, I passed the small grotto by my secret cave – a little pool for swimming on the far side of the outcropping. Slowing down only as much as necessary, I reached around and dug the crown from my sack. At the cave entrance, I paused and placed the tiara on top of my head. Sweeping the vines to one side, I slid inside.

The boy was gone.

CHAPTER 8

My jaw dropped. Stupidly, I blinked at the empty spot on the crimson, Old World rug.

I had left him right there.

Keroe...?

The full weight of a body slammed into me from behind, knocking me off my feet and onto the rug as I screamed. My crown crashed beside me, the clamshell breaking apart.

The body maneuvered itself over me, pressing and holding me face-down to the ground. Panic swelled like a tidal wave. I punched my arms and kicked my legs, twisting as much as I could.

"Help!" I cried, though I was far from the nearest guard post. That had been part of the cave's appeal.

"Somebody help me!"

My voice sounded wild, like it came from another mouth.

I heard a grunt – it was male – and in the struggle I managed to flip onto my back, desperate to face the assailant, fear practically choking me at this much forbidden touch.

My eyes widened.

The dark-haired boy from the beach.

Alive and moving. Fast.

His legs straddled my waist as he pressed his weight against me, pinning me to the ground. Two muscular arms tried to catch hold of mine, flailing wildly. I got in one scratch of my nails across his shoulders and chest, for which I was rewarded with his gasp of pain and the sight of the blood I drew.

It was my last attack. He captured my wrists and pinned them above my head, drawing his torso close to mine. I could feel every inch of his body, panting in unison as he hovered over me.

"Demon," I hissed. Then, louder, "Help, someone help me, please!"

Transferring both my wrists into one of his hands, the demon-boy clapped his free hand over my mouth. Our eyes locked. I swore my heart stopped at the threat in his gaze.

Dark green eyes.

For the first time, I noticed his eyes were deep green, like the foliage of the forest under the canopy. Where I played in secret since I was a child.

An idiotic thought at that moment, considering those eyes pierced mine with malice.

I swallowed, hard.

So this is what a demon looks like, I thought, with a shudder. Deep forest stare, hair darker than tree bark. I smelled his salty sweat and the tang of blood from cuts I drew across his chest... but I also smelled something I couldn't identify, before suddenly realizing it was *his* scent. So different, unlike anyone else I'd ever smelled, and yet, so... male and *good*.

I must have lost my mind.

He spoke. Carefully, menacingly.

"I will uncover your mouth, but if you scream, I will kill you. Do you understand?"

It was the strangest voice I had ever heard. Little coquina clams raced up my spine. I drew in a deep breath to steady myself, which only filled my nostrils more with his unusual scent as his hand pressed against my nose. I nodded in agreement.

"Good," he pronounced.

"Demon!" I seethed the accusation again once my mouth was free.

He gave a mirthless chuckle. "I've been called worse."

His voice had the most peculiar accent to it, neither royal nor common, nor similar to either. It sounded kind of funny, actually, and not at all demonic.

"Let me go," I commanded, throwing behind it all the power of all my years issuing orders to servants, with all the dignity I could muster, pinned to the ground. "You cannot touch me, it is forbidden. You will die for this. Let me go!"

"Might do," he replied casually. "First, you will tell me who you're with."

"With?" I asked, thrashing my head from side to side and still trying to squirm my body out from under his. The boy used his free hand to pin my shoulder to the rug, steadying me.

So much touching! Little fires lit along all our points of skin-on-skin contact, but somehow, gullbumps bloomed in the heat.

"No one came with me. I'm alone."

As soon as I said it, I realized how stupid that was to admit.

Why didn't I say that someone was right behind me, coming along any minute?

Cursing myself, I swallowed, then declared, "I am Braenese Zaria. It is forbidden to touch me; you will die for this."

"Who is your clan?" the demon boy demanded, ignoring my pronouncement.

To my horror, his hand pushed at the top of my dress, pulling it as far as it would go to one side and the next, lifting my shoulders up and searching behind them. I sucked in my breath. My back became as rigid as wood and for a moment I did not move.

Then my voice cracked as I whispered, "My clan? What is clan?"

The boy's free hand stopped pulling at the neck of my tunic. Instead, he cupped my chin and held my head steady. Those dark green eyes locked on mine, skewering me like a fishing spear.

"Who do you fight for? Whose mark do you bear?" His lips were inches from mine. I felt light-headed. Then, cocking his head, he asked, "Why do you say it's forbidden to touch you?"

"Mark? I bear no mark, I fight for no one. The guards protect me," I spat. "I am Braeni, royal!"

How many times did I have to say it?

"We'll see about that." He spoke in a clipped voice and then, suddenly, he lifted himself off me with a spring in his step. Whatever misfortune caused him to wash ashore, he looked to be in fine health now.

For a moment, I was paralyzed with disbelief at being abruptly released.

Then I scooted myself along the rough cave floor,

crawling backwards from him, like a scuttering crab. I rubbed my wrists where he held them.

"Stand up," he said, widening his stance to block any attempt to run past him.

Warning bells tolled in my head. Shakily, I rose.

"Why?" I was surprised to find my voice a whisper again.

"I want to see your mark," he replied. "Turn around and show me your back."

"*What?*"

"Show me your back," he repeated, evenly.

Hot anger coursed through my veins, setting a tingle to my arms. This boy, this demon - whatever he was - had *touched* me, had the audacity to *attack* me. And now he wanted me to... disrobe?

Incredulous, a guttural, boorish, half-snort escaped my mouth. More animal than human. Certainly not regal. I squared my shoulders and lifted my chin.

Mimicking my mother's tone, I replied, "I will do nothing of the sort. And if you want to live, you will stand aside, allow me to pass, and throw yourself on the mercy of The Queen. If you do this immediately, I will see to it that your life is spared, though I cannot save you from a hard sentence in the cane fields, where you'll toil until the day you're fish food!"

The boy-demon frowned.

"I don't know what kind of clan you've got here, *braenese*, was it? Like a princess? But I'm going to find out."

He positioned himself in front of the cave's mouth. Blocking the entrance.

Muscles tensed, he ordered, "Now, turn around and show me your back."

Perhaps I paled. Something in my face gave him pause.

The stranger held up his hands in an almost surrendering-motion, as if to show me he meant no harm.

"It's just your back," he said.

My eyes darted left and right, looking for anything to save me.

The cave's hollow, slightly bigger than my bedchamber, closed out in a rocky wall about ten paces from the entrance. There were no side passages save one tight tunnel along the back wall, not much wider than my shoulders. I shuddered, remembering the narrow space. I'd covered up that tunnel with a large boulder and ignored it since I was twelve.

There was nothing to use in my defense, of course. I had never thought to bring a weapon to my cave.

Not that I knew how to use one.

I could run to the top of Mount Flame. I could swim around the entire island. I could catch my dinner from the sea with a spear, net, or hand. But I had never been taught how to defend myself. Why would I need to?

"I will die before I comply."

I meant to declare the weighty words with dignity. Like my mother. But the vow came through gritted teeth, and my foot stomped in my old manner, a habit I never shook from my kinder years. I was the *chosen braenese*, daughter of Queen Pama. *He* couldn't command *me*.

Still, anyone else would cower before me. But the boy from the beach only chuckled, this time with real amusement.

"You know what? I believe you're stubborn enough that you might." He shook his head and walked over to the left side of the cave's mouth. Leaning against the cave wall, he casually crossed one leg in front of the other. As if this was something natural he did every day.

"But there's no need for anyone to lay down their life, princess. I'm going to give you two choices. You can turn around and let me see who you fight for. I will stand over here. I will not touch you."

He paused, but stared hard, baiting me. I tried to sound in control as I cleared my throat to ask, "And what is the second choice?"

He straightened into a central position across the cave's mouth once more, body tensed as if to attack.

"I'll be forced to come over there, princess, and bare your back myself."

I gulped involuntarily and so conspicuously I knew he had noticed.

I held my voice steady as I spat back with false confidence, "I'm going to give *you* two choices. You can either follow me back to the palace now and spend the rest of your days digging latrines - but at least have your life - or threaten me again and forfeit it."

My hands clenched into fists, chest pushed out, chin lifted.

It did not have the effect I wanted.

I *swear* he hid a smirk.

Well, if I could hear my nervous breathing, he probably could too.

Ignoring my proclamation, he raised an eyebrow in question and drawled, "OK, I will check for myself."

It took two steps forward for him to call my bluff.

"No wait! Stop! No, I'll do it. Stay there." My hands were raised in both defense and plea, and I had backed up two steps, matching his.

Why did I ever save this demon boy? Feverish heat spread through my head. How could I ever undo so much touch? Was I being punished for it now?

Slowly, I turned my back on him but made no further motion to comply.

"Aren't you a little old to be playing games?"

I looked over my shoulder. The stranger had picked up my shell crown, turning it over in his hands.

"I could ask the same of you," I muttered.

"This is no game, I assure you."

"Neither is the fact that you will die for this. Painfully."

He cocked his head at me, a command to continue. "I'm waiting."

I huffed through my nose. A dog's protest.

Closing my eyes, I pulled my arms through the neck of my tunic and lowered the top of my dress slightly, just to reveal the back of my shoulders. I was going to lift my dress up when I heard his strangely accented voice.

"Lower."

My mouth dropped. Whipping my head around, I narrowed my eyes.

"If I do this, do you promise to let me go?"

"I'm not making any promises," he replied. "Except that I promise *not* to let you go if you don't."

Fear shot through my heart, but I tried to reply coolly.

"It's your life you forfeit."

Teeth gritted, I slowly lowered my tunic, bearing a bit more of my back.

I revealed no more than a seasuit would show, and yet my whole body tingled strangely. Somehow, I felt more exposed to this boy's eyes than I had been to the entire village watching as Nasero judged me. The hair on my neck stood on end. My fingers tightened nervously around the seam of my tunic. Neither of us spoke for several seconds.

"Satisfied?" I demanded, through still-clenched teeth. I

did not wait for his reply. I pulled up my dress and turned around to confront him.

His eyes widened like sand tokens. "Where is your mark?"

"I *told* you, I don't have one."

"Are you freeborn?" he asked, brow furrowed. "A spy?"

"I am the braenese!" I exclaimed, and my foot stomped again. "And who are you? Are you a boy or a demon? Where did you come from? Why do you look like that?" The questions poured out of me now.

"I saved you from death on the beach and this is how you thank me?"

The boy paused, mouth parting. He did not answer but I could see he was considering. Frantically, I searched for an escape again.

This time, I saw the possibility upon my table. A small jar from the palace, heavy and white, of some polished material from the Old World.

"I found you on the beach. Yesterday, at dawn." I spoke in soothing tones.

That's it. This is your chance. Keep talking. He'll want answers.

"I wasn't sure if you were dying or merely unconscious. I dragged you to this cave to protect you. You are... different. You don't look like us. What you are, I don't know. But you owe me your life."

The boy ran his fingers through his hair as he stared at the floor, as if trying to bring back lost memories from the dirt.

I risked a step forward. Then another. "If it weren't for me, the guards would have found you. I don't know what they'd do."

Another step.

Just listen to me. Just a bit more...

"Here, you're hurt," I whispered soothingly, indicating the cuts from where my nails drew blood.

"Let me help you..."

Almost there...

I risked another step, arms raised to show I meant no harm. I reached for a scrap of cloth resting on the table.

At the last second, I grabbed the heavy jar. I charged forward and swung it with all my strength at the boy's head.

The sickening smack reverberated in the cave.

CHAPTER 9

Go.

My legs pumped faster than ever. Faster than anyone ever ran before.

And yet, he's gaining on me.

I heard the *thwack* of foot on dirt, closer behind me. I cringed, imagining hands reaching out to grab me any second.

Don't turn around. Don't lose time.

Faster!

The sea was safety.

If I could just reach the sea, I could outswim him. Maybe I didn't even need to make it that far. *Just get to the beach.* At this hour, there would be Steel Guard patrolling.

I heard the *crunch* of footfalls on dirt – now only feet behind me. Ahead, I could almost see the line of trees that gave way to the sand.

No!

My foot slipped on a gnarled root, cruelly placed in the middle of my path.

Nothing but useless air beneath me and then I hit the

ground. Hard. Palms skidding across tiny pebbles, legs splayed.

As I scrambled to right myself, pain signals from my leg, like someone had taken a torch to it, hit my brain.

I didn't recognize my own voice as it hollered. The primal cry of prey caught in its final moments, desperate for anyone to save it. Two red streams of blood dripped from my leg onto the rocks.

Crunch-crunch.

The unmistakable smack of feet hitting the path behind me. I watched my blood drip down my leg where rock had torn flesh. Warm to the touch, the blood made me dizzy. I dug my nails into the skin of my shin above the wound, trying to cut off some of the pain.

I wished I had never saved this boy-demon.

I wondered if he would kill me now. If it would be the last thought I ever had.

I heard his pant above me.

The stranger's shadow crept closer, overtaking the length of my body and blocking out what beams of sun peeked through the trees.

I turned and lifted my eyes, cringing. It was a pathetic plea for my life.

The boy-demon did not meet my gaze. Frowning at my leg, he swore under his breath.

When he dipped toward me, I cringed again and reflexively turned my head to protect it. I lifted my arm to shield my face, curling tighter into a ball, squeezing my eyes closed.

The blow didn't come.

Two strong arms reached around me, lifting me up and cradling me against a hard male chest. I gasped and pushed feebly against his arms, too weak to have any real effect.

The world seemed to lose focus, and I felt like I was losing my place in it.

"Let me go..." I croaked.

I suddenly realized I hadn't eaten much since yesterday morning. I'd barely touched the seafood stew for dinner. *My betrothal day.*

What a mess I'd made of it. What a mess I made of my life. However little of it remained.

Pain made me woozy, beckoning me to surrender to blissful darkness. The boy did not speak as he walked, other than grunting as he shifted my weight. Dimly, I smelled frangipani and registered that we were headed back to the cave.

The boy's bare hands seemed to burn the flesh on my arms and legs where they held me.

How did people do this every day?

Whatever test this was, I'd failed. Maybe I would even die for my sin.

Vines tickled my skin, parting around me as we re-entered the cave. The boy creature laid me down on the rug.

A reversal of yesterday.

We had come full circle.

How silent he became when absorbed, this dark-haired stranger with so many demands earlier. I looked up at his ears, just a bit too large and slightly tapered at the top. Like his contradictory lips, with their youthful pout juxtaposing those sharp lines that gave them a menacing quality. Part goofy, part sinister. Both boy and demon.

Ally and enemy.

His eyes ran up and down my body. He rose to his feet, looming over me.

Oh Keroe, here it is. He's going to kill me!

My body shook. Terror seized my heart, like the cold

fingers of some dark monster, gripping and squeezing. I couldn't get air. It was as if someone had sucked it all out of the cave. I felt sweat break out all over my body. Blood rushed from my head.

I lost ground in the fight to retain consciousness. The dark monster that squeezed my heart pushed me backwards, toward a sheer cliff. Breath would not come. My limbs felt as weak as a newborn's. I couldn't fight the strange boy; I couldn't even see. The dark monster raised one powerful foot and kicked me off the edge.

I fell down the sheer drop into the blackness of oblivion, into the waiting pool of the cool abyss.

"A STORM IS COMING,*" my mother told me, "You must leave, it's not safe here."*

I didn't want to go. Why wasn't the palace safe? It was the safest place on the island during a Black Squall. Jona and Gereth, she and father... why were they safe? I didn't ask. Raindrops dotted my skin, streaking down my arms and legs. I heard the crack of thunder at sea.

Queasiness churned in my stomach at the idea of leaving the palace, but my mother locked my wrist in her hand, pulling me through the forest, repeating that I must go, I must go, I must go...

I AWOKE IN A HAZE, dream and reality mixed, like a jar of sand and seawater shaken rapidly, not yet separated and settled to rightful positions.

I blinked to clear my vision...

... and I saw the boy-demon in front of me.

Oh god.

Was he going to torture me? Kill me? What was I going to do about all the touching? Would Keroe even still want me for his bride?

The boy sat across from me on the crimson rug, legs crossed. He'd re-fastened some of the strange joinders on his shirt, and rolled up the sleeves, revealing muscled arms.

Reflexively, I tried to back away, only to realize with stomach-sinking fear that my hands were tied behind me. *With what? The cloth from the table?* Fastened to a stalagmite that stretched nearly to the ceiling, my arms stretched behind me, giving me only a few inches to move.

The boy scooted closer. My heart raced.

I saw my leg had been cleaned and the pain dulled to a minor sting.

Had he done this? Why?

My façade of royal bravery crumpled.

"Don't hurt me," I begged.

He belly-laughed so loudly I jumped.

"Don't hurt *you?* I think you got that backwards *braenese.*"

He practically snarled the word. Pointing toward the cuts across his chest and then to his head, I could see a large, egg-shaped bump peeking out from beneath his dark hair.

"I'm hurt," I said.

"You did that to yourself." He *threw* the words at me. "Why did you run away like that?"

The boy exhaled a low breath, raking a hand through his hair and sweeping the ends from his forehead. "Look, I'm sorry. Really. I didn't mean to scare you. I found some alcohol to clean the wound..." he indicated my one old jug of sea-wine. Pointing outside the cave, he said, "And an aloe plant to help the healing. *Despite* what you did to me."

The boy grimaced. "I guess I sorta had that coming. And if you truly did save me this morning, I owe you."

"I..." *What was I supposed to say?* "Uhh... thank you for helping me. But then why did you tie me up? Let me go."

He shook his head. "I can't do that. I need some answers."

"What do you want to know? If I tell you, will you let me go?"

"That depends on the answers."

"Please," I implored. "Who are you? *What* are you?"

He ignored me. "Where am I?" he asked.

What would my mother do?

I looked at the boy's pale, bare feet, calloused and cut from running. He bled like a human. He spoke like a human. Perhaps it was as I once thought -- he had been born with strange features to a lesser peasant family, and they had hidden him away from sight until now. Either way, he seemed to need me, need information.

I straightened as best I could with my arms tied behind me. "I'll make you a deal."

The boy's eyebrows rose. Undeterred, I continued. "I'll answer one question from you and you answer one question from me. We take turns. Deal?"

"You're in no position to make deals," he replied.

I lifted my chin stubbornly and the boy chuckled. "OK, OK. I suppose some basic information can't hurt. I'll answer your questions as you answer mine."

He nodded his head in a sort of half-bow.

I grinned victoriously, surprising myself. Another surprise -- the boy broke into a smile in return. Then, realizing the slip, he quickly brought back his scowl.

"Where am I?" he asked first.

"You're in my cave," I replied.

"I can see that it's a cave," he said, jaw clenched. "Where is this cave, where am I?"

"My turn now."

"That did not answer my question."

"Then maybe you should be more specific next time." I couldn't help but grin again. *I must be crazy.* This was a stranger, a male. Who had *touched* me and tied me up. I didn't even know yet what I was going to do about all that touching. It was like it was too big to process and I could only ignore it in totality.

Also, something disarming about this boy's face had me lowering my guard. Was it compassion? He hadn't really hurt me yet and had gone so far as to help heal me.

"Who are you?" I asked.

"My name is Kirwyn," he replied. "Kirwyn Holt."

"Keer-win..." I drawled slowly, forming my tongue around the strange sounds. I had never heard a name like that before. I shook my head to clear it.

"That doesn't tell me anything. Who are you?"

"Uh-uh," he teased, waving his finger back-and-forth at me, smirking. "Your turn is over. Maybe you should be more specific next time."

My cheeks grew hot and I narrowed my eyes. I should be terrified, and yet, he was vexing me. The boy, Kirwyn, grinned triumphantly.

"Where is your cave located?" he asked, still smug.

"You're on the royal side of the island. And when the guards find you here, they will kill you-" I stopped, realizing that I was revealing more information than necessary for the game.

Kirwyn scratched his head. "I'm on an island...?" he murmured.

"My turn," I interrupted. I wanted to ask, *"What are you,"* but I was afraid I'd receive a clipped response like when I asked his name. "Human," most likely, which wouldn't tell me much.

"Where did you come from?" I asked.

"The North Continent. Different places." He replied only half-listening, eyes glazed, brow furrowed.

"What is North Continent?" I whispered. It wasn't my turn, but I was unable to stop the words tumbling out of my mouth.

"Enough!" he roared.

I jumped as much as the ties would allow. Kirwyn grabbed my chin, not roughly, but enough to hold my head straight, ensuring I met his gaze.

"The game ends now. You will answer my questions, all of them. Is that clear?"

CHAPTER 10

*P*oof.

Like blowing out a candle's flame, the playful tone vanished. Danger seemed to radiate from the boy once more, filling the air in the cave. Coquina clams climbed back up my spine. I strained my hands against the bonds while I nodded.

"Good," he replied, voice hard. He let go of my chin, but still crouched close to me, resting on the balls of his feet. "Where am I? Why aren't you marked?"

I shook my head. "I already *told* you. You're on the royal side of the island. I have no idea what you're talking about. Why would I be marked?"

"What island?" Kirwyn grit out, my own frustrated face reflected in his.

"What do you mean, what island? Are you... *are you a sea spirit?*" I whispered, eyes rounding. Little bubbles of excitement rose within me.

"What island?" he shouted.

"This... this is the island." I repeated, patiently. "Do you come from the sea? You're on land now. Did Keroe send you? I don't know where in the sea is your home..."

The boy stared at me like I was a mad-woman, but I continued helpfully, "If your home is very far, I could see how you might be confused... this is the island. Humans live here."

"I'm not a sea spirit and I know what land is!" Kirwyn shouted, face twisted in anger. "What I want to know is *which* island is this and how to get back to the North Continent."

"Which island?" *Oh no.* He was one oar short a full boat. "In all the sea kingdom, this is the only island."

Or maybe he suffered from some form of amnesia? I tried another tactic to re-establish my authority.

"I don't know what you are, but I'm Braenese Zaria." Pride colored my voice. "I can take you to The Mystics and they can help you find your way back under the sea. There are spells..."

Kirwyn cut me off, roaring, "Are you dim-witted or crazy? I don't live under the sea! I am a human, a man!" He pounded his fist against his chest to emphasize this point. "I'm freeborn, unmarked."

Kirwyn ran his fingers through his dark hair again, this time half-pulling the ends in frustration. His shoulders slumped and he rested his forehead against his fingers. "I'm from... the mainland, I guess, if this is an island."

"Main land?" I shook my head rapidly. "What are you talking about? This is... there is no other land."

Kirwyn shook his own head as he held it, as if fending off a headache.

"What are you talking about? You are crazy, aren't you? Is this a clan of freaks? I'm from the North Continent. The old America. Do you know history?" he asked hopefully, searching my face.

"I... don't know what you mean." I struggled to follow, as if I were missing one of my senses vital to understanding what lay before me, unable to move forward.

Kirwyn groaned. "OK, let's try a new tactic. Tell me your history. Your island's."

He wanted a history lesson now? Unbelievable.

But just maybe...

"If I do this, will you let me go?"

"I don't know," he admitted slowly. "But if you don't, I definitely will not. So you've got nothing to lose."

OK, then.

I licked my lips and began. "A long time ago the ancients lived here, the First Feet. They were human, but special. We – the Braeni, the royal family - have some of their artifacts. Others still stand. The concrete buildings, the Rainbow Rocks. The First Feet worshipped the Sea God so fervently and designed such magnificent objects to please him, that Keroe blessed them, and they entered the sea, joining his kingdom. But then the island had no people. Seeing the empty land saddened Keroe, so one day he rose to the surface and blew sea foam onto the beach. With his magical breath he created new humans – us. We worship him in thanks."

And I'm going to be his bride, I thought. But something stopped me from saying it.

Kirwyn stared, wide-eyed. Then scowled.

"That's a nice religious tale of your creation, now tell me your history."

He spoke slowly. Like I was too stupid to understand.

"I just did!" I exclaimed. "Do you mean the royal fami-ly's? We trace our roots back to the first humans Keroe created with his breath. You're on our side of the divide right now. Where you have no right to be."

"OK, braenese, I get it. I'm on your turf. Your guards will kill me, especially for touching you, a precious princess." Kirwyn raised his eyebrows and a slow grin spread across his face. "But first, they have to find me, and I can tell you wanted this cave hidden. So I'm guessing it will be a while before anyone comes looking for you here. Now let's just get through my questions and maybe I can even release you in time for your royal duties... whatever they may be."

Kirwyn reached out his hand, cupping and lifting my chin once more. A tingle ran through my body. How many shameful times had I'd been touched? One hundred? Was there any coming back?

"Where did the ancient people come from?" he asked.

"We don't know. They were always just... here."

"Does that make any sense?"

"Yes! I don't know! You don't make any sense! None of this makes any sense!" The words were tumbling out of my mouth again, unstoppable. I gulped back a sob. "Where do you come from? Why is your skin so pale and your face so... different?"

My lip quivered. Tears threatened to spill. I would not allow myself to cry. "I just want to go home. Please, just let me go."

In the middle of my breakdown, Kirwyn had gone over to the drinking pail. He scooped a cupful of water and knelt down before me again, pressing it to my lips.

"Drink," Kirwyn said. His gesture was gentle. His command was not.

Before, I would have spit the water right into his face. Now, I could barely pull myself out of the mire churning in my head, let alone muster a fight.

I allowed him to hold the cup to my lips, gently tilting it so that I could take a few sips. When our eyes met over the upturned cup, I quickly looked away. I licked my lips and wiped my chin on my shoulder.

"Please tell me what is going on?" I whispered.

Kirwyn withdrew and rolled back into a sitting position, crossing his legs in front, facing me.

I stared at his unusual face, unable to say exactly why it was odd. Something was just *off*. The features were pleasing, handsome even. He had nice symmetry, a strong jawline. But the curve of his lips, the dark green of his eyes, the slightly-too-large ears... and pale as a babe. *Different.*

Part of me wanted to touch his face. Just to be sure he was real.

I still wanted to scratch it bloody and free myself, of course.

Kirwyn stroked his chin and said, "My uncle and I were traveling south, hugging the coast. We were headed for El Puerto En Blanco and onto to the South Continent. There's a boat that trades, takes freeborn and others on the run down there. If you're able-bodied you sign up for three years of indentured servitude in return for your passage, and after that, you're free."

He spoke nonsense. *Definitely one oar short a full boat.* Or a pathological liar.

Kirwyn shrugged. "Or so we heard. We couldn't have been more than a week's journey from the launch point, if it indeed exists. We stick to the cover of night when traveling so that we're not caught by any warring clans, forced into joining. We found a band of misfits – escapees and freeborns – by an abandoned dock near Fort Cuttle. They'd heard of Southern-bound boats too but feared a trap and had no interest in chancing it themselves. My uncle and I were low on food and other supplies, so when the men needed an extra hand on their fishing boat, I agreed to take a short trip. My labor in exchange for food and supplies. Being out on open water is chancy. You've got nowhere to run if you're spotted, and yet to keep safe out there, you need a fairly large boat."

Kirwyn paused, lost in his thoughts.

I stared, not speaking. I couldn't. Nonsense words. *Free-born, Fort Cuttle, South Continent.*

"My uncle stayed behind. He lost three fingers and he... looks older than he is. The crew thought he'd slow them down, even though he probably could work harder than most of them. Anyway, the fishing was good... almost too good, you know? On the second day a storm came and we started taking on water. The waves... it was like nothing I had ever seen before. Huge swells, angry, ready to roll over you and swallow you up. I thought that it was the end, that this was how I was going to die."

Kirwyn's eyes became unfocused as the memory pulled him back. "Something flew at me, hit me in head, hard. I don't even know what it was. All I know is, I woke up here. In your cave."

My mouth dropped during his tale and remained open. *What was he talking about?*

There was no land outside of the island; the world was ocean. My brain couldn't process the concept. It began to shut down from trying.

Re-focusing, Kirwyn looked hard at me. "I don't know what's going on in your head or what kinda set-up you've got going on here, but there's a big, wild world out there. Princesses - braenese, whatever you call yourselves - are only in fairy tales and there is no such thing as the sea god."

Kirwyn looked at me condescendingly and declared,

"You're either crazy, or, if this is what your people actually believe, you're not very smart."

Fury flared in me like a lit torch. "And you're not very polite. I don't know where you come from, but where I come from, basic manners matter."

"Where I come from manners can get you killed," he shot back. "Logic matters."

"Well, we're not there," I countered. "We're here, on royal ground. So explain to me. What do you mean mainland? There is nowhere else and this is the paradise the Sea God gave to us. Of course there are royals. I have a sister, Jona, next in line to inherit the throne. And my mother, Braenese Pama. And my father, Braenar Darius-"

Kirwyn stood and began pacing. He threw up his hands for emphasis as he spoke. "Look, there is a world out there that's filled with islands. And larger land masses... we call them continents. They all have proper names, at least, they did when books were still being written. Now, there's a lot more fighting and a lot less art."

He stopped, gazing at the ground. "You're either mad or... somehow... somehow your island is isolated from the rest of the world..." He shook his head, disbelieving.

"I don't understand what you mean!" I cried. Tears of frustration nearly spilled over. I just wanted to lay my head down. It hurt.

"But let me go and you can see for yourself. I won't tell anyone about you, I promise. You can go quietly back to your sea-world, or wherever it is you really come from."

"Can't let you go, princess." He crossed his arms. "You'll go back to your guards or your clan or whoever and send them straight back to find me. I need to figure out where I am and how to get back home. I need you to help me do that."

My brain decided to start working again at those words. *His* need. *My* chance...

Once more I straightened as much as I could against the rock. I shook my head to flick behind me the curtains of hair that had spilled onto my shoulders.

"Honestly? Yes, this cave is secret. I can't expose you without exposing my secret. More importantly, if the guards find you, if they know what happened... I will be in almost as much trouble as you. I cannot be touched by a man. What they'll do..." I trailed off, closing my eyes against the memory. I knew what they'd do to *him*. I just wasn't sure about me.

I opened my eyes. Kirwyn stared, studying me.

Pressing on, I said, "I have as many questions as you do. More. But... there's no time."

Behind him, I could see the orange light of the waning sun through the spaces in the vines.

"At some point tonight, I will be noticed missing, and others will come looking for me. Tomorrow, I have some-where important to be. My parents will be wondering why I'm not home. Resting." I sat up even straighter. The move-ment hurt my arms. "So if you continue to keep me here, tied up to this rock, it's only a matter of time before we both lose."

Kirwyn stroked his chin, then squatted once more, resting on the balls of his feet.

"Or... or, you could trust me," I suggested. "The girl who saved you in the first place. The worst that could happen is the guards come after you sooner rather than later. The best that could happen is I'm telling you the truth. I will help you. I will return tomorrow morning and you can tell me about the... North Continent... and the clans."

Ridiculous. I was giving his lies credibility by even speaking of them. I wasn't that gullible.

"Before you think of using me as a hostage," I warned, "let me assure you, there is no way you will make it off the island against the Steel Guard and our highly-skilled archers." *Whose arrows had never been used, as far as I knew.* But I didn't add that.

Instead, I sealed the deal. "If you're as clever as you think you are, you could look at me and know that when a braenese gives her word of honor, she always keeps it."

Liar.

My earlier vow to Keroe echoed in my head.

Well... I never *really* uttered any vows. Not yet. Not until the wedding ceremony. But it was sort of *implied* at the betrothal.

I bit my lip. This didn't conflict with my vow to wed. Not really.

Wordlessly, Kirwyn rose and began pacing the short length of the cave once more, glancing over at me every few seconds. I held my breath waiting to see what he'd decide. Finally, he stopped, with his back turned to me.

"Okay," he sighed. "I'll let you go in return for your word of honor that you'll help me."

His shoulders rose and fell as he chuckled. "Did I say you're not smart? I take that back, princess. You're an astute negotiator."

I grinned and replied, "Did I say you're unkind? I take that back, boy. You're a paradigm of benevolence."

CHAPTER 11

"Alright. I'll wait here for you until you return," Kirwyn said, parting at the cave's mouth. "But if you tell anyone or send your guards, I'll kill you."

I don't know what demon seized my tongue, but I didn't appreciate being threatened.

Gliding through the entrance, I replied, *"Not if I kill you first."* Though it sounded more like a child's retort than the arch warning I'd intended.

Kirwyn seized my wrist. "Are you going to help me or not?"

I stared, pointedly, and he dropped it.

God, another touch.

"Are you going to apologize for attacking someone who tried?" I countered.

"I'm sorry," he grumbled. "I shouldn't have... attacked you."

I studied his face, trying to discern the depth of his sincerity.

"Good. But I'm not." I lifted my chin toward the lump on his head. "You shouldn't have touched me."

Now that I was free to go, I felt more than a little prickly at his treatment of me, and worse, panicked at all that touching. In the dark cave, it felt secret, hidden. But stepping out into the light made me wonder if imprints on my skin would somehow be revealed under the bright sun.

"Like I said," Kirwyn replied, spreading his hands in a gesture of acceptance, "I deserved that."

I pursed my lips and nodded, once. This was the best we could do, for now.

Ducking out of the cave and back into the forest, I pointed out to Kirwyn where to pick some fresh Pawpaws nearby, where he wouldn't likely be seen. In addition to the food still packed in the sack, he'd have enough to sustain himself. As much as my curiosity burned, there was no way I could return tomorrow, the day of my first wedding pageant.

I'd have to wait.

He'd have to wait.

Limping through the orchards at the back of the palace, I practiced my lie, worried that hints would spill like water through cracks.

"Zaria!" my mother cried as soon as I walked through the back door.

My father was a step behind her, not coming too close. He held Gereth back with the length of his arm. At three years old, Gereth was clumsy and forgetful.

Utterly pointless now.

If they only knew how despoiled I was.

My mother's long arms pulled me into an embrace, "Zaria, what happened? Are you hurt?"

"I'm fine..." I focused on the lie, trying to believe it

enough to somehow make it true, or at least *show* true on my face.

"I went for a swim around the island, only I forgot to eat breakfast this morning. When I passed the Eastern tip, I decided to stop and pick some mangoes, but I wasn't paying attention and slipped on that sharp hill by the Crossed Palms..." I figured this was believable. Everyone knew I was no good on land.

"I hobbled back to the village and a fishwife helped me, bandaged me. It hurt, but I was able to walk back home." I forced an uneven smile. "I'll be fine for the pageant tomorrow," I quickly added.

"We'll see about that. Let's get you upstairs, to bed," she commanded. "Mazriah, fetch the healer immediately."

"As soon as she finishes, you get some sleep. We'll send up a pot of clam broth. Are you still hungry?" my mother asked, lightly pressing the back of her hand to my forehead to check for fever.

"No!" I cried. "I mean, yes. I'm hungry. But I don't want to go to bed. I want to feast. With you."

My muscles ached and my eyes had trouble staying open. I wanted nothing more than to lay down in my bed sort through the storm of emotions inside me, to figure out who the boy-creature Kirwyn really was, and what was to become of me now that I'd been touched.

But I was too afraid another inconsistency would out my lies, as well as jeopardize my pageant tomorrow.

"I'm fine, Mother. Really. The fishwife did well."

"I'm sure she did the best she could within her abilities," my mother said, arching her eyebrows to indicate those abilities were quite limited in her view. "But we'll have the healer ensure you are well, and that the wound is properly treated with the best medicines in the archive. I will let Nasero know we are cancelling tomorrow's pageant."

"No!" I pleaded. New anger at Kirwyn swelled up inside me. If he caused the delay of my wedding… "I mean, I'm fine. Really. It's just an easy swim. The salt water will do my leg good. Please."

My mother's lips thinned. "Alright, but if you feel compromised, you must let me know first thing in the morning. I'll inform Nasero that you've been injured but, for now, are confident in your swim." She took one last look at my leg and then sighed, "I have to speak with him anyway. One of the villagers lost her family's prized buck last night."

"Another goat died?" My stomach turned as, unwillingly, the grotesque scene came to mind of our own dead bucks in the dawn's light, splayed on the ground.

My mother nodded. "We don't want to move all of the goats together, in case the illness spreads. But they don't seem to be safe anywhere now." As she spoke, she stroked the sparkling gemstone in her Old World necklace, her prized possession.

A few minutes later the healer arrived, a frail woman who'd been training other young healers at least twice as long as I'd been alive. She gave my wound a funny look but said nothing. Her black-and-white hair was matted into fuzzy rows she tied back, before pealing the cloth from my leg to begin her work.

Healers, like artists, occupied a space between the villagers and The Mystics in our hierarchy. They had their own training hall near the priests, not far from the palace. Everyone occupied a space inside the social strata, even Braeni.

Everyone except Fire Maidens.

The shrouded group of priestesses made their home at the top of Mount Flame and rarely left, much like stilt-dwellers never left the sea. The maidens tended an eternal flame, continually burning in their hall on the promontory. Although no one was ever allowed into the innermost chambers of the temple, night or day, a fire blazed at the entrance. That way, anyone who needed a hearth fire had ready access to a flame. In the cool season, nights were a bit chilly with the ocean breeze, but mainly, the people used the fire for cooking.

As the healer worked, I felt like my lie had been accepted, and I let my mind drift back to the cave.

Kirwyn-the-boy-demon was lying.

Obviously.

What I couldn't figure out was *why*. What could he hope to gain?

The best thing to do would be to let him continue. Eventually, I'd catch him in an inconsistency and I'd force him to confess. Then I'd find out what was really going on. Where he came from and what he wanted.

Pleased, I nodded to myself. The touching was past, and no one knew. Everything was going to be fine. I'd solve the mystery of the boy-creature, marry the Sea King, and live the rest of my life happily, under the ocean.

A pat on my leg told me the elderly healer had finished. She gave me one chalky, white pill from the Old World, for now, and one to take tonight, before bed. I thanked her and joined my family, already having started night's feast and not wanting to interrupt Gereth's sleep schedule.

It wasn't until I sat at the water table that I was stunned to realize I had forgotten about my prized shell crown.

It lay broken, with Kirwyn, back at the cave.

CHAPTER 12

When I woke, I remembered a hint of my night-dream; but pieces of it were already missing, jettisoned like fallen goods off a boat into a foggy sea. It was something about the palace again, not being allowed inside. But as it slipped away, I felt the sun warm my face, caressing me into wakefulness.

I shot up in bed, looked down at my leg, and twisted my ankle left and right. *No pain.*

No reason to miss the pageant.

It was simple, really. The weakest child or the frailest elder could swim the cove if needed, albeit much slower. But the pageant was a traditional part of the ceremonies, to ensure Keroe had a healthy bride for the sea.

I counted on my fingers and clapped happily to myself. *Just twenty-eight days, including today, until my wedding.*

Twenty-eight days to figure out where the boy from the beach really came from.

Kirwyn.

I tossed the sounds around my head and snorted to myself. *What a silly name.* What funny-looking features.

What a strange tone of voice. I wondered, for the umpteenth time, what he *really* was.

Only one way to find out, I thought, springing out of bed, and testing my weight on my ankle.

But not until tomorrow.

Today was all about my first pageant.

PERCHED ON THE ROCKY LEDGE, the sun warmed my scalp, exposed down the middle for the crown braid Mazriah wove into it that morning. Below, turquoise waters sparkled, beckoning me. I tensed my toes against the curve of rock, eager to dive. Nasero intoned another extended speech, this one about my physical stamina, but I didn't even hear half of it. He seemed a gentler High Mystic than the last one, but also a more long-winded one.

Behind me, as my mother and father beamed, I resolved to make them proud with the fastest swim by a chosen braenese, ever. Gereth and Jona stayed at the palace, under Mazriah's care, so my only other company were the few Mystics standing with my family further back atop the cliff.

Almost everyone on land swelled to crowd the rocks on the far side of the cove. I shaded my eyes against the sun as I looked across the waters, even though I knew I wasn't likely to make out a face amongst of the thousands of people from my side. Tomé was in there, somewhere, eagerly waiting with jug of fresh water. Far to my right, bobbing in boats beyond the mouth of the cove, the stilt-dwellers had paddled over to view the pageant without having to set foot upon the sinful land.

About a half a mile, end-to-end. I shook my injured leg. It wouldn't stall me. It didn't even hurt.

Shut up already, Nasero. I just want in. I'm only getting hotter by the minute.

I cracked my neck and rolled my shoulders.

"...Braenese Zaria may begin!"

My feet left rock before he finished the sentence. I dove like a dinbird into the sea, thirty feet below. Leaping to my future.

The warm, saline water enveloped my body and I broke into a quick pace, easy in the calm current.

The world disappeared, even time itself dissolved into the sea, and it was just me and the water.

Head down, breath up, head down, breath up. I found more meditation in the rhythmic pattern of my strokes on the surface than I did in the excruciatingly boring sitting exercises during Sunday services with the Mystics.

I belonged to the sea.

Even though they mesmerized me, if I lived as a Fire Maiden, eternally cloistered high upon the mount, I was sure the air would dry out my body, and, once brittle, it would burst beside the flame. I could never be far from the sea.

Head down, breath up, head down, breath up.

Out of the corner of my eye, I saw something move in the water beside me. A dark shadow under the waves. Something huge.

I stopped and righted myself, bobbing as I scanned the surface. I was about two thirds of the way to shore. My spine tingled. *What was it?*

There, it moved again! A shadow below me.

My stomach clenched and my heart exploded into a pain so sharp I thought I might die of fright.

Shark.

Exactly like the pictures in the books.

How? There were no sharks in these waters. Not anymore.

I realized I was scared stiff. I could hear people screaming now, shouting at me, waving their arms, but there was no one in the water to help me. I forced myself to move, whipping my head around. No boats bobbed close enough; the stilt-dwellers were too far.

There was no way out but straight ahead -- the rocks at the finish line. I could make it in a few minutes at my hardest pace.

You have to move. Swim.

Swim for your life.

My only choice. Keep moving.

Go, go, go!

I broke into my fastest stroke, pushing straight for the shore. I couldn't outswim a mythic shark, but maybe I could make it to the rocks before it decided to attack.

Frantic, I willed all the strength I could muster to swing my arms faster than ever before, to kick my legs harder than I thought possible.

Less than two minutes and I'd be safe.

Please, Keroe, please don't let him eat me.

My hands shook as I swam. I couldn't look, but I imagined the shark circling me, like the tales they taught us in school.

Don't think about it, just swim.

One minute.

Faster, faster, you've got to swim faster.

The rocks were just a few more feet. *Please don't eat me, please don't eat me.*

Villagers screamed. I pictured the shark opening wide jaws with jagged, razor teeth to clamp down on my stomach or my kicking legs.

Push, push.

Almost there...

Don't bite me...

Here!

I scraped myself up onto the nearest rock, scratching my body. With a half-gasp-half-cry, I quickly swung my legs up beyond the reach of teeth. The hands of half a dozen village women reached out and pulled me higher, further scraping me over the sharp and slippery, algae-covered rocks.

I looked down at myself.

I bled from my chest and hands.

But I was safe. Whole. Unbitten.

I hadn't noticed before, but several men had jumped into the ocean on either side of my path, shouting, splashing, and throwing rocks. Trying to beckon the shark away from where I swam. Even the stilt-dwellers had paddled closer in a fruitless attempt to rescue me. I searched the water for the creature. Maybe the commotion scared it away; I couldn't see anything moving now.

"Braenese Zaria, Keroe saved you. I saw him in the water, fighting off the shark!"

I turned my head in the direction of a snaggle-toothed woman next to me, shouting over a crowd of women swelling to encircle me.

Where was Tomé? I looked over female heads, part of me thankful these women hovered near because I could barely stand on my own. My legs were wobbly jellyfish, my stomach; hollow -- like the shark had actually reared its head through my middle, tearing a hole. I needed Tomé.

There -- pushing his way forward. I wanted to cry in relief.

"There's blood in the water," he said.

What?

"Aye, yes, the blood! From where Keroe fought the shark!" It was the same woman, one large snaggle-tooth protruding from her gummy mouth. Her eyebrows were bleached into non-existence from the sun, her hair whitened at the temples.

"No." Tomé's voice was deep and firm. "The blood was there before the shark." He paused, then explained, "I was alone on the beach. I hadn't made it to the finish line yet. You probably couldn't see from this angle," he pointed down, indicating where we stood, "but I saw clouds of red from over there. The blood was there before."

I tried to make sense of Tomé's words while the women argued over him. They pushed past him, ushering me inland. Cheers and shouts grew louder, as if danger inflamed the crowd's euphoria, heightening the buzz in the air by my near-death experience, by Keroe's triumphant rescue of his bride-to-be.

I couldn't understand what Tomé meant, why the shark was in the water, or even what was expected of me now. All I could do was put one foot in front of the other as I allowed myself to be led away. I didn't have my sandals, but I didn't even feel the rough cove below my feet.

I sat. I was made to sit. I do not know. A rock formed a stool under me, and Tomé handed a woman the water pitcher. It was the same woman who saw Keroe fight the shark. She bade me drink like a doting grandmother, smoothing loose strands of hair behind my ears. This encounter would be a story she'd retell to generations of offspring.

I had almost died, but this was the lucky day she helped the chosen braenese at her first wedding pageant.

I let out a delirious laugh-cry. Uneven, high-pitched.

I couldn't die. I was getting married in three weeks.

Every child heard tales, but no one had seen a live shark for ages. Suddenly, it was swimming under me. Appearing out of nowhere. Just like Kirwyn had appeared on the beach. *Did he have something to do with the shark?*

What was he doing, right now, back in my cave?

The corners of Tomé's mouth still pulled into a frown, but he did not speak.

Nothing extraordinary had happened my whole life. Now two impossible events occurred. Were they related?

Was the shark a punishment, or perhaps a warning?

The tall, pale-blonde head of my mother emerged through the fussing women, immediately parting as they saw her. Before I knew what I was doing, I ran into her arms.

Confession danced on my lips.

"Shh..." she soothed, though I swore her hands shook. "Everything is okay now. You're safe. Your father is leading a hunt, it'll be dead by sun down."

Her word carried throughout the crowd, up to those standing back by the trees. *A hunt! There's going to be a hunt! Braenar Darius will spear the shark!*

Maybe Keroe no longer wanted me, a despoiled bride. Maybe my mother could help. I hiccupped, longing to confess, refusing to cry in front of everyone.

She squeezed me tighter. "Shh..."

I needed to tell her I had been touched. I opened my mouth...

"Is the braenese alright?" Nasero interrupted. With the long sleeves of his ceremonial robe, he dappled the sweat glistening on his dark face.

I nodded, gulping air. The moment to confess had passed.

"Are you hurt?" Nasero pressed.

I didn't want to speak. Not for a long time. Maybe not ever. I wanted to stay silent, to swim in the Sea of Sorrows. But a royal couldn't take the sacred vow for anything less than the death of a loved one.

I whispered, "I'm... okay. I'm not hurt."

I wanted to believe it.

He exhaled, continuing to pat his brow. "Praise Keroe."

"Conclude the pageant," my mother commanded. Turning, she whispered in my ear, "Let's get you home. I'll boil some tamarind tea."

She gave me one last squeeze, then stepped back. The rest of the crowd backed away at her cue.

Suddenly, Nasero and I stood alone on the stony outcrop between the crowd and the sea. Wind whipped fallen strands of my hair about my face and neck. I looked up at the High Mystic, momentarily holding onto his kind eyes. Those brown eyes warmed me in a way I'd always wished my father's had.

He turned to face the crowd.

"Demonstrating her physical aptitude, the chosen braenese has successfully swam the Wide Cove."

He bellowed deep, aiming to reach the thousands of villagers stretching along the sandy banks below, or further back upon the rocks, though the usual *oomph* in his voice had diminished.

From the corner of my eye, I saw a boat beyond the cove ride out to sea -- presumably my father hunting the shark. Nearby, two young boys, bored by the proceedings and with no sense of danger, shoved each other with raucous laugher. Daring one another to stick a foot in the water.

The waves continued to caress the beach. The scorching

sun beat down from the very height of its arc. Bees buzzed happily between nearby palm trees.

I had just faced a shark, but the world continued unchanged, uncaring.

I turned back to Nasero as he proclaimed, mustering a bit more enthusiasm, "Your physical worthiness proved, I present your second crown!"

Ever so careful not to touch me, he placed the coral crown upon my head.

Its crimson, jagged edges were sharp like shark's teeth, covered in blood.

CHAPTER 13

omé leapt from the floor cushion as my mother and I entered the front hall of the palace.

"I saw blood in the water," he said. "And it wasn't from the Sea God."

My mother's lips made a wry smile. "No, I wouldn't think so."

"That's what the villagers are saying. But it looked like there had been a fresh kill, a large one, that attracted the shark. Maybe there was another shark, a fight? Maybe they are coming back?"

"That's not possible." My mother dismissed the idea with a wave of her hand. "We hunted the sharks out of these waters long before you were even born. I haven't seen one since I was three or four. And we caught that one and ate it, too." She sat down on a wooden chair along the wall, to relieve some of the extra weight she carried. One hand rubbed her round belly.

She was right. I'd been weaned on stories of the great shark hunters of ancient times, when shark meat fed the village for days. We still had dangerous brushes with the sting of the Goodnight Fish, a burn with live coral, or the spikes of the sea urchin, but these encounters were accidents. Our only predators in the sea, sharks, no longer existed to feed on humans – or we on them.

And yet, one remained, promising to haunt my nightmares for the rest of my life.

Suddenly, another image popped into my mind, twisting my stomach like a fish flop in the gut. *What if the boy from the beach disregarded my command to stay put, waded into the ocean, and was attacked?*

"But there was blood in the water," Tomé insisted. "Something brought the shark there. Maybe something died?"

My mother frowned, toying the sparkling, Old World jewel at her throat. Worry on her face made *me* worry more than anything else.

"The blood came from Zaria... I told her she was not ready to swim. Look, her wound re-opened."

Everyone looked at my leg, myself included, and saw the bandage had soaked red. I hadn't even noticed or felt any pain.

"But, this shark is troubling. Very troubling. I will speak to Nasero about it after tomorrow's morning service. *Mazriah*," my mother called, and Mazriah scurried into the room, silent and obedient. "Fetch the healer."

My mother rose to her feet.

The discussion was over.

While waiting for the healer to clean and re-bandage my leg, I sipped a calming cup of tamarind tea my mother had brewed, and then another.

The concoction worked its magic.

My shoulders began to relax and my mind drifted away from the memory of the shark, from the sharp edge of fear.

Miraculously, within a few minutes, I felt almost light-headed, hopeful. My thoughts turned to my wedding, now one step closer.

Two of the four crowns were mine.

I lifted one side of my mouth into a dreamy smile as I pictured the final crown I'd wear on my wedding day.

LATE AFTERNOON SUN cast golden beams through our tall windows as the old healer finished, but my father and the hunting party had not returned. If they didn't kill the shark soon, they would have to resume the chase tomorrow.

My perking-up convinced my mother to continue with our celebratory night's feast, and she left to oversee preparations.

As soon as her white tunic disappeared beyond the columns in the front hall, Tomé whispered, "Something is wrong, Zaria. I saw the blood in the water. And it was more than a few drops from your leg. Also, your wound hadn't re-opened during the swim. I would have noticed, someone would have noticed the blood. That shark was there for a reason. I think there are more out there than they're letting on. It's just too much coincidence that a shark hasn't been seen for decades and suddenly is there for your pageant? I think they've come back."

My giddy mood evaporated instantly and my stomach sank like a rock in the sea.

How could we swim with sharks in the waters? And if we couldn't swim, what would I do? I fought back a shiver as I pictured the hungry rows of jagged teeth.

I needed to warn the boy from the beach. Didn't I?

I badly wanted Tomé's advice, but couldn't bring myself to tell him.

"But how can you be sure where the blood came from and when?" I argued. "I was bleeding from the rocks when I escaped."

"No, your bandage was clear, the wound hadn't reopened yet. You cut your chest and hands only. I remember. And anyway, there was more blood out there than could have pooled from a minor wound."

Of course Tomé noticed what others hadn't. And if *he* worried about more sharks returning, I should worry too. No one had a mind like Tomé's. I needed his counsel on the boy in the cave. My secret rested on the edge of my tongue...

"Wait," I said, with a sudden realization. "Why weren't you on the cove with everyone else?"

"What?" Tomé asked.

"You said you saw the blood because you were still crossing the beach. Why were you over there?"

"I was late," Tomé admitted, sheepishly.

"How could you be late for my pageant?" I asked, exasperated. He knew how important it was to me.

"I'm sorry. Marcin needed another set of hands for a new carving at the workshop. It was too heavy to lift alone. No one else was around to help and we lost track of time."

Before I could argue, he continued, "Don't worry. We'll find out where the shark came from. There's no huntsman like your father. If there's more, he'll kill them all, and we'll feast for weeks."

Tomé paused, looking as if he wanted to reach out and hug me, or take my hand, or soothe me in some way. I felt a familiar surge of anger that the simplest act of affection and support from my only real friend was forbidden.

Instead, Tomé said softly, "I'm sorry I was late and I'm

sorry this happened. Only, don't let it spoil what you've earned." He smiled, brightening. "You looked pretty in your crown. Where's the shell one?"

"I... oh..." I looked down at the pillows. "I, um, gave it to Jona to play with." I silently cursed myself. Why did I say something so unbelievably careless?

"Mm..." Tomé trailed off, and I chewed my lip, hoping he wouldn't push the matter. "Well, two down, two to go, eh? One of sea glass and then a pearl tiara for your wedding day, right?"

I nodded.

"What's the next pageant? Something to do with your mental aptitude? They do know who they're dealing with?" he joked. "I hope they make it something easy, like sorting fish, perhaps. Or maybe you can tell stories of village tales and folklore. I think you could do a great rendition of one concerning... stones under the bed."

I searched for something nearby to throw at his head, found a wooden bowl, and chucked it. It missed by several feet.

He laughed, not even bothering to duck.

For a moment, I laughed too.

"It's our goddess, who fights off sharks!"

Marcin stood beside the water table chewing on a sugarcane. His hair was tied back in a goat's tail. Muscular arms flexed under bronzed skin, the product of repetitious scrollwork in the garden sun. Tonight, he wore shoes -- corded leather crisscrossing up his legs.

I flashed a brief smile. I wasn't yet ready to joke about the ordeal, but at least he didn't credit Keroe.

"It's my father who kills them," I pointed out.

My father had returned victorious a few moments before. Traditionally, the hunter would claim the choicest cut of meat from the prey, but knowing I did not want to see the shark again, he had offered it up to his men. Just to be safe, word spread that swimming was banned for the next three days, until a thorough search could be completed, making sure the dead shark didn't have any friends.

I didn't mind the short ban as much as I thought -- I had more than enough to occupy my time with the dark-haired boy. I wondered if he poked around the cave and I hoped he didn't find the silver egg I'd hidden.

Tomé and Marcin sat in the extra chairs while my mother, father, and I, took our usual places at the water table. Gereth and Jona had separately been fed a dinner of scallops and mushy Pawpaws earlier.

In celebration of my first pageant, a spiked, purple-rose hibiscus punch was served in beautiful Old World glasses, etched with patterns in gold. Occasionally, my mother did permit a glass of something boozy at a festivity -- or was she was loosening the rules as my departure neared?

"To the Goddess!" Tomé toasted and we drank the sweet concoction.

As a special first course, the cook surprised us with a dish of plump bee larvae dripping in freshly-gathered honey, complementing the larvae's bacon-mushroom flavor. Large plates, bowled at the edges to float, were set upon the water with our next course of gingered Mahi, topped with seared pineapple.

"My favorite," my father remarked, when the main course was served. He kissed my mother on the check. The dish, commonly known by the macabre name of "Mommy with a Baby," was a seared chicken stuffed with a soft egg.

"Delicious," he declared, cutting his piece. The runny egg dripped onto the plate.

He was right, but the name turned my stomach. Though a favorite of mine when I was young, I didn't touch it now. I ate chicken. I ate eggs. But the gory image the presentation created made me grimace and I no longer cared for the dish. I guessed my mother hadn't noticed. I picked at the edges of the meat so she wouldn't be hurt.

"Darling, here. Finish mine," my father insisted, offering his plate to my mother. In her sixth moon of pregnancy, she'd quickly polished off her piece.

"No, I had it prepared with you and Zaria in mind," she protested.

"And it would give me greater pleasure to see you eat it," he countered, kissing her hand.

Tomé rolled his eyes with exaggeration. "These two. So *adoring* after so many years of marriage. It's unnatural. Me? I can barely tolerate someone after a few months."

Marcin laughed, nodding his head in agreement, and I smiled as well. My parents *did* dote on one another with such politeness.

Dessert, a sugar cake topped with a coconut-and-rose infused cream, melted divinely on my tongue, and made up for the chicken.

"How about another round of punch?" Marcin asked, hopeful.

"Well..." my mother sighed, looking at my father, who shrugged, sipping his soursop tea. "I suppose one more glass would be acceptable, on such an occasion."

"To the High Braenese. Long live Queen Pama!" Marcin toasted.

After their drinks were emptied, he and Tomé bent their heads in conference.

"'T'wod not be right to leave out a member of the royal family, least of all the High Braenar," Tomé announced, borrowing a tongue from an Old World fairy tale book to show off his smarts. "Methinks we should have one more drink. To toast the King's health."

My father held up his hand and gamed along. "'T'wod be a sin. Observe this healthy body. So robust, it would be pure greed to ask for more. Nay, methinks it wise to remain *quietly grateful,* so as to not anger Keroe."

Surprised by my father's jovial mood, I laughed. Tomé chuckled good-naturedly at being taken down a peg and mock-punched Marcin's arm.

I'd often thought to be near Tomé was to bask in the sun's glow; and Marcin, with his equally blinding smile, made the boys shine together like a pair of twin suns. If such a thing existed.

"Worth a shot," Tomé grinned, shrugging.

CHAPTER 14

"You're actually braver than I gave you credit for. Or foolish. Or both."

Kirwyn leaned against a wall of the cave, one leg crossed over the other, relaxed. His pallor had improved, skin beginning to deepen into a light tan. His hair had been cleaned and combed. He must have explored, and immersed in deeper water somewhere, ignoring my instructions to stay put.

But he was alive. No shark bites.

"I could say the same about you."

Kirwyn lifted one shoulder in a shrug.

Actually, I didn't know what to make of the dark-haired creature before me. Which is why I'd hidden a knife in my tunic and buried one fifty yards out.

"At first, I didn't think you had a deceptive bone in your body," he said.

"And you don't have an honest one in yours."

Kirwyn grinned, wide. It was a charming smile, I'd give him that. As my eyes adjusted to the dim cave, I could see he had grown a little stubble without a scraping blade, and

I thought it suited him. It would have to stay. I certainly wasn't going to arm him with a knife.

"Then we'd both be wrong," he said. "See, at first I thought you couldn't possibly deceive, not well, anyway. No offense, princess, but you wear your emotions on your face. So halfway through the traps I set for your guards out there-" at this revelation, I whipped my head around to the cave's entrance, "-don't worry, I didn't bother finishing."

Kirwyn paced the Old World rug as he spoke. "I've had a lot of time to think over the last two days, about whether I should stay in this cave or not. And I realized a few things that don't add up."

He tapped his fingers to his mouth before continuing, "You can't tell your people about me without getting yourself into trouble, so that buys me a bit of safety. But here's what's more interesting. You talk of honor, but... you *did* deceive your family... yet you did not deceive me. Other than when you hit me on my head, of course," he absentmindedly touched the bump, then continued pacing.

"You say that you have never been touched by a male before, a very serious rule you followed your whole life – until now. So, we know you lied to your own clan. But not me."

He squared himself in front of me, inches from my face, arms folded. My muscles tensed, ready for a fight. I fought the urge to step back, forcing myself to look him in the eyes. I pictured the knife in my pocket.

Be ready. He might attack again.

"Why?" he asked.

I opened my mouth and closed it, like a fish. I did not expect the question. My gaze drifted and I stared into the dark recess of the cave.

I had done wicked things. All my life, and more so

recently. I desperately wanted to marry Keroe, and yet I had done things that might prevent it. And I couldn't even understand why.

Kirwyn nodded, smirking.

"What?" I asked, annoyed not to be in on some joke.

"You're easier to read than an open book! You don't even know, do you? In this short time, I know you better than you know you. Because I know that you don't know and you don't know that you don't know."

My mind took few seconds to catch up with what he just said. In the meantime, Kirwyn practically skipped back to his post on the wall, resuming his lazy pose once more. My shoulders relaxed, no longer anticipating an attack.

"You don't have a plan, do you? You think I'm like your 'artifacts' over there. I think you're a naïve little girl who's hiding something she found to play with, disregarding the dangers."

"I can handle my mother," I protested, with an angry wave of my hand. "If anyone found out, there might be a cleansing ritual, but they won't put me to death for touching someone, borne out of one act of compassion."

Kirwyn scoffed. "I don't mean the dangers of your people. *I mean me.*"

Something in his tone made my heart skip a beat, followed by a hot flush blooming on my cheeks.

"I thought you might be Keroe," I blurted, defensively.

"Who's Keroe?"

I rolled my eyes, exasperated with his pretense. "The Sea God. You look so different. There is a story so old it's but a whisper, that the First Feet, the Gods, looked different. I thought you might be the Sea God, you know. Come to life. In human form. That's the reason I saved you." I didn't add, *one of the possible reasons.*

"You thought I was... God?" Kirwyn asked, eyebrows raised. "Me? I'm chuffed. That's a new one. I thought I was a demon last you checked."

He began to laugh. Again. I shifted my weight and frowned, feeling I was existing too much for his amusement.

Huffing through my nose, I took several steps back and leaned against the opposite wall, facing off across the cave. We both folded our arms and studied one another. A breeze blew the vines hiding the cave's entrance, sending light patterns dancing across the stones between us.

"Back to your original point, *boy*. How would I be wrong to call you deceptive? You're not honest."

"And how, *braenese*, have I deceived you?"

"You lie about your origins."

Kirwyn shook his head. "I don't. And there's your foolishness. Believing that there's no other land in the world? That some sea god fashioned you out of ocean foam? I'm telling you, there's a big world out there. Bigger than even I've seen or ever will see, and I've covered a lot of ground."

His blasphemy set my cheeks on fire again. "Let me get this straight," I grit out. "I'm foolish because everything I know to be true, everything every single person in the world knows to be true, doesn't agree with the lies some stranger is telling me? I can't place your origin, I'll give you that. But I'm not foolish enough to change my mind about everything true in the world just because some washed-up creature tells me to. That *would* be crazy."

I expected an argument. A snarky retort at the very least.

"You're right," he replied slowly. His eyes focused somewhere distant, on some spot above my shoulder.

"I'm... *what?*"

"You're right. I don't know what kind of clan you've got here on your island," he shook his head. "But if all your people believe the same thing, if you've all been living your lives the same way for so long, how can I expect you to trust me?"

I eyed him warily. Was this a trick? Kirwyn walked to the center of the room and sat down on the crimson rug, legs bent in front, elbows resting on his knees. He looked up.

"Maybe you could show me around, at least where it's safe? Tell me about this place? Then maybe we can come to understand each other and I can figure out a way to get back home."

I realized at that moment, for all his condescending banter, Kirwyn was powerless.

And really had been the entire time.

Reliant on my charity to help him. If I was telling the truth, he couldn't make himself known or he'd be killed by my guards. If I was not, that still didn't help him get back to wherever he wanted to go.

Deep green eyes studied me. Funny how they could look so full of danger and yet soulful at the same time. Like the very forest they resembled.

I sat onto the rug, facing him, but still several feet away, legs crossed in front of me.

"You tied me up."

"I know. I apologized."

"You threatened to kill me."

Kirwyn looked at the ground. "I didn't mean it..."

"Yes," I interrupted sharply. "I think you did."

Kirwyn gazed at the cave wall behind me as if not paying much attention, but he straightened his back and cocked a one-sided smile. "Ok. Maybe I did. A misunderstanding, princess. I promise I won't threaten to kill you in the future."

I tilted my head, catching the key word. "Or *actually* kill me. Or attempt to."

Kirwyn chuckled. "All of the above. None of the above. I promise. Now. No more talk of killing?"

What I said next was a firm command.

"One more thing. Don't. Ever. Touch. Me. Again."

This time, Kirwyn's eyes swept to mine. A charge filled the space between us, like the air before a lightning storm. A wild thought popped into my head, that I *wanted* him to protest, that I liked feeling him touch me. Afraid he'd read the illicit thought in my eyes, I struggled not to lose this staring contest. I studied his eyes in return, though I could read nothing in that impenetrable green forest.

"Ok, princess. I won't touch you," Kirwyn agreed. "And... thank you. For not exposing me. For coming back."

I felt a strange disappointment that... *what?* He'd agreed to what I wanted. I shoved the thought away.

"OK. I'll show you around, but only where it's safe. I'll tell you about my people. And you tell me about where you're from. The *real* story."

Before he could protest, I added, "We can't go far. We can only stay on this side of the island. And we must be careful."

"Why?" Kirwyn asked.

"Your face!" I threw my hands up in the air. "It would give you away immediately."

"What's wrong with my face?" Kirwyn asked, raising his eyebrows. "I think it's handsome."

"It's... different!" I exclaimed, not sure how to explain it. "Besides, no one here knows you anyway. You'd be taken by the guard immediately."

Kirwyn frowned, rubbing his chin.

"If you've been isolated here long enough, perhaps there isn't a large enough gene pool to go around," he whispered, musing to himself.

I was about to ask what he meant when I noticed the furry body of a tarantula climbing over his shoulder.

"Don't move," I commanded, voice low.

Kirwyn shifted his gaze to me, eyes sharp with anticipation.

Quickly, I reached over and grabbed the spider between its second and third pair of legs. I lifted him off of Kirwyn.

"*Ah!*" Kirwyn jumped when he saw it in my hands. Then he bolted upright and did a dance, looking over his shoulders for more spiders.

I laughed as I carried the little guy safely out of the cave. I walked far enough into the brush for him to not return anytime soon and placed him gently down on a rock.

Kirwyn no longer danced, but he was still engrossed in a full-body check when I ducked back into the dim cave.

"I'm impressed," he said, begrudgingly. "He could have bitten you. They're dangerous."

I chuckled and sat down on the rug to face him. "Yes, but not really. It's the Black Titan you have to watch out for. He'll make you scream in pain, and the toxin will swell whatever area he bit to twice its normal size."

"What's a Black Titan?" Kirwyn asked, alarmed. "Another spider?"

I shook my head. "It's a centipede. A giant one, as big as your arm from palm to elbow. More orange than black, really. Aggressive, too. Its venom can kill a small child. If you see one, just walk away. Fast."

"I'll keep that in mind," Kirwyn replied.

"Come on," I said, tilting my head toward the mouth of

the cave. "I'll show you some remote places on the royal side. We'll go to the grotto first."

I stood, dusting off my tunic.

Kirwyn jumped to his feet. The smirk was back.

"That algae pool down the path? Already seen it."

CHAPTER 15

"You grew up in a library? Big enough to sleep in? To live in?"

Unbelievable. Just like everything else Kirwyn said.

We had a few books and scrolls, mostly used for schooling purposes, in the Hall of The Mystics. Books were not removed from the premises, and special permission was needed to enter. In the world Kirwyn described, libraries overflowed with novels and tomes, more than a person could read in a lifetime, more than a person could read in *several* lifetimes. And no one even went into the libraries. Not because they were sparse or forbidden, but because they *simply didn't bother.*

"That's why my uncle and I were safe living there," Kirwyn shrugged.

For a liar, he was very easy to talk to.

Although I guess that's what made liars so good: conversational ease.

Wading through the thick, inner forest, waist-high with growth, Kirwyn and I headed toward the northwestern ridge that opened up onto one of the more secluded beaches, Little Shade Beach. It was only a narrow strip of sand, ten to twenty feet wide, protected by silver coconut trees on all sides. It was the safest option, aside from Lover's Lookout, and that required a boat or an ocean swim to access, blocked by steep cliffs on all sides.

Obviously, it wasn't an option, as we'd be spotted in the daylight.

Although... the name really deterred me, as much as the risk.

"My mother and father died when I was six months old. They were travelling with my uncle across the plains, heading west," Kirwyn said, straining to be heard over several parrots making a ruckus nearby. I shuffled closer to better hear.

"They moved around a lot, staying in one place for only a few days at a time. The plan was to find somewhere deserted in the far westlands, beyond the Cold Mountains. Or in the mountains. Or in the desert. They debated on their journey, according to my uncle."

Kirwyn looked far ahead as he spoke, as if he could see into the past.

"But they never made it. Somewhere in the plains, another band of travelers came along the same direction, just behind them. An unfriendly band. Most are."

He paused, wiping sweat from his brow.

"My family was armed, of course, but didn't want a fight if they could avoid it. They hid in some nearby wheat fields. The others would have passed us, but..." Kirwyn trailed off, closing his eyes against the merciless sun.

"What?" I asked, feeling a tingle at the back of my neck.

"Nothing," he shrugged. "In the fight that followed my parents were killed. So were three men and one woman from the other band. One younger man got away. My uncle and I survived."

As he finished speaking, Kirwyn sat on the edge of a mossy log, beneath the shade of a towering, broad-leafed tree.

My tunic stuck to my back, but to shade myself I'd need to be too close to Kirwyn. I sat down on the sunny end of the log. The far end.

Kirwyn wiped the sweat from his brow again. Raking his dark hair, he continued, "After that, well, my uncle had a baby on his hands he knew little about caring for, no longer had the safety of numbers, and, I think, a broken heart."

"He headed back east, back where he knew the territory better. Found a small town in the Green Mountains. It had been picked over long ago, so there wasn't much to lure any clans or traveling freeborns. It was so isolated and half-reclaimed by the forest that it was hard to find in the first place. Other than a church, an empty grocery store, about a dozen old shops, and three or four dozen homes, there wasn't much there. At one end, up the road a bit, was the library. We made it our home. Figured no one coming through for supplies would bother with it, and we were right."

Throughout Kirwyn's tale, I barely breathed, mesmerized by his story. The ease with which his words rolled off his tongue made me want to believe him.

"I wasn't born in the library, but I might as well have been. I spent the first seventeen years of my life there. We hid our existence as best we could, but we needed to farm. My uncle cleared some land further out and we grew crops. Potatoes, lettuce, blueberries, strawberries so sweet one taste was a bite of heaven. We couldn't risk raising livestock, so we hunted for game. Mostly the deer who tried to eat our garden."

Kirwyn threw one leg over the log and swiveled to face me, leaning forward on his hands. "My life fell into a pattern. I spent my days on our little farm, or hunting in the forest, and my nights in the library. Years passed this way. Just the two of us. We spied on travelers who got close, but we were mostly isolated. Just my uncle, myself, and rooms full of books. When I grew to where we felt we could protect ourselves enough, we risked occasional trips for trading. That's when we heard about the ship, the one that takes people south. Rumor is you can barter passage for three years of indentured servitude. As we heard more stories over the years, we decided to head for the coast. I agreed to one short trip on that fishing boat. And that's how I wound up here." He smiled wryly as he finished.

My head spun, aching to grasp meaning in his words, marveling at the depth of his make-believe worlds.

"You must be worried about your uncle," I said softly, eying him to see if I could catch any honest emotion in his response.

"I'm more worried that he's worried about me. I need to get off this island and find my way back to Fort Cuttle."

Kirwyn lifted his head and hopeful green eyes struck mine.

Praise Keroe, he was handsome. Whether he was smirking or looking at me like... *that.* Somehow both pleading and determined at the same time. Sensuous lips parted. I hadn't noticed until today that he had two very pointed canines, giving his mouth a feral quality. Ready to devour me.

I turned away, looking in the direction of the beach. Not that I could see it from here.

He lied through those teeth and obviously something was wrong with him.

"Zaria?" he asked softly. I whipped my head back around. It was the first time he called me by my name and it made something flutter in my stomach.

Suddenly afraid of what he might ask, I sprang to my feet. "Come on. I'll show you the beach."

As I turned to go, I spotted a juicy caterpillar on the edge of the log. I scooped it up and popped the fuzzy body into my mouth.

Kirwyn's eyes widened into sand tokens and his jaw dropped.

Was there something on my face? Self-consciously, I wiped my mouth with the back of my hand.

"Did you - did you just - eat a caterpillar?" he stammered.

I blinked. *So what?*

"Yes. Oh! I'm sorry. That was rude of me. You must be hungry. I should have offered to share."

"No, no, no! I do *not* want to eat a bug!" Kirwyn exclaimed, jumping to his feet and waving his hands in protest. "And certainly not a caterpillar. They become butterflies!"

"Well," I grinned, patting my stomach, "Not that one."

WE MADE slow progress wading through the thickening forest toward the deep ridge. There were no paths to follow since no one ever came there. Below, a short valley led to the sea, not too long of a hike, but steep. A bit further up the island, the ridge dropped sharply once more, into a tiny beach protected on all three sides by the tall cliff. *Lover's*

Lookout or Lover's Cove. No one normally used that beach because it was on our side of the island, plus there were plenty of longer beaches more easily reached.

"That was just... wow. Gross. I mean, I know you can eat insects, but my uncle and I never. Just gross. Do you eat butterflies, too?" Kirwyn asked, as we descended further into the valley.

"Of course not. The nutritional value is in the larval stage. Athletes fill up on dozens of them before the Solstice Games."

"What else do you eat?"

I thought about it. "Mmm, well, fish, mostly. Mollusks, too. Lots of fruit. Dinbirds. Thumperfeet and goat breed quickly, so we often feast on their meat. Except a lot of goats have been dying lately, and we can't risk eating those."

"Why have the goats died?" Kirwyn asked. "What's a thumperfeet? What's a dinbird?"

"Well, um, you know. Thumperfeet." I moved my right foot up and down rapidly against the ground and used my fingers to make ears above my head.

"Oh, rabbit!" Kirwyn chuckled. "Yeah, I guess that makes sense."

"And a dinbird is, you know, those birds you see around the shore?"

"The gray and white ones?"

"Yes. They can be annoying, pestering people even. And they're rather dim-witted creatures."

"Yet anything that flies can shit on the rest of us," Kiwyn remarked, wryly.

"As for the goats dying... we don't know. It's an illness we've never seen before."

As soon as I said it, I wondered if their deaths had

something to do with the old priest being land-buried. Did the Mystics blame the mysterious illness on him? I'd heard stories that had happened once, long ago, when crops failed and the High Mystic died around the same time. A council of royals and Mystics decided he was to blame for the poor harvest and damned his soul to the dirt.

I walked ahead, but the ground became pebbly and loose on the downward slope of the valley. I was always better in sea than on land. My foot slid on the rocks, and I started to fall.

Instinctively, Kirwyn reached his hand out to me.

Instinctively, I didn't take it.

"*Landdammit,*" I cursed, having tried to brace myself and gaining only pain shooting through my pot-marked hands. Stupid rocks.

Kirwyn looked down and shrugged. "I tried to catch you."

Ignoring him, I picked myself up and continued toward the beach. I might have let a few branches I pushed aside whack Kirwyn in the face, behind me. Accidentally.

After a few minutes, the trees thinned and I could see the crystalline waters ahead. As always, they beckoned with a dance of sparkles. Especially inviting after sweating through the valley.

I plopped down where the dirt met the sand, not daring to go too far out. The tide had washed ashore a large amount of seaweed; there must have been a storm at sea last night. That meant that this beach, already plagued, would have even more sand fleas than usual. But it also made it a safe choice.

Kirwyn sat beside me, grinning from goofy, pointed ear, to goofy, pointed ear.

"So," he began. "You'll have to excuse me, but I haven't

met many princesses in my time, outside of fairy-tale books. And they're certainly not like you. They don't eat bugs, for starters. And they don't... they don't entirely look like you. They're usually waifish and helpless and not crushing any competition in long-distance swims."

I frowned. A waif wouldn't make a good fishwife, let alone a braenese.

"Then they don't sound like very good princesses. In your book version."

"Not that I mind," Kirwyn amended. "I rather like your version." Then he *winked,* and the strangest tingle began in my stomach and seemed to shoot up through my chest.

"But what's the deal with the no touching?" he asked. "Is it a royal thing or just a princess thing?"

"It's a me thing," I sighed. I wanted to explain that I was thrilled for my destiny, I just hated the way it isolated me. But I could never be so honest with a stranger and a liar.

I cut to the facts. "No one can touch me because I'm fated to marry Keroe."

Kirwyn stared at me, unblinking. "Your God? You're... going to marry a God? Uh, how are you going to do that, exactly?"

"During the next Hidden Moon. I mean, he's not at the ceremony, of course. But he's out there, watching, in the God Sea, the Blue Beyond. No one is allowed to go there, but me. That night, Nasero and I - he's the High Mystic - will ride out to sea, but only I can cross the threshold. Nasero will return, and I'll make the journey alone."

Kirwyn frowned as I spoke, remaining quiet for several seconds after I finished. If he wanted to say something snarky, he held back.

"So... if this Mystic comes out with you, but you take the last part alone... are you swimming? Does he have a boat tied to yours?" he asked. "I mean, how do you go alone, if you're in the boat together?"

Oh. I wasn't sure I knew.

"Um…"

Maybe I misunderstood my mother? I would have to ask her the details later.

"Wait a minute!" Kirwyn exclaimed, holding up his hands in a "stop" position. Suddenly, he looked like he was going to burst with laughter and could barely get out his next words.

"You said you thought *I* was Keroe when we first met. I mean, that's why you saved me, right? So you thought *I* was your husband?"

He belly-laughed, head thrown back in glee.

Utter mortification seized me. I knew my face turned the purple-red of a star apple. It spread, and even my scalp was hot. My whole head felt like an apple, and I wanted to pluck it right off my body and hide it in the forest undergrowth.

I realized I'd squeezed my eyes shut, but I was smiling a painfully embarrassed smile. With great reluctance, I opened my eyes.

Kirwyn stood, wiping his strange trousers with a flourish. He turned side-to-side, then posed, hands on hips, head pointed to the sky, like a garden statue.

"How do I look, braenese? Am I everything you ever imagined your God-husband to be? Do we raise… what are they called? Little baby godlets together?"

If I had something within reach to throw, I would have. My hands itched to pluck *his* head off his body and drop kick it into the forest. I allowed myself a second to appreciate the fantasy.

Without thinking, I hurled words instead.

"Your ears stick out like sapotes. If I married you and had your children, I don't see how I could possibly birth them. With ears like that, they'd rip me in two."

What?

Oh, god.

Why did I say that?

It was out of my mouth before I realized the image it provided him.

Kirwyn halted, mouth agape. Then the corners of his lips pulled up in a smile and he let out an appreciative chuckle.

"Wow. Do they teach princesses to talk like that in royal princess school?"

With a groan, I dropped my head into my hands, covering my eyes. *Inconceivable.* I had made it *worse.*

"No, I'm glad." Kirwyn continued to chuckle. "Don't think princesses in story books have much of a survival rate where I come from. I like your braenese version better. You're... fiery."

I was stunned. That made two compliments today. Not that I was counting.

"Only royals are allowed on this side of the island, right?"

The question pulled me out of my thoughts. Kirwyn, now still, stared at a spot over my shoulder.

"Yes. Why?"

"And you said the guards don't come here?"

"Not without good reason," I replied. "In fact, they've been bulking up on the borderline lately. Some kind of training. Why?"

He walked past me. Knelt in the dirt.

"Because there are footprints here. And they're fresh."

CHAPTER 16

Gullbumps prickled all over my skin. I slouched, trying to shrink into myself. Quickly, I glanced over both shoulders, suddenly afraid that someone could spot us at any minute. I cursed myself for being so careless.

"Well, that's... that's not usual," I hedged, trying to calm myself more than Kirwyn. "But there's nothing really to keep the guards or other members of our family from coming here, if they want to." I chewed my lip. "We should head back to the cave to be safe."

For once, Kirwyn didn't argue. Without speaking, we made our way back up the valley and into the scorching afternoon sun. This time, we stepped quietly, carefully ducking below branches and straddling rocks on our way uphill. My ears strained to hear any human sound around us and my heart raced with every natural noise the forest made. The journey took twice as long, causing me to be later than I liked.

As soon as the vines closed behind us, secreting us in

the cool, dark, cave, Kirwyn broke the silence by throwing rapid questions at me.

About the footprints.

The guards' schedules.

Access to the royal tip of the island.

But puzzling over the questions wouldn't bring me to answers I didn't have, and the sun gave warning with its low angle. Not only would my mother expect me at night's feast, I needed time to find out if any more sharks were spotted. Fishing boats had been permitted to work with the rise of dawn, but two days remained on the swim ban.

"Maybe a guard had taken a stroll after duty," I reasoned. It wasn't explicitly forbidden. Just unlucky.

But I couldn't stay to debate.

Late the night before, Mazriah had trouble sleeping and busied herself by making a marmalade of sour oranges, as well as a lathering soap from the leftover fruit and leaves. I had borrowed some of each to give to Kirwyn so that he could eat and wash up. I also brought him a chewstick twig for a toothbrush. The end became frothy when gnawed, cleaning the teeth, but he crooked an eyebrow when I presented it to him -- he wasn't at all familiar with the simple concept. I made a mental note to add a powdered toothpaste, made from dried stems of the same tree, for next time. Additionally, I left Kirwyn a night's feast of coconuts, unleavened cassava bread and salt-cured mackerel.

Lastly, and with hesitation, I gave him the final item I'd brought.

Kirwyn let out a low whistle as he surveyed the supplies. "Thank you. No one's ever given me anything like this before. Except my uncle."

"You're welcome. In return, maybe soon you'll tell me

the truth about where you come from." Before he could protest, I cut him off, "And remember your vow not to try to kill me."

I spun on my heel and turned to leave.

"It was me," Kirwyn suddenly whispered.

I turned back, tense. "What?"

He reached around, rubbing the back of his neck. "The other band of travelers would have passed my family the night my parents died. They'd still be alive. But I began to cry in my mother's arms. They heard me. Turned back. It was my cries that killed my parents."

The air felt heavy around us. Why had he suddenly confessed a private event to me? To make me believe his stories? To make me feel sorry for him?

"It's... not your fault," I said, cautiously. "You were just a baby."

Kirwyn lifted one shoulder in a half-shrug. "That's what my uncle says. I reckon he regretted ever telling me the story."

I shifted my weight, unsure what to say, toying with the vines that hung beside me.

"It's not your fault," I repeated.

It must have been the wrong words. Kirwyn shook his head, like he was shaking something off.

"I know," he said coolly, busying himself with organizing the provisions I'd left. He nodded his head in the direction of the forest.

"You better get going. It won't do for a princess to be late to supper."

～

ALONE, I walked the easy path through the forest and back to the palace, my guard still raised as I listened for any human footsteps around me.

Having provided his hidden dwelling, meals, and grooming utensils, I almost felt like Kirwyn was a sort of secret pet I kept.

Well, maybe more of a feral pet.

That could turn on me at any second.

Maybe I shouldn't have given him that scraping knife for his beard.

"Mother?" I called, passing through the front courtyard and into the palace.

"She's in the temple, braenese," a tall, long-nosed guard replied, breaking his stiff stance to bow.

"Thanks," I murmured, and ambled down the path, a ten-minute walk to the Hall of the Mystics.

Afternoon services were over by now and the temple should be empty. Only the very devout attended prayers daily, and usually only selected one of the two services. Typically, they were the elderly villagers, who weren't occupied with fishing, deep diving, or other work at that time. Sunday Services were a livelier event, though I hadn't regularly attended since my schooling ended. I worshipped Keroe in my own way, I didn't need to hear the priests drone on about it.

And to be honest, sometimes I even slept past the morning bells.

On those Sundays I couldn't escape, I joined the crowds spilling out the doors of the Hall, forcing latecomers to find seats on the grass or under the forest canopy. Freshly-picked sugar apples were brought in from the royal orchards, and one of the gardeners distributed the treats to the children. You could hear the Mystics chant-sing as far as the palace, depending on the wind. I had to admit, when the music swelled and everyone joined in familiar hymns, even I found that part entrancing. Plans had begun to expand the hall, after the wedding.

Not that I would be around to see it.

Nearing the building, I sniffed the air. I could smell incense wafting from within, a mixture of Old World Frankincense and Santo oil, woodsy and slightly sour. It had seeped into the stone walls and wooden benches, giving the room an earthy smell, even when it wasn't burning.

As expected, the temple was empty. Without hundreds of bodies pressed inside, creating heat, the stone walls of the shaded structure kept a slight chill in the air.

Searching for my mother, I passed the dark rows of backless wooden benches, then the dais with the enormous carving depicting an image of Keroe blowing sea foam into human forms. I popped out the small door behind the altar and headed for the cloisters where the Mystics lived, ate, and slept. One dozen or so thatched cottages, each nestled into a small nook off the path, made up the pious village.

Hearing voices to my left, I walked toward the High Mystic's dwelling, the largest of all.

The door was open.

Pentyr, the handsome, young Mystic, stood before Nasero's writing desk.

As I appeared in the doorway, both men *abruptly* stopped talking, eyes shifting in my direction.

If they had continued speaking, I would never have noticed anything amiss.

But the guarded look on their faces signaled an alarm in my brain, and the sudden silence that followed, pricked my ears.

For a split second, no one said anything.

I looked from Nasero to Pentyr.

Nasero caught the mistake, smiling too brightly. It didn't touch his eyes, which almost looked sad.

"Ah, Braenese Zaria. What brings you to temple? Afternoon services are long over, though I don't recall your attendance ever before."

Chastised, I blushed and looked down. My eyes fell upon a row of reed pens on Nasero's desk. A scrap of parchment next to them caught my attention, which I could barely make out from across the room.

Nasero quickly shuffled the parchment so that the piece on top was moved below.

"I was looking for my mother," I said, feeling uneasy.

"You just missed her. I imagine she's back at the palace by now."

It was a gentle dismissal. Pentyr, usually bubbling with more cockiness than was good for him, looked at the wall, away from my eyes.

"Okay. Thank you." I took a step backward, eager to escape the tension. "Bye," I mumbled, scurrying away.

I had heard something I shouldn't.

And I wouldn't have even known it if they hadn't stopped speaking so abruptly. Looked guilty. Looked as if they had been caught.

But what did the words mean?

They were written on the scrap of parchment, too, the one Nasero tried to cover up. I had seen it before he had time.

What did the words mean?

I turned them over in my head.

Daughter of Elowa.

Who was Elowa?

CHAPTER 17

I had no opportunity to ask my mother if she knew any more about the sharks, let alone a woman named Elowa. The High Braenese never made it to night's feast; she never even made it downstairs. The baby caused a nerve pain in her back and the healer immediately recommended bed rest. Although she'd had three successful pregnancies before, the chances of a stillborn or of dying in childbirth always lurked nearby, like a Black Titan hiding in the rocks, ready to strike without warning. No one wanted another tragedy like grandmother.

Over floating bowls of fried conch and green figs, the question of Elowa danced on the tip of my tongue, but every time I opened my mouth to ask my father, I closed it before I got the words out.

Preoccupied with the well-being of my mother, he was even more taciturn around me than usual. A quiet supper passed where my thoughts alternated between wondering what Kirwyn was up to in the cave, and the mysterious woman named Elowa.

Perhaps I wouldn't ask Mother, I thought. She already had

enough to worry about. But I would definitely bring it up to the smartest person I knew.

Tomé.

"Have there been any more sharks sighted?" I asked my father, breaking the silence over a dessert of sea grapes, rolled in a sticky paste and coated with cane sugar.

"Not a one," my father replied with confidence.

Silence descended once more.

"Will the swim ban be lifted?" I asked.

"I'm sure of it," he said.

I rolled a grape around my tongue, trying to decide if I would feel safe entering the water again in two days.

Keroe would protect me, though. *Wouldn't he?* Two more pageants to go and we'd be wed.

I excused myself from night's feast as father and Jona splashed their hands together in the water.

Despite crawling into bed early, I had a fitful night's sleep.

Bing, bong, bing, bong.

The melody of the bells woke me the next morning and I immediately shimmied into my tunic and headed down the stairs. I stopped only to check in with my father about my mother's condition. He said she'd improved but was continuing to rest for the day.

Under a cool and cloudy sky, I headed straight for the library, eager to explore the scrolls for mention of Elowa.

Surely, she'd be in the Book of Records. Everyone who ever lived went into that book, all the way back to Milton, the first of the new men Keroe created.

It was a quick walk to the library -- a small, Old World

building of concrete, nestled against a hill in the pious grounds of the Mystics. I pushed the thick door ajar and slid into the dim chamber. Direct sunlight hurt the preservation of the scrolls, and especially the Old World books. As did too much handling.

Of course, my family had unrestrained access, but I didn't come here often anymore. Of the one hundred or so scrolls, most were formulas for building, records of harvests, psalms, psalms and more psalms. I'd heard those every week in Sunday school. Besides, I preferred the Story Gathering, where fresh tales were told around a fire at night, over the handful of Old World fairy-tale books I'd committed to memory long ago.

As I stepped into the small room, my eyes immediately settled on the lone figure sitting on a bench with a long braid falling down her back.

Lida.

I frowned and folded my arms. How much permission had *she* been granted?

Hearing the door open, Lida turned around to look at me. Slowly, almost bored, she turned back to the book lying open before her.

"Braenese Zaria," she said, still looking at the book.

I felt a prickle of irritation, like the bites of sand fleas. It wasn't unlawful to not bow before royalty, but it was just something that was *done.* Out of respect. Maybe not for a Mystic or Fire Maiden, but certainly for a commoner. At the very least, polite people acknowledged one another face-to-face and feigned friendly greetings.

What was her problem with me, anyway?

"Lida," I replied in the same, even tone.

"I was just leaving," she said. But she made no move to go. Instead, she lazily turned the page on her book, finished the chapter, and closed the Old World fairy tale with a sigh. Finally, she rose and strode toward the door. But when she was about two feet from where I was standing, she stopped. It was as if she changed her mind, couldn't hold something back.

"I'm surprised to see you in here," she said, flipping her braid behind her shoulder. "Shouldn't you be frolicking in the forest, like a braenese is suited to do?"

Okay, that was *definitely* meant to be rude. A spark of fire flared inside me. It wasn't her words, as much as her tone. But what could I *do*, exactly? Report her for improper tone? It would sound childish, weak. I could handle my own battles.

I drew myself stiff and tall, like my mother. I was taller than Lida anyway, if only by an inch.

"I'm surprised to see *you* in here," I retorted, holding contact with her deep brown eyes. "Shouldn't you be gutting fish, or whatever it is a commoner is suited to do?"

Lida's face flushed and I knew I struck a nerve. I brushed past her and, with my head high, I carried myself over to the shelves of parchment which I pretended to examine, hoping she'd just leave.

But she didn't.

"You have to forgive me," Lida said, her voice dripping like sticky sweet honey. "It's just that you showed such little interest in the scrolls before, I didn't even know you could read."

My mouth fell. *What was her* problem *with me?*

The flames inside me raged into a wildfire and I know she saw her success in provoking me when I turned around, eyes wide.

I instantly regretted letting her read my fury. Lida smiled a tight, bitchy little grin. Her smirk fanned the wildfire throughout my body, but I forced my own face to relax.

"You have to forgive *me*. I didn't know you were capable of such a shit-eating little grin -" I waved my hand toward her mouth, "but of course it makes sense, for a person familiar with the job of digging latrines."

It was both an insult and a threat, of sorts. Latrine duty rotated throughout the villagers, but I could get her assigned to it more regularly if I chose.

Well, maybe not. But she didn't know that.

"I bet you go running to the High Braenese for everything." Lida hissed the word *braenese*.

Then her tone changed. Her eyebrows raised.

She looked me right in the eyes and said evenly, slowly, "Oh, wait. I bet you *don't*."

Coquina clams ran up my spine. There was something about the way she said it that made me queasy.

What did she know? It was a threat. *Wasn't it?*

Lida turned without another word, her thick, long braid swishing. She opened and closed the library door, leaving me staring.

I stood there for a few seconds, mouth agape, before I came to my senses.

Don't think about it now, I scolded myself. *Don't even think about Kirwyn right now. Forget her. Focus on finding Elowa.*

I grabbed the Book of Records, plopped onto the bench, and forced myself to concentrate.

But after one hour and one sore back, I couldn't find Elowa's name on the pages of parchment that made up the recording.

I put it away and brought down several Palm books, fanning out the long, narrow pages of dried leaf, to see if any recent accounts of harvests, disputes, or transfers of goods and services mentioned her name.

But two hours later, I pushed them all aside and rubbed my temples in frustration from a morning wasted, staring at boring ledgers.

The fact that Nasero clearly wanted Elowa and her daughter hidden intrigued me. Not being able to find her existence in the Book of Records, or any parchment for that matter, *really* got me fixated. I had a feeling about Elowa I couldn't shake, again that uneasy nudge at the back of my mind.

She couldn't be in our family. I knew all my relatives, and royal daughters were so often physical copies of their mothers, parentage was obvious from birth. I myself was a miniature version of my mother's broad shoulders, her wide-set eyes, and her soft, round face.

Elowa also couldn't be with the Fire Maidens. While I didn't know their inner workings, I knew which unmarried women were selected from the village to join them.

So who was she? And who was her daughter? Were they still alive?

I shook my head, disappointed.

At least I can see Kirwyn now. One upping him in a debate about land and getting closer to his truth might raise my spirits.

I left the dim library and reemerged into bright sunlight. By now it was late morning and the clouds had passed. Another scorching day ahead.

"Running off for a swim around the island again?" Tomé taunted, causing me to jump before I even turned around.

I smiled nervously. "Maybe. Coming to read some boring manual for hours on end?"

"Definitely," he teased in a husky voice, an octave lower than usual.

I rolled my eyes and moved to pass him, but he held up a hand to stop me. In the other rested a thin sugarcane, for chewing.

"Zaria," Tomé said. "In all seriousness, I wanted to read about some ancient herbs and tinctures. Marcin has a cousin who feeds the goats. He says the goats aren't dying of a disease. He thinks they're being poisoned."

I shook my head vigorously. "No. That can't be. Who would do that?"

Our food supply was always kept in careful balance. To threaten that was to threaten *everyone*.

"And besides," I added, "only a few goats have died since we moved the pasture."

"I know. Whoever is doing it – if someone is doing it – seems not to be able to get near the palace very easily."

I searched Tomé's bright blue eyes. His playful nature reminded me of Kirwyn's, but the similarity ended there. Nothing dark lurked underneath, his open face reflected his open heart. Along with the shark, this was only the second time in *years* I'd seen him anything but carefree.

Cautiously, I asked, "What do you think is going on?"

Tomé cocked his head, a bird-like movement on his long neck. "Something is off. I don't know what exactly, but there are things, Zaria... that just don't add up..."

It was like cold water flooded my gut. At that moment he sounded *exactly* like Kirwyn.

As usual, my face must have shown my feelings because Tomé quickly said, "But don't worry." He smiled that big grin that lit up his face like the sun. "Nothing to jeopardize your wedding."

Tomé waved his hand, dismissively. "It's probably environmental factors, or the hay. In fact, I'll probably be waist-deep examining goat manure, while you're making passionate love to the Sea God in a bed of undulating kelp, voyeuristic fish swimming circles above."

Tomé moved his body, acting out the love-making scene, and I snorted a laugh.

"Do spare a thought for your odorous cousin, oh great Sea Queen. Perhaps you can whisper in the Sea God's ear and send a lover my way, too. After I get cleaned up, of course."

I nodded, still grinning. "One lover. Coming right up. At least, I promise I'll do my best."

I started to leave and then remembered why I came to the library in the first place.

"Tomé?" I asked, hesitantly, turning back. "Do you know who the daughter of Elowa is?"

He shook his head, biting down on the sugarcane. "Nope. Who's that?"

I shrugged. "Do you think, if you happen to find anything in your research that mentions her name, could you let me know? But... don't tell anyone, okay?"

Tomé bowed formally, in the manner of the Steel Guard. "A secret mission from the braenese. I accept."

He slipped into the library and I headed toward the royal forest. Once under the cover of trees, I began jogging.

Not because I was eager to see Kirwyn, of course.

Well, I was, but not *because* of him. Only because I wanted to learn the truth *from* him.

An important distinction.

CHAPTER 18

Landdammit.

Kirwyn's curious lips were the problem. And his strange-but-attractive features.

Elowa's name haunted me through the hot afternoon, but I couldn't focus on *that* mystery, with *this* one before me.

We'd settled by a softly babbling stream, running a few hundred feet ahead into the ocean. We lingered close to the cave, for safety. If the wind blew right, I could almost smell the frangipani that grew by my hiding space. Cupping our hands, we drank from the freshwater stream.

After my trip to the library, I had spent the rest of the morning telling Kirwyn about my family. The loss of my aunt, Braenese Enith, along with her husband, in their boating accident when I was only a few months old. I told him of Queen Alette, the chosen braenese of the last generation, right now waiting for me to join her under the sea.

Kirwyn spent the hours lying in return.

I couldn't get him to waver from his tale no matter how

we argued. He made me want to pull at my hair and scream.

My gaze fell upon his sculpted mouth as he wiped the last droplets of water from his lips.

He made me want to use my tongue in other ways too.

I began braiding my hair away from my face, for something to do.

Kirwyn cocked his head, listening to the call of parrots and dinbirds flying above.

"It's such a surreal paradise here." He swept his gaze to the bend in the stream ahead, where the breeze blew leafy branches of low trees down to kiss the water, and then set them dancing back up in the air. "Where beautiful princesses rescue you and feed you fresh coconuts on unspoilt beaches."

He called me beautiful.

That was *definitely* a compliment.

I played with the hem of my tunic. Should I thank him? Return the compliment? I folded my legs under me, debating.

"I admit, I'm enchanted by this turquoise sea, these myths you insist upon, this world your people have created here. I almost believe *I'm* the crazy one, that I hit my head and made up that whole ugly world out there."

Kirwyn's expression changed and he shook his head, angrily. "If, you know, I didn't suspect this is all an evil lie or sick experiment. It's weird. How'd you get here? Have generations of inbreeding narrowed the gene pool? Why don't you know about the rest of the world?"

His eyes flashed as he continued, "This is an illusion, a lie. Because there *is* a world out there. You've got to believe me. There is no Sea God controlling your fate. Your land isn't the only land. It's chaos in much of the real world.

Somehow... somehow your people are protected. You've been able to build this society here, away from the wars."

He shook his head again, in frustration. "Someone is lying to you."

"Let's say for a minute you were right," I replied, eager to counter his argument. "Let's say there's something beyond the island. That doesn't mean that there is no Sea God. It just proves that our island is blessed. Keroe would protect us from anything bad out there. From these other boats finding us."

"I can't win with you!" Kirwyn exclaimed. "No matter what I say, you'll just say that Keroe did it." He shot to his feet and smacked his face. "Where do you think this came from?" He lifted his shirt with the strange fasteners, then pulled at his pants, *"and this?"*

"I... don't know." While his skin had begun to tan in the past few days, I couldn't explain his strange features or his funny clothing. "But I will find out. Just because I don't have an answer doesn't mean I'll believe yours."

Kirwyn's chest rose and fell in a heavy sigh. "That's... wise. But can't you see that's what you're already doing? Maybe it's these Mystics, whoever they are. You're believing their lies."

He ran his fingers through his hair, smoothing it back into place. "OK. Let me back up and start from the beginning."

I tilted my head down and stared up, ready to listen closely, to catch him in an inconsistency.

Kirwyn sat down once more, stretched his long, lean legs in front, and rested his elbows on his knees. He didn't seem to notice that he sat two feet closer than before.

"Many years ago, the clans formed. Hundreds of years?

Don't know. There's not an accurate history. I guess it got too difficult to record when everything was changing so fast, falling apart. And those recording anything tend to be those in power, so who can rely on what they say?"

"As the world changed, cities fell to anarchy and looters swooped in. Eventually, production and distribution ceased, money lost its value, and fighting very quickly turned from stolen jewels and technology to water, food, and medicine. That's when the clans began."

"Everyone belongs to a clan now. That's what the mark on your back indicates -- who your people are. Who you fight for. If you're caught by an opposing clan you might be killed, or you might be ransomed. But no mark, no protection. You'll most likely wind up a slave. Death is preferable."

"But you don't have a mark," I pointed out.

Kirwyn nodded. "I'm a freeborn. My parents, my uncle. We belong to no one. And we were going to get out, if only that ship hadn't gone down. Things have begun to change in the Southern Continent, we hear. More space, more democracy. Less people, less fighting. You can make a life there, a safer one."

Kirwyn looked down. "By now my uncle must think me dead." His shoulders slumped, and his defeated posture almost made me want to reach out and put my arm around him.

"What are these marks?" I asked, changing the subject.

"Oh, um, there are countless. Here," he reached around and patted the upper right area of his back. "You wear your allegiance with a tattoo here -"

"*Shh!*" I whispered, cutting him off.

I'd heard a rustle to my left, about twenty yards over.

Kirwyn didn't move a muscle.

I looked only with my eyes, keeping my head straight forward. I couldn't see anything moving amongst the multihued greens of the trees. Slowly, I let my eyes rove from the ferns below to the canopy of palm leaves, but everything was still, everything belonged.

Had a guard come into the forest?

There were no posts this deep. Kirwyn and I both cocked our heads slightly, listening for another sound. I mentally kicked myself for becoming so bold. We should have stayed hidden in the cave. They'd kill Kirwyn.

There!

The rustle came again, further away, but louder. It didn't sound like a small animal, it sounded heavier, though not quite boar-like. Human.

Kirwyn sprang to his feet, pulling the beard-scraping knife from his pocket in one fluid motion. He spread his left arm in front of me, protectively, keeping me behind him while the other brandished the knife.

Unbelievable.

He was the one they'd kill and he was trying to protect *me?*

Bewildered, I stood up behind him, ears straining, ready to run. A full minute passed as we waited, muscles tensed to bolt.

Silence.

The scuffling noise didn't return. It was as if it had disappeared into thin air.

Kirwyn looked back at me, brow furrowed, and I shook my head. I didn't understand it either.

Unmoving, we waited another minute, but the noise was gone. Slowly, Kirwyn's shoulders relaxed, but his eyes continued to scan the trees in all directions.

Cave, I mouthed, when he looked at me again. He nodded, and spread his arm in front, indicating I should lead the way.

We walked as quietly as we could through the thick undergrowth, cringing at every pebble rolling beneath our steps, pulse racing at the soft *whoosh* from branches moved to make passage. We took a circuitous path, stopping to listen every few hundred feet, looking over our shoulders, and twice doubling-back to throw anyone off our trail.

It was all unnecessary.

No one followed.

The further we walked, the more I realized that whatever we heard, it couldn't have been human. The most likely explanation was that an animal had gone into a hole, its underground home, and my imagination had made a bigger deal of it than it was.

Pausing to check over my shoulder one last time as we crossed beneath the frangipani trees, I satisfied myself that no one was nearby, and we ducked inside the cave.

"What did you hear?" Kirwyn's voice was a sharp whisper. He stood so close to me I caught his masculine scent.

"I – I don't know. It sounded too loud to be animal, but it must have been, the way it disappeared entirely. Perhaps a boar hiding, or something burrowing underground... maybe it was more scared of us than we were of it."

Kirwyn narrowed his eyes. "It sounded like human feet, but you're right. There was a shuffling and then... gone."

"Can we talk about something else? This is giving me the creeps." I had an eerie feeling, similar to when I awoke from one of my night-dreams. "Let's just... stay here. And you can finish telling me your story."

"Alright..." Kirwyn agreed, reluctantly. "Where was I?"

He plopped down on the Old World rug and I joined him. "Oh, right. The clans."

"The Blackjacks are the biggest. They've got a tattoo of a spade on their backs, from the card deck. They control the largest city in the Eastern midlands, Spade City, and it's got electric power. You're set for life, as long as you're born there, an original. Everyone they've conquered is a slave, and they've a lot of slave labor to keep things running. If they catch you, if any clan makes a slave of you, they tattoo over your symbol. Not just over, they cover your back with an X, with a smaller branding of their symbol above. You're forever marked. Even if you escape, you better not get caught. If you're found, you'll be tortured. If another clan finds you, most like as not, they'll trade or sell you to back to where you escaped from, and you'll be tortured upon your return."

I shuddered. I could see why Kirwyn wanted to leave such a place.

Not that I believed him.

"There's Copperheads," Kirwyn continued, "With snake tattoos on their backs. Fewer in number, but not one whit less deadly. They take their name from the snake near their wooded river, south of Spade City. You don't even want to cross there – you'll never see 'em coming. They hide in the trees and hunt with poison-tipped darts.

Between the library where I grew up and Fort Cuttle, my uncle and I had to pass through Biohazard territory."

Kirwyn let out a low whistle. "People mostly leave them alone. They took up residence in an old radioactive plant, so no one wants to go anywhere *near* it. Life is dangerous for anyone, but..." he shifted uncomfortably, not meeting my eyes, "more so for women. The Biohazards learned this a long time ago. Their clan is *only* women. I've never seen one, but I've heard stories. They say they have eyes of every color, from the radioactive waste. Red, yellow, even black. Not sure I believe that, but I don't want to get close enough to find out. They capture men and... well, I don't know what they do to them," he paused, shaking his head for emphasis, "but they're never seen again."

There were so many words Kirwyn said that didn't make sense. *Electricity. Spades. City. Copperhead. Radioactive. Biohazard.* My head was dizzy, swimming in circles and pulled downward as if caught in a tidal pool. Too many words to address. How did he make up all this stuff? He'd be the star of Story Gathering, if he were able to tell a tale around the fire one night.

Seizing upon the only information I could readily grasp, I asked, "What do *you* think happens when a Biohazard catches a man?"

"Like I said, I don't ever want to find out. It's best to steer clear of their territory. Although you," he looked me up and down, "they might assimilate. You're strong enough. At least physically."

I frowned at his compliment, wrapped in an insult.

"Me? Probably slit my throat before I could blink."

A silence descended between us and I realized that aside from when we'd heard the noise, we'd been talking non-stop all day. I'd never met a boy who talked as much as Kirwyn. Not that I'd been around a lot of boys, outside of Tomé.

I switched my focus to the table of Old World objects along the cave wall. My gaze fell upon the shiny token, whose markings had rubbed off long ago, and I got up to examine it, thinking I might ask Kirwyn if he knew more about the coin.

Kirwyn rose as well, walking to the back of the cave and scooping a mouthful of fresh water from the drip.

I tensed, hoping my silver egg remained well-hidden under the rocks. As a present I was giving myself for my wedding day, I didn't want to share it with him, and I silently cursed myself for not taking it out of the cave before he woke up. But then, I didn't expect him to be staying.

The air was cooler in the cavern, but still humid, and Kirwyn waved the bottom of his shirt in and out, trying to create a breeze. His clothes weren't made correctly, I realized. They were too heavy for the heat, and the past few days had been unusually dry. By this late in the hot season, we ordinarily received frequent afternoon rains.

With each pull of his shirt, Kirwyn revealed a section of his smooth, muscled torso underneath.

I didn't realize I was staring until he caught me.

I quickly averted my gaze, feeling my cheeks grow hot. I knew he saw something in my stupid face that showed everything.

But I didn't know what could have caused the change. Something in the air shifted, something darkened, and I didn't understand what I had just done that made it so.

"What's the tunnel behind this boulder?" Kirwyn asked, pointing at the heavy, rough stone. His tone was off, almost flippant, and I was now *sure* something changed.

"Oh, that." I suppressed a shudder. "I don't like tight spaces. Hate them, actually. I don't know where it leads and I don't care. I sealed it up with that rock years ago."

Kirwyn gave a wry smile. "You must really hate tight spaces if it curbed *your* curiosity. I'd want to find out where it goes."

"Be my guest," I said, waving my hand. "In fact, I'm surprised you haven't already."

Kirwyn flashed his devil-may-care grin. "Maybe I have."

Cocky. I huffed, refusing to be baited. *Why was he suddenly being antagonistic again?* He wanted me to ask, to find out if he really crawled through there, and what he might have seen inside.

I folded my arms across my chest, refusing to ask, to be provoked.

Even though I *was* dying to know where it led.

He was probably lying. He lied about so much else and I could barely fit into the tunnel. How could he?

Kirwyn began pacing the rug.

"So. When does your wedding take place?"

My mouth fell. I wasn't expecting that question out of the blue. Why did he care? And why did he suddenly seem... kind of hostile?

"Twenty-six days, counting today," I said automatically, and a bit wistfully.

"Mmm..." Kirwyn mused. "And you'll be the blushing bride, I suppose. You know, men prefer an experienced woman, someone who knows what they're doing... And a god? Well. I'm sure he has high expectations. You don't want to let down a deity."

Kirwyn stroked his chin in mock thought as he paced. "I'll tell you what, princess. I'm feeling charitable today."

His voice became sultry as he squared himself above me. "Let's reenact the day we met. You can lower your dress, and I'll teach you a few things to impress a god."

What? Why was he being an ass all of a sudden?

I shot to my feet, blood boiling.

Before I could form a retort, one side of Kirwyn's mouth curled into grin. "I bet you want to smack me now, don't you?"

His smug face was well within reach of my hand. My palms tingled.

"But you can't touch me," he concluded.

Infuriated, I turned on my heel and stomped out of the cave, throwing aside the vines. I grunted loudly to a silent audience of frangipani trees.

Kirwyn's laugh, echoing from inside the cave, set my cheeks on fire once more.

Unable to stop my own feet, I threw aside the vines again, stalked back into the cavern, and stood toe-to-toe with Kirwyn.

"I'll make an exception," I declared, drawing back my hand and smacking him hard across his face.

I could barely make out, in the shadowy light of the cave, the mark of my hand. First white and then an angry red, as it splayed across his cheek.

Kirwyn's head hadn't done more than move a bit to the right, and his smirk told me he'd gotten exactly the reaction he wanted. I immediately regretted letting him get under my skin.

And then, I felt my skin tingle as the mood changed *again.*

Something alive, something hungry, sparked from Kirwyn's dark green stare. I heard his ragged breathing. Saw his arm muscles tense. It seemed...

No.

But yes, I thought wildly.

He was going to grab me and kiss me.

My heart pounded in my ears. I suddenly realized my posture, my body language, was *telling* him to touch me. I had leaned subtly forward, my chest arching out towards him, my lips parted. Ready.

Move back, I told myself.

But I was a prisoner of my body, caught like prey in the net of his gaze.

Our breath mingled. His woodsy scent filled my nostrils. I felt dizzy.

And then he...

Sat.

Abruptly.

Kirwyn folded his body and sat down on the rug at my feet. Suddenly leaving me towering above. Confused as possible. Staring at the wall behind where he once stood.

My jaw dropped. *What just happened? Was it all in my head?*

My god, I was just like every other crazed cuspate girl, adolescent urges raging, pushing us to act like idiots.

But.

Kirwyn wasn't any different.

Something had just happened between us. I felt it.

I looked down. He reclined back on his arms, looking as if he hadn't a care in the world.

Well then. Fine. I could play that game, too.

I couldn't read his thoughts *now,* but I knew what they were a few seconds ago.

I affected an air of nonchalance to match his. Actually, I truly *was* indifferent. Why would I want to kiss him anyway, when I had just slapped him? I must have had a temporary lapse of sanity, brought on by boiling anger. It was ridiculous to think that I, the destined Sea Queen, could be stirred by some discarded village boy to anything like desire. Nonsense. Preposterous.

And even if I was, I wouldn't let it happen again.

"On your wedding day, you're just going to go out there, sailing off alone into the horizon," Kirwyn said, mostly to himself.

Oh yeah. That's what we were talking about.

I nodded, making sure to beam proudly.

He didn't seem to notice. "So, what's out there, in your Blue Beyond? If you don't believe me that there's more land, what do you think is out there if you were to sail on and on? Tell me."

"I can do one better," I grinned. "I can show you."

CHAPTER 19

The next day I practically skipped like a schoolgirl, too happy to care. I had the map in hand and a sack full of fried plantains, crusty bread, and other provisions for Kirwyn.

I had twisted half my hair up and secured it with a pretty shell comb. As I left the palace, I sniffed the air, getting a nose full of goat manure. No beasts had died in the last few days and everyone seemed to be in a good mood with the illness passing, my mother in particular. I debated again asking her about Elowa, but the ache in her back healed, and she had hurried off to Sacred Beach - a small, blessed crescent of sand two leagues from the palace - to oversee a tribute to Keroe.

It was on Sacred Beach the Sea God had blown the foam that became the new humans, and on this beach we sailed boats laden with fruit, dried strips of wild boar, clayware, and other artisanal weavings and carvings, as offerings bound for the Blue Beyond. The next shipment was scheduled for the day after my next pageant, and it was particularly full of freshly picked almonds, pots of sour orange marmalade, and low-coral dwellers. Many of the sea urchins and abalone had been gathered by revered deep-divers of the village, capable of holding their breath longer than anyone else, for a special wedding tribute.

I could hold my breath with the best of them, but it wasn't fitting work for a braenese.

Lifting spirits further, no sharks were sighted and the swim restriction concluded. Everyone seemed to be in good humor. Me, especially.

Final measurements were taken to adjust my wedding dress – an Old World gown I was dying to see - and over night's feast, my mother, and even my father, drilled me on the lengthy vows. I tasted different desserts Mazriah baked, to select my preference for the wedding feast. The leading dish was a traditional cake of creamed cheese with a gooey passion fruit sauce on top that melted dreamily on my tongue.

I wish Kirwyn could see me in my dress, I thought, as I walked. *What would become of him when I left?*

A fish flopped in my stomach, but I pushed the thought away. I'd... consider it another day. Or perhaps... perhaps the Fire Maidens could help. Perhaps they had the answer. Perhaps Kirwyn and I could sneak out one night to find out.

I took a slightly different route each time I walked to the cave, not wanting to trample an obvious, well-worn path. Though it was unlikely anyone would bother trekking through the dense, royal forest, other than the creatures who lived there. My quick pace sent little green lizards scurrying from underfoot, climbing nearby trees for safety.

I arrived with a sheen of sweat, though Kirwyn leaned against the side of the cave entrance, looking cool, one leg folded in front of the other.

"What have you got there, princess?"

"You'll see," I grinned.

We sat on the worn, crimson rug, and shared a breakfast of two overripe and slightly mushy avocados I took from the kitchen, along with two boiled eggs. Kirwyn licked his fingers clean as we finished.

"I want to apologize for yesterday," he said, jarring me.

I stared. *Was he going to say it? Mention that he almost kissed me? It wasn't in my head, right?*

"I shouldn't have made those comments about your wedding night."

Oh. That.

I waved my hand, dismissively. "I haven't even thought about it."

It wasn't a lie, exactly. Like flying fish, images of what transpired yesterday kept breaking the surface, then diving back under the waves, to hide. Or maybe I shoved them back under the water. Same thing.

"Okay, show me," he said, nodding to my sack, green eyes dancing with anticipation.

I scooted closer and unfolded the map I borrowed from the library. *"See?"*

Kirwyn stared at the map a long time, expressionless.

It should have taken only a few seconds to see the endless waterfall to the west. The giant tidal pool to the south. The ferocious sea monster to the east and the infinite ice wall to the north.

Why wasn't he ashamed? I wondered, frowning. He didn't seem the least contrite. He looked disheartened, if anything.

When he finally looked up, I saw pity in his eyes.

"And everyone here has seen this map, believes this to be true?" he asked.

"It is!" I exclaimed. I wondered what it would take to

prove to him what the world looked like. Would we need to plummet off the boundless waterfall ourselves? Would he need to see the bodies that had washed ashore, shredded from the monster's claws? One terrifying look and every child had nightmares for life.

"Alright," he said. "I've seen enough to know how they keep you in."

Kirwyn leaned back, resting his weight on his hands. "What I can't figure is, how are they keeping others *out?*"

CHAPTER 20

Whenever I wasn't called for a wedding task, I slid into the forest to meet Kirwyn with enough food for a small breakfast, lunch, and his night's feast. I was always expected back at the palace at dusk.

The portions were meager, but the forest supplemented with freshly-fallen coconuts, or ripened sea grapes by the beach. Kirwyn gratefully ate everything I offered, except insects. I didn't know what he had against bugs in particular, but when he refused even a crunchy, smoked beetle kabob, I gave up and ate every last bite myself, licking the stick with exaggeration as Kirwyn scrunched his face in disgust.

As I began to relax a bit about getting caught, I became more worried about puzzling out the truth of Kirwyn before I left land for good. My best theory on his origins – that he was a strange, discarded village boy – had several holes. How did he get the Old World clothes? How had he remained hidden for so long?

My best plan to help his request – to sneak an old boat

onto the beach at night – also had several holes. It was unlikely I could bring one without being spotted. Even if I did, what was the point? Where would he go? Back to the land he wove stories about each day?

Tantalizing stories of magical inventions, impossible creatures, people crowding the ground in numbers never seen before.

I watched his sensuous lips as he spoke and after a few days, I had trouble telling if I was enraptured by the stories, or the man.

One especially humid afternoon, after several days passed without any unusual sounds or footprints, we dared a quick dip in the waters off Shady Beach. I was surprised to learn Kirwyn had never seen a conch before, when low-tide brought a few mollusks onto the sand. He spotted them scurrying with their funny hop-walk, and pointed, his face quizzical.

"Oh, those?" I said. "Well, we use them for everything, really. Sweet and Spicy Conch Stew is my favorite. All boats have an empty shell on board. You crack a hole in the top to make a horn. Fishermen blow each morning to signal their departure, and when they arrive at home at dusk, to signal their return. And the musicians use them for celebrations. There's a popular song I like-"

I began to hum the tune, but stopped, biting my lip. "I'm not a very good singer."

Kirwyn grinned. His white teeth stood out against his newly bronzed face. He had recently scraped his beard free of stubble with the knife I provided. His dark hair glistened blue-black when wet.

"Will you play one for me sometime?"

I shook my head. "I'm not musical. I never even learned how to blow one, to be honest. I'm much better at physical games, especially swimming. I can swim around the whole island," I said, aware that it sounded a little boastful. "And you? Are you a good singer?"

Kirwyn shrugged, ducking under the shade of a tree. Facing the ocean, he smoothed back his wet hair. He wore only the strange black trousers, rolled up at the legs. I watched the water drip from his bare chest onto the underbrush for a few seconds, before I caught what I was doing and focused on a very interesting leaf.

"Not really," he said. "I like reading, but I guess that's not much of a skill. Although – and don't take this the wrong way – growing up surrounded by books probably helped me to become good at deciphering what people really want... and good at persuading them to get what I want."

I tossed my hands into the air, exasperated. *Really? He just admitted a talent for deceit?*

"Come on!" Kirwyn laughed. "If I was lying to you about the world, would I admit what a good liar I am?"

"Yes. Maybe that's exactly what a liar would do. I wouldn't know. I don't lie."

"Except to your family," Kirwyn pointed out.

I lowered my gaze and Kirwyn said, "I'm sorry. I didn't mean... it's just, I'm not entirely sure why you're helping me. Believe me, I'm thankful. And I get the curiosity and you're rebellious, but, this... it seems like a big risk, considering the consequences. And the fact that your wedding is only a few weeks away."

I bit my lip harder as a heavy, sinking feeling pulled at the pit of my stomach. I *did* want to be a good bride for Keroe and to make my parents proud.

"It's not that I mean to lie to them, or to the priests," I said. "It's just that, I don't know... I was so bored growing up, so lonely. Everyone in the palace mostly ignored me, like I was already gone."

I heard a loud dinbird squawk, as if it called me a liar. "I don't know, maybe I was angry."

"You..." I wasn't sure how to explain the confusion churning inside me, it was like a disturbance on the seabed, and I couldn't see clearly through the cloud of sand swirling around.

"I really did think you were Keroe when you washed up on the beach. At least a part of me did... enough to make an excuse of it to myself, to touch you," I admitted.

The pesky dinbird cried again. Suddenly, the dam broke.

"I didn't make up these rules, you know! I want to marry Keroe, of course. But I don't understand why no man can ever touch me. I didn't decide that. It made everyone afraid of me. Rightly so, because if you knew what they do to any male who touches me..." I broke off, squeezing my eyes shut against the memory of that poor, young boy.

I shook my head to clear it, opened my eyes, and started again.

"It doesn't seem right that Keroe wouldn't allow even my father to hold me. I – I think the Mystics got that part wrong."

I averted my eyes, shamed to have said it aloud. "Maybe. Maybe because I want to believe that. Besides, you seemed... safe. Like, I could touch you and if anything happened, no one would ever believe you anyway."

"Gee, thanks." Kirwyn tossed his head back as he chuckled. "But why do you keep coming back to help me?"

I realized Kirwyn and I were only a foot apart. My whole body hummed, as the real reason I came danced at the edges of my mind. Saying it aloud was out of the question. I barely let the idea fully form privately, in my head. I tried banishing it beneath the waves, but it kept bobbing to the surface, buoyantly refusing to sink.

I want you to touch me.

I swear, like an animal, Kirwyn could tell, could smell it on me.

Which only made the heat inside me grow.

Without a word, that feeling permeated the air again between my eyes and his deep-forest-stare. *Landdammit,* those eyes could trap me like a little lost child in the wood. It was just like back in the cave, but without all the anger behind it.

Gullflesh broke out on my arms. The longing in his eyes was real, I was sure of it this time. The ache grew between us, around us, separating us from the outside world, wrapping us in a cocoon of yearning.

I remembered the steel grip of his hands on my wrists the day he attacked me, and I visibly gulped, picturing them upon my body again, holding my hands above my head, this time to kiss me...

Then darkness suddenly passed over Kirwyn's face.

"Zaria, I think something bad is going to happen to you," he said, slowly.

Just like that, the moment was gone. *Again.* Kirwyn still held my gaze, but the spell was broken.

"There's no sea god," he said. "I think those Mystics are going to hurt you. Or kill you. It sounds like something I read about in ancient times. Like a maiden sacrificed to the sea to appease an imagined god. There's a world out there. Really, I swear there is."

His eyes searched mine, pleading. "Let me take you with me. I can protect you there."

"I can protect you here," I countered.

"For how long?" Kirwyn asked. "Zaria, let's just say for a

minute there is a sea god. You don't marry someone you don't love-" Kirwyn spoke over me when he saw that I was going to argue, "-and you don't love someone you don't know. I don't blame you for being naïve. An entire world here seems created to perpetuate this lie they're selling you."

"My mother-"

"I think your mother is being lied to, as well. I think these Mystics are duping her and duping everyone else. That first priest you told me about? The one who didn't want you to get married? I think he was on your side. Maybe he was trying to save you."

"No! Stop it." I shot to my feet. "What you're saying is blasphemy and it's not true. I'm marrying Keroe. I *will* be the Sea Queen." My foot stomped. The old habit. "It's been done this way for hundreds of years. I won't listen to you. I won't come back if you keep talking like this."

No matter how infuriatingly cute you are when you smirk.

Kirwyn held his hands up, "Okay, okay, I'm sorry. I won't mention it again. But something is wrong. You have to admit that. The dying goats, the old high Mystic, the shark, *me.* These are things you can't explain. At least, let's try to find answers." He stood up, facing me. "Together."

His open, hopeful expression tugged at my heart.

I pursed my lips. "There is something else..."

I told Kirwyn about the "daughter of Elowa." Not that I thought he'd have heard of her, but it was worth a shot.

Discouraged, I plopped back down on the grass and gazed outward, into the Blue Beyond. The sunlight caught the azure sea, casting endless sparkles, like millions of my mother's Old World jewels tossed about the waves.

All I ever wanted was to live out there. To spend every day swimming in the enchanted dream-world beneath the

God Sea. The hush of the waves seemed to call to my soul, singing in a secret language only I knew. I felt the ache deep in my bones, a pain like the arthritic limbs of the old.

The ocean was the very reason my heart beat.

I belonged to the sea. If that wasn't true, then *I* wasn't true. I didn't exist, or need to.

Nothing Kirwyn said could be right. He didn't know my mother. She was the strongest person I'd ever met. The Mystics couldn't be lying to her. And my father? No one would dare. They couldn't deceive everyone.

Could they?

If so, who was left? I sunk my head into my hands.

An idea sparked once more in my mind. There was one option remaining.

Fire Maidens.

I would journey up the mountain and see what I could learn from them.

But I couldn't go tomorrow, I suddenly realized. Tomorrow was the second wedding pageant, the exhibition of my mental abilities.

How was it that I'd almost forgotten?

CHAPTER 21

louds blocked the sun, tenting the entire sky in white, and the day had a slight chill -- more akin to the dry season than the usual heat this time of year.

At least it would rain soon.

Mazriah styled half my hair up, into another crown braid, only this time the rest hung loosely down my back, whipping my face in the wind.

"Children of Keroe..." Nasero welcomed the villagers, guards and Mystics, jostling for the best view in the court-yard at the back of the palace. My family, along with Tomé, Marcin - and, to my dismay, Lida - all eagerly waited on a raised platform with servants pouring water and wine.

Smiling her tight smile that never touched her eyes, I was sure the little social climber was thrilled to be in such a position of honor. Lida had her hair pulled tightly back into her usual thick braid.

Well, good, I thought. *Enjoy your close-up view of my next crowning.*

I would give her a special smirk once the High Mystic

placed my next crown – blue and green sea glass – upon my head.

Nasero stepped to the front of the platform and held up his hands to silence the crowd.

"Children of Keroe, welcome to Braenese Zaria's second wedding pageant! The braenese has been given an encoded map she will use to find three secret locations, picking up a token from each..."

A thrill rose in my chest as he spoke. Looking over the heads amassed together – *my people* - I knew Kirwyn was wrong. There might be things I couldn't explain, like his existence or the daughter of Elowa, but that didn't have anything to do with Keroe, and my wedding.

"...And when she returns, she'll receive her third crown," he held up the shining tiara, "of sea glass!"

I tore my eyes from the stunning tiara and looked at the parchment in my hand. Once again, the task was ridiculously simple, as I had already been given the code right on the back of the map. I was beginning to wonder if Keroe had really low standards or if the Mystics thought so little of the chosen braenese, they had devised the simplest of challenges so that we not fail.

My mother rose and kissed the top of my head, bidding me luck. "Do you need anything? An extra skin of water?"

I shook my head. The air was neither hot, nor the task, arduous. It wouldn't take long at all. The code was a basic letter-for-letter inversion, so that "A" equaled "Z," "B" equaled "Y," and so on. All I needed to do was use it to spell out the hidden locations on the front, using the key on the back. Four-year-old Gereth could practically do it.

Much like the first pageant, there was no special dress for this occasion. I did wear my sporting sandals at my mother's recommendation. Hardened leather came up around my ankles, and pliable ties secured the shoes around my feet, better supporting them. Athletes used such shoes for the Solstice Games. As soon as I decoded the first location, I saw why she suggested it.

D – z – g – v – i – u – z – o – o

W – a – t – e – r – f – a – l - l.

Waterfall.

The surrounding banks would be a mire of mud and puddles.

Well, feet, let's go.

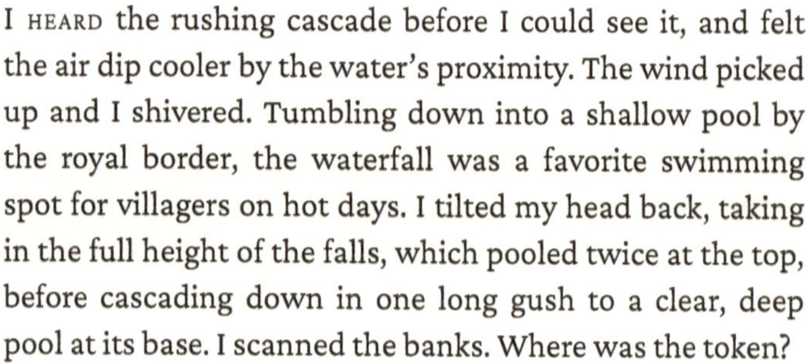

I HEARD the rushing cascade before I could see it, and felt the air dip cooler by the water's proximity. The wind picked up and I shivered. Tumbling down into a shallow pool by the royal border, the waterfall was a favorite swimming spot for villagers on hot days. I tilted my head back, taking in the full height of the falls, which pooled twice at the top, before cascading down in one long gush to a clear, deep pool at its base. I scanned the banks. Where was the token?

There. Something straight and wooden stuck out by the rocks to my right.

I ran closer to find a miniature carving of Keroe, the kind villagers often placed by the doorways of their homes, for luck.

Okay. Easy enough. Next I'd head to...

I used the decoder on the back of the map to spell out *Felled Tree,* the second location, and then I went ahead and spelled out the final clue, *Orchard Back Gate.*

My mouth dropped.

Unbelievable.

I was practically going in a straight line along the island

divide: from the waterfall, down to the large tree that had recently fallen across the stream, back to the wrought-wood gate at the Pawpaw Orchard behind the palace.

What a pageant! I tossed my hands in the air and laughed to myself. This was even easier than the swim across Wide Cove. *Why, yes, I can follow a map's key and walk in a straight line.* I'd be done in half an hour.

Taking a well-worn path along the stream, I came to the felled Silver Palm. It had been so unusually tall, everyone grieved to see it topple in a storm six moon cycles back, and we left the blessed tree where it lay, refraining from using the dead wood for any boats or carving.

The wooden statue of Keroe rested against its mid-section. Easy. I shook my head.

Onto the orchard. The entire pageant would be completed in no time, I thought, shivering once more. I wasn't even able to work up a sweat.

The wooden Orchard Gate wasn't so much a gate as a marker, because there was no fence surrounding the cultivated acre of trees, just the tall, wood-woven arch that indicated where the orchard ended and the wild forest began.

The excited tingle that had started in my stomach at the beginning of the pageant spread throughout my humming body as I hiked the downward slope back toward the palace. In mere minutes, the next crown would be mine. I pictured the translucent blue and green sea glass, wondering if Kirwyn would think it pretty against my light hair. I'd sneak out to see him as soon as I got the chance, conveniently wearing my tiara.

I continued trekking toward the orchard, picking up my pace as the ground leveled out and the dense forest thinned. I stopped at the dusty clearance before the archway and listened. From there, carried on the cool wind,

I could make out the sounds of the cheering crowd behind the palace. The exuberance sent a thrill through my body and my fingertips tingled as I spotted the token, leaning against the foot of the gate.

I bent down to pick it up and as I straightened, I heard a fast-moving rustle from my left. I whipped my head toward the sound.

Through the Pawpaw trees a figure emerged.

Solan, the old High Mystic.

The *dead* High Mystic.

Alive and moving.

I blinked, disbelieving what I saw. Solan was dead. Land-buried.

How could he be here, racing toward me?

I lost my grip on the Keroe statues and they clattered to the ground. A spring of cold water filled my belly. My mouth fell open, ready to scream if it weren't suddenly so dry.

Madness in his eyes, the dead man ran toward me -- brandishing a gleaming sword from the Steel Guard high above his head.

CHAPTER 22

I stood, dumb as a goat before the slaughter, mouth slack.

My mind registered danger. It tolled like the horrific warning bells the Mystics rang for a Black Squall. But my limbs didn't seem to receive the message, couldn't manage to act in response.

The old High Mystic wore the same robes I'd last seen him in, now torn. Like his face they were filthy, caked in dirt.

I couldn't accept what I saw. He was dead. He looked like a dead man: sallow complexion, cheekbones jutting out sharply beneath thin skin.

Precious seconds passed while I remained still.

While the tall, bony man, lunged to attack me, it was as if time slowed, distorted, and dragged out in length. Then, my wits came back to me and my brain began to work out the terrible fact that I was in mortal peril.

Someone screamed – I think it was me, though it sounded far away to my ears.

Next thing I knew I was running through the orchard,

ducking under the Pawpaw branches, stumbling, screaming for help.

Behind me, fueled by madness, Solan caught up.

His body slammed into my back and I fell to the ground, skinning my hands on dirt and pebbles. Frantically, I flipped over, crossing my arms in front of me as flimsy protection against the sword.

I was going to die.

The old High Mystic was going to kill me.

Why?

A guttural cry of triumph echoed in the orchard as he pushed himself off me, enough to back up and swing his sword.

"No!" I begged, screwing my eyes shut and turning my head against the blow.

This is it.

A high-pitched whistle sang on the wind, then *thwump*.

I popped open my eyes.

The ghastly sight of Solan's head with an arrow through its center filled my vision. His expression was frozen mid-way between the ecstasy of bloodlust and the horror of his own death.

He slumped to the right and fell, dead in the dirt.

This time, for real.

"Braenese!" someone called. It was the voice of Nasero, struggling to keep up with half a dozen guards and palace archers who ran toward me. "Braenese, are you hurt?"

I shook my head, dazed for a moment. But then I surprised myself when a sob tore from my mouth and tears suddenly escaped my eyes. I never cried in public. Was this shock?

No one knelt to soothe me. No one offered a hand to

help me rise. No one wrapped their arms around me and told me it would be okay.

How could they? They were men.

A tense, helpless circle formed around me, watching as I sobbed.

"Your mother will be here shortly. I am so sorry, braenese, braenese? Are you hurt?" the High Mystic asked again. "Have you been touched?"

I lied, shaking my head. I couldn't bear the repercussions of that right now. I had been *more* than touched, I had almost been *killed*. Someone touched me in an attempt to *kill* me. My brain struggled to accept it.

I was twice-touched, I realized suddenly.

Once in trying to save a life, once in trying to take one.

"Zaria!" My mother was on her knees, hugging, kissing the top of my head, running one hand over my limbs as if to make sure I was still all there, whole. I breathed in the heavy fragrance of her enigmatic flower scent.

It suddenly occurred to me that all my life, she was more physically affectionate than other mothers, perhaps to make up for what I was lacking from my father. From everyone.

"I thought he was dead," I whispered between hiccups. "How could he still be alive?"

Kirwyn was right. The Mystics lied. Anger at the deception took root in my stomach.

Except Kirwyn was wrong, too. The old High Mystic didn't want to help me, he wanted to kill me.

"I'm taking you to my chambers," my mother said, conscious of our audience. "We'll speak there."

"Nasero, let the people know the braenese has completed her pageant, but that she has... sprained her ankle at the end and won't be crowned until tomorrow.

Then meet us in my chambers, please." She turned to my father, who stood back, with the men. "Darius, dear, stay here and oversee."

What did my mother know of this?

I allowed myself to be escorted through the palace and into her chamber, but I did not speak, fury building and replacing shock.

Or maybe seizing on anger was the only way I could sort through what had just happened, because I felt like if I let go of it for a second, the horror would claim me and pull me under to a place where I couldn't breathe.

It felt odd being helped into my mother and father's bed. Wrong. I wanted my own bed.

A servant about my age came scurrying inside with a pot of tamarind tea and bowl of clam broth but I did not touch it.

A moment later, Nasero entered my parent's chambers.

Anxious, I glowered, waiting for an explanation. I noticed Nasero and my mother exchange a look, and Nasero nodded slightly to my mother, as if bequeathing permission to speak.

"Solan did not die on the day of your betrothal ceremony." My mother whispered the evident fact tentatively, as if this revealed a secret.

Obviously, I thought. I ignored her and turned to Nasero.

"You said you buried him," I accused.

His warm brown eyes filled with sadness. But I didn't fully trust it now. He'd lied about Solan and he was hiding something about Elowa.

"We fabricated the story of the land-burial because we had no body."

The confession sent my mind running in all directions. I had to force myself to focus on what he said next.

"He suffered a heart attack during your betrothal. When we were cleaning up his chambers, we found evidence that... that is, it became clear that he had descended into madness. Braenese, I am sorry, but he did not believe you were fit to marry Keroe. He planned on denouncing you, unworthy."

I knew it.

My mind flashed back to that day, to the look of disapproval in his eyes. Now, I thought, *maybe it was hatred.*

Nasero continued, "He was unconscious for hours, or he must have been pretending. On the eve of your betrothal, he disappeared from his sick-bed. We sent out guards, but no one could find him. Perhaps someone has been hiding him, someone loyal, a friend. Just to be safe, we bulked up patrols along the royal border. We knew he didn't believe you a worthy bride for Keroe, but we didn't know he was this far gone. We never thought he'd try to kill you."

"You were wrong." I spat the words, pausing only a moment to see I'd wounded Nasero. I turned my glare on my mother. "Why would he want to kill me?"

My mother sat down beside me, facing me. "He was deranged. He thought he could stop the wedding by denying you. It seems that when he failed, he became..." she shuddered, "Insane. Murderous. If he couldn't deny you, he'd kill you. We never thought he was mad enough..." My mother's voice cracked as she spoke.

The question "*Why did he want to deny me?*" was on the tip of my tongue, but I bit it back, thinking of Kirwyn. *Did the old High Mystic know? About my cave with the Old World objects?*

My mother wore the same pleading look Kirwyn wore yesterday. "We didn't want to tell you and upset you. Please understand. I chose to protect you. I would do anything to protect you."

"He's dead now," Nasero added.

Again, obvious, I thought.

"We're questioning every villager, even the stilt-dwellers, but we do not believe anyone else less than worships you. No one else will ever harm you," Nasero said, solemnly. He seemed to make the promise both to me and my mother, as his eyes flicked between us.

Something else nagged at me, something that didn't add up. I couldn't put my finger on it. My brain struggled to make sense of too many lies, too many impossible things happening.

Bowing, Nasero backed out of the room, "I'll leave you alone and prepare the arrangements for the morning."

"Thank you," my mother said, watching the High Priest as he left.

When she turned back to me, she kissed my forehead. "Sleep here tonight, with me. I'll go tell your father to stay in another chamber. I'll be right back."

She turned to leave.

"Wait!" I shouted, suddenly realizing what bothered me. "Was Solan poisoning the goats?"

"Poisoning?" my mother asked, bewildered.

"Tomé said they might have been poisoned. If so, could Solan have been doing it? If he didn't want me to marry Keroe, if he was willing to kill me, why wouldn't he be willing to kill the goats, as well? Endanger our food supply and kill us all?"

My mother closed her eyes, covering them momentarily. Then she used her hand to smooth the hair away from her face instead.

"I will speak to the High Mystic," she said. "I suppose

it's possible, but... it seems unlikely they were deliberately killed, and that has no bearing on your wedding. Regardless, he's dead, and the goats are now protected."

She turned again to leave.

"Wait!" I called once more, unable to hold back the burning question any longer. Truths seemed to be tumbling out, making now the perfect time to ask.

"Who is Elowa? Who is her daughter?"

My mother frowned. "Elowa? I don't know who that is."

"Mother," I said, pressing on. "You lied to me about Solan. I heard the High Mystic say the name *Elowa* and try to cover it up. I'd ask him, but he'd just deny it."

"Are you sure you heard correctly?" my mother asked.

"Yes, I'm sure! Tell me the truth. Please. Swear to me, swear on... me. You don't know who Elowa is?"

She crossed the room and sat beside me once more. With one hand on her belly, protruding under her tunic, she said, "I swear on our whole family, even your little brother or sister. I don't know who this person Elowa is."

She kissed my forehead again and as she leaned close, my nose caught her scent -- vanilla, with sweet flowers I could not name. Tilting my head back, I saw for the first time that her eyes had begun to develop slight creases on the edges.

"I only lied about Solan to protect you. I hope you can understand that, and trust that I will always keep you safe."

My mother left the room and I closed my eyes. Even though sunlight still shone through the windows, I had just begun to succumb to sleep when I caught the hint of something rotten in the air that I had been too distracted to notice before.

I opened my eyes, wrinkling my nose.

The Dahlias on the bedside table. My mother had let

the flowers die; the water had gone putrid. She hadn't even called the servants to change it.

Now that I thought about it, she hadn't re-styled her hair today, despite the pageant. Or the day before that. The elaborate up-do was days old, wisps of hair had begun to loosen and fall.

Guilt about my anger crept up inside me.

This wasn't easy for her either. Saying goodbye forever to her first-born daughter, and now two threats on my life, all while nearing the delivery of her fourth child.

At that moment, I vowed not to make it more difficult for her.

Did I have any right to be mad at her anyway?

Wasn't I just as guilty of lying, if not more?

IT TOOK me a minute to realize where I was when I woke up the next morning, and then the horror of yesterday hit me like a tidal wave.

I looked through the doorway into the bathing room and saw my mother stepping out of her bath. Her necklace – an Old World diamond nestled between little pink conch pearls – sparkled as she towel-dried her hair.

Close the curtain, I thought. *Let me go back to sleep for at least an hour.*

But I needed to get out of bed. Meet the crowds. Be crowned.

A strange mixture, like clashing tides, churned inside me. I almost died yesterday. Shouldn't I be left alone? To recover? This all seemed... wrong.

I don't even know if I want to marry the Sea God anymore.

For one heartbeat, that blasphemous thought seized my mind. And then a sudden, ridiculous idea.

I just want to see Kirwyn and tell him what happened.

A preposterous notion.

What comfort could he give? And I couldn't get away today anyway.

I banished the foolishness underground as I dragged myself into a sitting position. I was my mother's daughter. I could do this.

Get dressed, Zaria.

The world is waiting on you.

CHAPTER 23

arcin broke the surface of the water with an unbridled whoop, hand shooting up in the air, grasping a net full of oysters he hoped contained a pearl.

I'd been watching as he and Tomé alternated bobbing heads for the past hour, practicing their dives. I'd been too distraught to join in and too distraught to do anything else but stare at the school of vibrant rockfish swimming through the reef below me.

After the crowning that morning, my mother had forbidden me to go into the forest today, as expected.

Just to be safe, she said.

I agreed without arguing, keeping my vow from the night before.

In an effort to keep my mind busy, I tagged along with Tomé and Marcin for the afternoon, but jittery fish darted about my belly whenever I thought of Kirwyn.

Which was about every other minute.

What would he think had held me up? Would he have enough food to last until tomorrow?

With an ache in my chest I didn't fully understand - or want to - I turned and gazed beyond the cove, over the tall palm trees and into the direction of the cave.

I heard Tomé splash as he surfaced once more. He swam quickly back toward the rocky shore where I sat, passed me the heavy net chock full of sandy oysters, and I tossed an empty net back.

Lida was held up on some errand or other and wasn't able to join. I didn't remember the exact reason, and didn't care, other than to be thankful it occurred.

Tomé dove back into the calm seas, leaving me to the peaceful *shush* of the ocean. I reached up and gently rubbed a piece of smooth sea glass from the crown on my head. I had to admit the polished blue and green tiara was stunning. It wasn't heavy, either, like the coral crown. Decorative Old World metal had been wrought in between the pieces of sea glass to hold it together, making it even more extraordinary.

I wondered if I could bring it with me when I met Keroe. The bridal boat would be laden with fruits, sea wine, pots of dried herbs, and other tributes for the Sea King. Surely, I could take along a few items as well.

What I most want to take with me is Kirwyn.

The absurd thought popped into my head and I looked around nervously, as if someone could hear me think blasphemy.

"Zaria!" Tomé cried, surfacing again. His hand waved a strange, rectangular object. Marcin's head bobbed up behind him. They were talking excitedly to one another, but I couldn't hear from my post on the rocks.

"What's that?" I shouted.

"Look!" Tomé called, waving the object again. "It's an Old World book!"

I jumped into the waist-high ocean, scattering neon fish in all directions. Sloshing forward, I walked as fast as I could against the water while Tomé and Marcin quickly swam back.

A new book hadn't been found in *hundreds* of years. *Imagine, a new story!*

The three of us climbed back onto slippery rocks and Tomé carefully handed me the water-logged volume. It would be turned over to my mother, who would then release it to the Mystic's library, of course.

Of course.

But we had it now... there was no reason we couldn't examine it beforehand.

"How is it so well-preserved?" Tomé marveled.

I shook my head, bewildered. He was right, the book was in exceedingly good condition for having been submerged in water for... thousands of years? How had it held together that long?

"It must be some kind of magic," I mused.

We sat in a circle on a smooth rock, legs crossed, heads bent. The mushy pages, stuck together, would need drying out. The front cover read, *Cat's Cradle, Kurt Vonnegut,* so I guessed that it might be a nursery book for the kinder years. Maybe a long fairy tale. I peeled back the sopping cover, the only page that could safely be turned, for now.

I gasped.

Kirwyn Holt, blurred, but distinguishable, was written on the inside.

The world around me seemed to swim and the book alone came into greater focus.

Was this... Kirwyn's book?

Marcin let out a low whistle. "Sweet. It's inscribed with

an Old World name. Ca-ire-wine... Ca-ire-win? Key-er-win? Weird. Let's head back, show it off."

"No!" I blurted.

Marcin and Tomé looked at me, surprised.

"I mean, we should give it to my mother, and let her decide on the official announcement. She might want to examine the book, read it thoroughly to uncover more secrets about the Old World. Before sharing the news."

Marcin grinned, "She thinks like a queen already. Okay, just make sure we get the credit for the find."

"And first rights of reading," Tomé added.

I nodded, stunned, as I possessively clutched the sodden book to my chest.

"Come on," Marcin grabbed Tomé's arm with one hand and his net of oysters with the other.

"I'll race you to the beach."

I exhaled, relieved at his boundless energy - already carrying him to the next activity - but my heart kept up its speedy beat.

How could an Old World book belong to Kirwyn? How was that possible?

Was this some sort of trick he played?

But how would he know that we'd be here, today, deep diving?

For the umpteenth time in the last few weeks, my head had more questions than it could hold. As if we had all seen wrong, as if it would change, I looked back down to the inside cover.

Kirwyn Holt.

I stared at the letters making up his name until they began to dance in front of my eyes, making me dizzy.

Tomé and Marcin hooted in the distance and I looked up. They raced from one end of the beach to the other, exuberant in the find and confident that they'd receive credit when my mother shared the treasure.

Guilt crept up inside me because I didn't plan on turning this over to my mother. As soon as I could, I would bring it to Kirwyn and question him.

Still sitting on the rock, legs folded under me, I fell into a sort of trance staring at his name on the wet page. Maybe a few minutes had passed, maybe an hour, I couldn't even tell. All I saw was the name *Kirwyn Holt.*

Crack.

I heard the sound and whipped my head toward the beach.

The boys were playing some sort of game with a coconut and a stick. Tomé would toss the hard shell at Marcin, who would then smack it with the stick, sending it as far as he could.

For a moment, I watched them toss and hit the shell back and forth. Marcin had tied his hair back once more with the leather cord into his usual goat's tail. He stood taller and more broad-shouldered than Tomé, but both boys' hair shone golden in the sun, both had the same wide smiles, and I was struck again by the image of twin suns.

I looked back down at the book, studying the name as if clues would leap off the page. *Could it be a different Kirwyn, from the Old World?* But what a coincidence that would be...

Thwack.

A *sickening* thwack sounded from the beach.

"Ah!" came the accompanying cry.

Ripped from my daze, I saw Tomé lying on his back in the sand, cradling his head. The coconut lay beside him. As Marcin ran over, my stomach dropped. Tomé looked badly hurt.

Still holding onto the book, I leapt over the jagged rocks toward the beach, thankfully without stumbling once.

"Owww…" Tomé moaned, rocking back and forth. Marcin, standing nearby, sympathetically sucked in his breath.

"Landdammit," Tomé swore.

"He might have a concussion. We need to keep him talking," I urged, coming to stand beside the two boys.

Ignoring me, Tomé wailed, "You clocked me. That's gonna leave a bump."

"Sorry, man."

"What?" Tomé asked.

"I'm sorry," Marcin replied. His hands spread out, helplessly.

"What?" Tomé asked again. "I - I can't hear you. Oh, Keroe, I think I lost my hearing! Come closer!"

Marcin stepped toward Tomé.

Lightning fast, Tomé caught Marcin's legs between his own and, twisting them, knocked him onto his back. He jumped on top of Marcin and began pummeling the older boy half-playfully, half-purposefully, with his fists. The two of them *wrestled* and *laughed,* despite whatever injury Tomé suffered.

I stared, mouth agape, shaking my head.

Boys.

Seeing Tomé was *mostly* fine and intending to leave them to their play, I turned to walk up the beach, wanting to muse over the book again.

I made it three feet before stopping in my tracks.

Ominous black smoke rose from Sacred Beach, the next cove over. It wasn't like the white clouds that billowed from the beaches when villagers burned leaves to smoke out the mosquitoes. It ran black and gray, as if something caught fire. Something that wasn't supposed to.

"Tomé!" I shouted, breaking up the fight and pointing in the distance. Both boys jumped to their feet.

"What is it?" Marcin asked.

I shook my head, a sick feeling forming in the pit of my stomach.

We looked at one another in silent question and then, at the same time, broke into a run in the direction of the smoke.

It took about ten minutes to get inland, around the rocks, through the forest, and then back out to the next cove. The trees were a blur, I didn't notice anything as we ran. I trailed slightly behind and pushed myself to keep up with the strong, long strides of Tomé and Marcin.

By the time we arrived, a crowd of villagers formed a semi-circle with half a dozen Steel Guards holding everyone back for safety.

I covered my mouth in horror at the pillows of angry smoke.

The tribute boat for Keroe, the shipment my mother had gone to oversee the other day, *had been set ablaze.*

The pots of marmalade, the low-coral dwellers, the special weavings, all of it. Burned to nothingness. The remains of the charred boat smoldered, wrecked beyond repair, scenting the air with an inappropriately warm-and-woodsy smell in contrast to the abomination before us.

Who would do such a thing?

My hand fell to my heart. The old High Mystic was dead and yet threats to our food continued. Food not even intended for us.

This was an attack on the Sea God.

I shivered, despite the hot sun. Whoever did it was still out there.

Who knew what they'd do next?

CHAPTER 24

"Oh. Hey."

Kirwyn looked up with only a quick glance when I arrived, lounging on a patch of grass beside the cave's mouth, licking the Pawpaw juice from his fingers. The scruff was back, he hadn't bothered to scrape his beard in a few days.

I arrived at the grove of frangipani trees, sweaty, having run with a sack doubly full of food after scrambling out of bed before the bells.

"I'm sorry," I gasped, hands on my knees as I caught my breath. "I wasn't allowed to leave because-"

"Hey, princess. It's no big deal," Kirwyn said. "I don't need a babysitter."

I scowled. My fingers itched to remove the Old World book from my sack and confront him, but he was being such a goat's ass. "I'm sorry-"

"You don't need to be," Kirwyn cut me off again. "I know wedding plans are a time-consuming ordeal." He took another bite of the syrupy fruit.

I snapped my mouth shut. It seemed he thrived in my

absence. Too busy to even shave, picking Pawpaws and sunbathing.

And I thought he'd be worried. Silly Zaria.

"I'm glad to see you're well," I snapped. "I'm not. I was almost murdered."

Kirwyn sat up. "What do you mean? What happened?"

I took a deep breath and related everything that transpired the past two days. Kirwyn's demeanor changed from a prickly hostility to alarm – the concern I mistakenly expected he'd feel with me missing the day before.

So that's what it takes to soften this strange boy, I thought, remembering how he treated my ankle when I fell. *I only needed to have a brush with serious danger, or death, to get him to care.*

Not that I cared if he cared.

I was only here to find out the truth.

"Zaria..." Kirwyn sighed, in a way that made me tingle to hear my name from his lips. "What about these fire women you mentioned? You've not had much contact with them before?"

"Fire Maidens?" I asked, and Kirwyn nodded.

"Servants fetch fire if we need it, though we're more than capable of starting our own, and one is almost always burning in the kitchens. I've seen the Maidens before, of course, when they're on errands or gathering wood outside their temple. But I've never gone inside. And I've never met the Arch Priestess. They love their secrecy more than the Mystics. Only the brightest and most studious of unmarried women are invited to join them." I licked my lips, a little embarrassed. "I was never really that interested, until recently."

"Let's go see them. Tonight." Kirwyn insisted.

"I can't sneak away at night right now. It's hard enough

to get away during the day, and I'm only allowed on the royal side of the island. Let things cool down a little."

Kirwyn shot me a look of displeasure but nodded reluctantly.

FOR THE NEXT THREE DAYS, we fell back into our routine -- sharing a breakfast of avocados on bread, or sugar apples and nut butter. We chatted through the mornings, though I never came closer to catching Kirwyn in any inconsistency and the mystery of his existence only grew.

At my mother's command, my final pageant had been pushed back seven days, to the week before my wedding. She'd ordered it done so that I had time to recuperate, as well as to make sure enough protection was put in place against any unusual circumstances.

Part of me felt *more* anxious about the decision – I wanted to know what the final pageant was and get it over with – but a bigger part of me delighted in spending more free time with Kirwyn.

I still hadn't shown him the book. I had changed my mind when he didn't seem to care that I'd been missing, and for some reason I'd held off since.

I was now keeping secrets from everyone.

Late one sunny afternoon, we lounged upon the rocks by my cave's grotto, drinking a cool hibiscus tea I'd brought, sweetened with sugar cane juice. The grotto's freshwater pooled in a figure eight, both outside the mouth of the cave and inside the echoing chamber as well. This provided a quick place to hide on the off-chance anyone came this way. We'd grown bolder in our exploring, not foolish.

The breeze picked up and the air had that heavy, expectant feeling. It would likely rain come nightfall. But as we sat on the rocks to dry off, the wind was pleasant, shaking the branches slightly and helping to rain down a shower of frangipani petals to rest beside us, or float upon the water.

The more Kirwyn wove his tales, the more I felt entrapped -- as if in a maze, unable to find my way out to the truth.

He called our lakes, *ponds.* He called our mountain just a hill. Kirwyn spoke of mountain ranges so wide they took weeks to pass and so tall they kissed the clouds.

I wanted to stand on the top of one of those peaks, to reach up my hand and run my fingers through a passing cloud. I wanted to catch a handful of a fluffy one and put it in my pocket, proof that I had touched the sky.

Kirwyn chuckled when I told him.

"Clouds don't work that way. Even the thickest and heaviest aren't something you can hold on to. They'd slip through your fingers, like mist in the trees."

"You're like a cloud," I said, before I could stop myself.

I gulped, as if I could swallow back my words.

Kirwyn narrowed his eyes. "What do you mean?"

"I mean..."

Well, there was no stopping it now.

"I don't know where you come from really. Maybe the clouds," I said, raising my hand toward the sky. "And I feel like... well, you can't stay long. I can't... I mean, I feel like I can't grab you, hold you down."

I smiled, embarrassed, looking around as I spoke -- anywhere but his eyes.

"You'll slip through my fingers, and I'll never know the truth of you."

That didn't reveal too much, right? I mean, it could be interpreted any way.

"And you're like the sun," Kirwyn said, smiling. "And not just because your hair is golden. But because I always feel... warm around you. Even when you're just here, not doing anything in particular. But when you turn to me, full on, when you engage... I feel the heat." He shook his head. "But like the sun, the closer I get, the more dangerous it is. And if I touch you, I burn."

I *felt* like the sun as he spoke because a warmth spread over my whole body.

Touch me?

The words made me blush -- and not just because it was forbidden... but because it was the idea of *Kirwyn's hands* doing the touching.

"I... I... don't mean to burn," I stammered.

"The sun can't help what it is." Kirwyn shrugged. "A ray might be safe though. The sun's rays aren't as deadly."

I wasn't sure what he meant. Kirwyn shifted beside me, coming closer, staring at me with those deep green eyes. The skin on my arms and legs tingled. His strange face was too beautiful, his gaze too intense. He didn't look like any of the boys I'd ever seen before, and he certainly didn't act like them.

I looked down, shyly.

Could he read longing in my eyes? Hear my wicked heart?

My whole body was betraying me, betraying everything I'd been taught. *I should go, move away to a safe distance where he couldn't affect me.*

I raised my eyes to his. *Too late.* I could no more move from the thrall of his gaze than I could jump out of my own skin.

"May I touch your hair, princess Zaria?" he asked, eyes locked on mine.

I didn't move at first, then nodded, not daring to speak.

He reached out and rubbed a lock between two fingers. It wasn't the same as touching me, my skin. But it was one step away. Self-consciousness crept over me. My tresses, weathered by the sun, brittle from the sea, couldn't feel silky. I never soaked my hair overnight in coconut oil, never brushed and styled it regularly, as my mother did.

Kirwyn didn't seem to notice.

"Beautiful," he whispered.

Gullbumps rose on my skin. His body *nearly* grazed mine. He hadn't been this close since he attacked me. His scent filled my nostrils, woodsy and fresh, like a breeze through the forest, or the mossy trees themselves.

"That's the puzzle of you," I murmured. His eyes were on my lips. I wasn't imagining it. Not this time.

"What's that?" he asked, voice husky.

"Part of you is tangible, and that part is *so* solid, like the ground underfoot. Nothing breaks you; others break against you. And those dark forest eyes. You're as solid as the earth itself… But you're part mystery, too. One that can't be pinned down. Like the clouds, the air."

I smiled, self-conscious. *Did I sound silly?* Like a simple-minded schoolgirl, not a queen-to-be?

But I couldn't stop the words. "I feel you could be a dream I made up. Which is the truth? Which is the real you? Earth underfoot? Or air above?"

"I could say the same about you, with polarizing elements." I felt his warm breath on my face as he spoke.

What's polarizing? I thought. Not trusting myself to ask, I raised my eyebrows in question.

"You're not only fire, the sun that will burn me if I get

too close... you're like water. The ocean you can't seem to stay away from for very long."

His sculpted lips were inches from mine.

"I can't stay away from it either. That nourishing, sparkling sea, that promises to cool me down on this island when I get too... *hot.*"

My eyelids fluttered with desire at his last word and he saw it.

God help me, he saw it.

I parted my sinner's lips, willing.

Kirwyn's mouth claimed mine.

CHAPTER 25

The Coquí frog croaked its nocturnal mating call as I climbed down the tree outside my window. It wasn't easy – either for my first-ever leap from my window to the nearest branch, or to get a foothold in the subsequent branches down to the ground. But I'd never before had proper motivation to try.

Such as meeting Kirwyn at the ancient Ceiba tree.

I'd been as giddy as any other cuspate girl as I waited for the palace to sleep. I twirled in circles in my room, dancing, holding my fingers to my lips as if I could still feel Kirwyn's there.

This is what everyone else had, *this* is what I was missing out on.

Would he kiss me again? I wondered, as I ran through the orchard and into the wild forest.

Would Keroe see?

My feet hurried for another reason, as well. I worried that somehow, someone still wanted to hurt me. Imagining a madman lurking behind each tree, I spooked at every sound. My familiar forest had become a stranger. The storm

I predicted earlier held off, but the air held a charge that promised it wouldn't be for long.

Kirwyn's dark head poked out from the massive tree trunk as I approached. He hid, nestled in one of the tall, vertical folds of its base.

As soon as I neared he grabbed my hips, pulled me to the trunk, and pressed his lips to mine.

Delirium swept through me as he didn't hold back this time, stroking my sides and my back.

Then, out of the blue, Keroe's face popped into my mind: enraged, shouting words of damnation.

I stopped kissing.

"What is it?" Kirwyn whispered, voice husky.

"It's just... I hope Keroe can't see this far inland. In the dark."

Kirwyn groaned.

"What? I am going to marry him, after all. I am going to be the Sea Goddess."

"The Sea Goddess?" Kirwyn asked, mock-astounded. "You're *my* goddess."

He threw himself down at my feet with exaggerated prostration and planted loud kisses on my toes.

"Oh fair goddess, oh beautiful queen."

He worked his way up, kissing my knees, my thighs, turning my giggles to full-blown laughter, even as warning bells tolled in my head.

How had this happened? Days ago, we hated each other. And now...

"Let this strange, peasant boy worship you, let him kiss you..." he kissed me very close to the area between my thighs and I threw back my head, gasping as I jerked. But Kirwyn quickly worked his way up to my stomach.

"Let him place his unworthy lips upon your divine skin," he teased, brushing the top of my chest.

So much touching made me light-headed, ready to swoon.

"Let him have you," he whispered, turning serious as he kissed my neck and made my knees weak. Then he met my eyes.

"For whatever time together you say we have."

I pictured a thousand scenarios of getting caught, shaming my family, of damnation for us both.

But I answered by returning the kiss.

To avoid being seen, we took the steeper, overgrown route, up the spine of the mountain.

Kirwyn donned a crown of leaves, doing the best he could to hide his face. Combined with the white tunic I'd given him, he looked like a dryad. Late at night, it wasn't likely we'd run into any villagers but didn't want to take any chances. The hike on the mountain's back would take more than an hour up and at least an hour down, plus whatever time it took to speak with the Maidens. *If* they would actually entertain us. Having never been into the temple itself, I had no idea what to expect. Maybe my mother could command them, but I doubted they'd listen to me. They existed in a bubble, outside of our authority. They always had.

A lantern would have been helpful, but we couldn't risk the light. My imagination ran wild in the darkness. I worried that at any moment, guards would jump out and capture us, having witnessed Kirwyn touching me under the Ceiba tree. I played out the scenario, picturing my mother's face upon learning I despoiled myself, cancelling my marriage, disgusting the entire island.

More than a few times on the long journey up the mountain, I thought of turning back, locking myself in my room and never seeing Kirwyn again.

We spoke little as we hiked, focusing on our footing in the darkness and trying to listen for any unusual sounds that might warn us of others nearby. As thankful as I was for the cover of night and thick trees, it made for slow progress uphill.

Finally, my heartbeat quickened as we neared the top and a worn, dirt path started to form. After a few more minutes I could see the back of the flat, rectangular-shaped structure of the Fire Maiden's temple. Concrete, from the Old World, rough and hard to the touch. I ran my hands along the outer wall. The surface scratched my palms. It wasn't smooth, polished like the inner walls of the palace.

Why did the First Feet build with something so drab and painful? I wondered. Just another Old World mystery. Well, it did withstand the odd Black Squall and certainly contained fire better than wood.

Kirwyn and I walked toward the front of the building, but I approached the forbidding, wooden doors alone. The carvings were New World, depicting a scene of a fire illuminating a great hall of books. Kirwyn stayed hidden in the shadows of the trees, about ten paces back.

"I'll be back soon," I whispered.

I lifted my hand to knock on the towering doors before me.

They opened, creaking, before I could touch knuckle to wood.

A pretty woman, about twenty-five or thirty years old, stood in the doorway. She was a few inches taller than me, and her hair, which fell just past her shoulders, had a slight wave. Her large, round eyes captivated me. Their pale, green hue, set against her darker skin, made a striking and unusual combination.

"Braenese Zaria. Come in." She had a raspy, sultry voice. She turned, indicating I should follow, and then added, "Bring your friend, too."

A fish flopped in my stomach. "I- I-"

But she continued walking. I turned back to Kirwyn, helpless. His eyes remained narrowed upon the woman's back. He stepped from the shadows, tore off his crown of leaves, and we walked together behind her.

The Fire Temple, a massive, cavernous structure, seemed to swallow us. The ceiling appeared even higher than it had from the outside. Half of it was open to the sky, a large circle cut from the center. Below, a crackling fire - the eternal flame - burned in a stone pit. It threw shadows on the wall, creating an effect that was both eerie and dramatic, but warmed the cavernous room with a comforting, homey scent. Symmetrical wooden doors on each side of the hall led to unknown rooms, left and right. Neither were as tall as the entryway, but they each had ornate carvings, this time of the usual labyrinths wrought into heavy wood.

"This way," the woman said in her throaty voice, indicating we should follow her through the back of the hall, opposite where we entered. Her voice echoed, as did our footsteps.

Through an open doorway, we came into a small chamber, furnished with simple floor cushions, a few wooden settees, and a patterned weaving on one of the walls. The woman stopped, turned to us, and waited. She didn't seem the least alarmed or curious by Kirwyn's strange appearance, and that made me even more alarmed.

Nervously, I looked at Kirwyn. He seemed equally confused.

The woman appeared to be waiting for something, but for what I could not tell.

Finally, she spoke.

"Men are not allowed in the inner chambers of the sanctuary."

"I'm not leaving Zaria." Kirwyn's voice, low, forceful, surprised me. He did not touch me in her presence, but he moved his body slightly in front of mine.

"We mean no harm to the braenese," the woman said.

"I'm not leaving her," he repeated.

The woman bowed her head, once, without argument, leading me to believe she had prepared for this.

"Very well. You are not from here, so we will make an exception. My name is Elizabette, and you'll find I do most of the speaking, but it is she who will give you what you need, or not. Be fair warned, however -- her vow, her path, is the *Tongue of Light.* She speaks in such a manner as to illuminate the truth within you."

I didn't listen to her warning.

My ears rang, my heart pounded.

You are not from here, she said.

Casually, as if Kirwyn lived on one side of the village over the other.

Was it all true?

If she knew he wasn't from land, did she know where he was from?

I opened my mouth, but Elizabette spoke before me.

"Wait here," she ordered, and disappeared beyond the door.

I turned my wide eyes to Kirwyn, but I was too afraid to even whisper -- the walls seemed to have ears here. He must have felt the same, because he remained mute as well.

I shook my head, unable to believe what I'd just heard. Kirwyn may have guessed at my thoughts because sadness touched the edges of his eyes, and he nodded slightly.

When the woman returned a moment later, I opened my mouth again to speak and she silenced me with a wave of her hand.

I scowled at such a gesture in my direction – I was a braenese, after all - but before I could protest, she beckoned us forward and I stumbled after her.

We emerged into a large, ceremonial room, similar to the throne room in the palace.

Unlike the two chairs where my mother and father sat, however, there was only one throne here.

Occupying the tall, dark chair was a woman I'd heard of but had never met. She was maybe seventy or eighty years old and quite thin. Her hair faded to white and hung loose over her shoulders. The skin around her small, wise eyes wrinkled as she watched us. Deep lines creased either side of her mouth.

The Arch Priestess.

Most people had been up to the temple at some point or another, but I had never known anyone given an audience with the Arch Priestess, even my mother.

Another woman sat on a bench to the side of the room. She couldn't have been more than twenty. Her hair astounded me – colored unnaturally red and cut to the shoulders. I'd seen berry-dyed hair in streaks, but it was startling to see all over. She wore dangling earrings made of something like Old World fishing tackle and tattoos of strange symbols climbed her arms.

Those arms sat neatly in her lap -- her posture formal. But her face glowered.

"Arch Priestess," Elizabette said, breaking the silence in the echoing chamber, "May I introduce Braenese Zaria, and the stranger." She bowed, then added, "These two have grown close in their acquaintance."

I bristled at her commenting on my relationship with Kirwyn but focused on the woman before me.

"Arch Priestess," I said, bowing slightly to mimic Elizabette. Was that the correct way to address her? A bow could not offend, at least, and for someone of my station, it showed great respect.

I felt as if my mother took over my voice. "Please forgive me for being so direct, but I must ask urgent questions. How do you know... my friend... isn't from around here? We came here seeking answers. We don't believe... that is, my friend and I aren't sure we can trust the Mystics, and my mother and father aren't aware of the truth. Things have been happening that we can't explain, terrible things. Do you know why the goats are dying? Who would burn the tribute boat? Why did the old High Mystic want to kill me? Can you tell me – who is Elowa?"

All the questions tumbled out of me and yet I had more to ask.

The Arch Priestess leaned back in her chair, silent for several seconds. I worried I had barraged her with too many queries at once, and that she might not answer or even speak at all. Then, slowly, she replied.

"You've come to the right place. But you are the wrong person." Her voice was deep, soft.

What?

"What do you mean?" I asked.

"Excuse me – priestess, your highness," Kirwyn interrupted, awkwardly. "Can you help me get off this island? I need to get back home. And maybe convince her-" he pointed his thumb at me, "to come with me. She thinks she's about to marry the sea god. I think she's about to get herself killed. I don't know what's going on here, but I know it's a lie," he narrowed his eyes, "and I think you do, too."

I heard Kirwyn's voice at a distance.

I was the wrong person? What did that mean?

The Arch Priestess settled back in her chair and folded her frail, birdlike hands in her lap. Feeling like I had been dismissed, desperation swelled inside me.

"Can you help me?" I asked Elizabette, spinning to face her. Before waiting for an answer, I whirled to address the surly woman on the bench. "Can you?"

"Danaire cannot speak," Elizabette replied on her behalf. "She swims in a Sea of Sorrows."

Oh. I wondered what had happened that, drowning in pain, the red-haired woman could not speak.

"I'm sorry," I told the redhead, shifting my gaze back to the throne, in respect of her grief.

The Arch Priestess looked at Elizabette and it was as if something passed between them.

"In this temple, we have a thousand answers to a thousand questions, some of which you seek. Others, even our flame cannot illuminate," Elizabette said. "I can tell you this, and this alone. Many, many generations ago, when the books were sent to be burned in our fire - we did not burn them all."

I stared. *Books?*

Like those shown on the door's carving? Like Kirwyn described in his library? Row upon row that filled every wall and stacked to the ceiling?

"May I see the books?" I asked. If I couldn't get answers here, I'd read them for myself.

Elizabette shook her head. "We cannot interfere with the affairs of the island."

Was it my imagination, or did her eyes flick toward Danaire?

"With you, least of all. We tried once, in the past. The cost of it proved too high. We wait, silent, and in return we may guard the sacred knowledge in peace."

What did she mean the cost proved 'too high?' Had someone done something to them?

"I know you know there's more out there!" Kirwyn yelled, sharply. "Why can't you do something about it? They're going to kill her!"

At Kirwyn's shouting the Priestess spoke, and her words sent coquina clams up my spine.

Fixing her dark eyes on me she said, "Caution, braenese. Just because someone walks your path, doesn't mean you have the same destination. Just because someone has the same destination, doesn't mean they walk your path."

What?

What did that *mean?*

She bowed her head deeply, an official dismissal this time.

Elizabette addressed us, kind, but formally. "Your audience has concluded. We will forget that we ever saw you. We can give you no more. We ask that you do not repeat what you have heard here and that you do not return."

My mind swam in circles. *Why?* Everything was happening too quickly. *All this for nothing.* I could hear Kirwyn raging beside me, but he sounded distant, the words not making sense in my head.

Elizabette tried to escort us out and Kirwyn protested, "No! I want answers, you can't leave her to die."

Numbly, I let myself be led toward the door, dimly hearing Kirwyn's protests of my upcoming marriage.

Wait.

I planted my feet and turned.

"Please," I pleaded, one last time. "I'm to marry Keroe in a fortnight. Is my wedding real? Or am I being lied to?"

No one moved. The Arch Priestess regarded me silently. I watched the torchlight flicker, sending light and shadows across her stoic face. The tension in the air pressed heavy around me, building as if to erupt.

Say something.

Kirwyn tensed beside me.

Say something. Say something *real,* not riddles.

Danaire flicked her eyes back and forth between the Priestess and I, just as anxious for a response. Only the Priestess remained calm.

"Just because someone wants what you want, doesn't make them your ally. Just because they don't, doesn't make them your enemy."

What the...? What in the sea kingdom did that *mean?*

CHAPTER 26

Like a dreamwalker, I followed Elizabette back through the private chambers and into the main hall. Kirwyn fired off a string of questions she did not answer. His demands became increasingly colorful, swearing punctuating each, but he might as well have been talking to the concrete walls of the shrine.

Without another word from Elizabette, she escorted us outside. The looming doors of the temple closed tight behind us.

"That was helpful," Kirwyn declared dryly, speaking to the trees as much as to me. He nodded his head toward the silent temple. "I see why you never bothered to come up before. Riddles upon riddles. Useless."

"No, no. I shouldn't say that," he said, changing his mind. "We did learn *some* things. We know that they are lying to you. Do you believe me now? Enough to talk to your mother and father? Zaria, if the Mystics are deceiving you, if they plan to kill you, your parents need to know. You've all been weaned on a lie of this sea god."

"Stop!" I yelled, surprising even myself.

I ran off toward the woods at the back of the temple. I couldn't begin to sort out what just happened, I couldn't handle another onslaught of arguments and questions, and we were too exposed by the doors.

"Zaria!" Kirwyn called, running after me.

"I can't argue with you now, it's too much," I cried, pulling at my hair. "Let me just... make sense of what she said. These riddles. I don't know what she means."

"I do."

The voice came from the forest, causing both of us to jump, then tense -- ready to fight or run.

A rustle of leaves broke the air as someone stepped out from behind a thick cluster of bushes. I squinted in the darkness.

Danaire.

What was she doing here?

"I thought you were swimming in a Sea of Sorrows?" I whispered, confused.

Danaire snorted. "I'm not sad. And I'm not sorry. I'm angry. *Livid.* I could scream. I could burn down this whole place."

Up close, I could smell the alcohol on her breath, her skin.

"Will you please tell us the truth?" Kirwyn demanded.

Danaire laughed, hysteria bubbling out of her lips. "Will *I* tell you? Will *I* tell you?"

She seemed to be talking more to herself, than us. "No, no, I will not break that vow on top of the others. I will confess my sins, oh yes. I will confess. Absolution. Maybe I am sorry. Maybe I do seek forgiveness. Maybe not. Maybe I still want a way out. Poor things. Poor things. I'm sorry you poor things."

Was she mad? Confess *what?* I could see Kirwyn tense as she became more unhinged.

"It was me." Danaire's mouth twisted before continuing, like she struggled to get the words out. "I poisoned the goats and burned Keroe's tribute."

Her declaration hit me like a punch in my gut. Why would she kill those helpless animals? Hurt the balance of food? Attack *God?*

"Why?" Kirwyn's sharp demand asked the question for me.

Another hysterical laugh. "Because it was better than killing *her.*"

Kirwyn grabbed Danaire by her shoulders so hard I thought he might leave bruises.

"Why would you want to hurt Zaria?" he asked.

"Go ahead and kill me if you like. I won't break more vows," she swore.

"I won't break more vows," she repeated.

"I won't break more vows."

It was like Danaire passed into a fevered state, laughing as her head lobbed back-and-forth.

My own head began to pound. I just wanted to get away from her.

The wind blew stronger.

"Leave her!" I shouted, pulling Kirwyn's tunic. "She's drunk. Probably mad. And I have to get back."

He let her go and she fell limply onto the ground, laughing.

"Let's just go," I begged. But I didn't wait for Kirwyn to reply before I took off toward the dirt path.

Seconds later, thunder boomed in warning. The sky broke into a heavy rain, pouring forth everything it had held back for days. Kirwyn and I were soaked in seconds, and within minutes, the ground became a slippery mire. The storm pounded the leaves, drowning out our voices. We were too preoccupied with not falling to talk much.

Instead of making good time on our return, it took even longer to get down the mountain.

Dawn couldn't have been more than an hour away by the time we took shelter in the tall roots of the Ceiba tree. It wasn't completely dry, but provided some coverage, at least.

"We have to be methodical," Kirwyn said. "Let's recap the facts."

Dripping, he paced the small distance from one fold of the trunk to the next.

"What do we know?" he asked, then answered his own question.

"Someone here wanted to burn all the books -- the Mystics, likely. These Fire Maidens kept some. So, they probably know ancient history, they know about the world. They're up there, studying the past, speaking in riddles, shrouded in secrecy. But they're isolated... I bet they don't know what's going on *now*."

Kirwyn paused, running his fingers through his hair, then started pacing again.

"Or, they know some things, but they can't tell us what they know because in the past, they paid a price for it. Maybe someone was hurt for interfering. Maybe they even killed one of the Fire Maidens..." Kirwyn stopped again, gazing into the darkness.

"But it's Danaire who's been killing the goats." He shook his head, puzzled. "But what does that have to do with sparing you?"

Kirwyn paced again, rattling off lists and theories. I watched, the pounding in my head worsening. I needed to get back into my room and I was nervous that I couldn't climb the tree in this rain. It was easy for Kirwyn to be logical. None of this was happening to him. If the Fire Maidens were telling the truth, all he needed was to find a way off our land, to get back to wherever he came from.

But... did it even matter if there was land beyond the God Sea? It didn't change my wedding. It didn't change anything. Not really. Not for me.

I could *not* get caught out here. I had to sneak back into my room, and soon. I had my final pageant next week. And after that, I was getting married. Everyone expected me to do these things. Even if it was real, what did Kirwyn's world matter, anyway? It was his, not mine.

"Kirwyn, I have to go."

"Right, I'm sorry," he said. He swept me into his arms, kissing me once. "But you believe me now, right? You believe I come from the world out there?"

I nodded... but I didn't really. I didn't know what to believe and it didn't change my fate.

"And you don't believe in the sea god anymore, right?"

I didn't say anything.

Kirwyn ran his hands though his hair and swore.

"Please, I have to get back," I said.

"OK, promise me I'll see you tomorrow? We're not done discussing this." His tone was that of a parent speaking to a child.

I *felt* childish at that moment, but not for that reason. As he kissed me goodbye, I knew I somehow wanted to keep him. Even as I clung to it harder than before, part of me – shamefully - didn't want to do my duty as the first-born braenese.

Childishly, I wanted it both ways.

Kirwyn and my marriage.

We broke apart, Kirwyn sloshing back into the wet woods towards the cave. I watched until he disappeared, then ran back to the palace.

The tree outside my window had become impossibly wet. I couldn't find purchase anywhere in the slippery truck. My head throbbed worse than ever. All I wanted was to get a good night's sleep so that I could try to solve the priestess' riddles in the morning, and I was starting to panic that I'd never make it back to my chambers.

Clinging for all I was worth, I tried again and again. Holding on until my arms shook, swiping the rain away from my eyes until slowly, miraculously, I made it to the high branch nearest my window.

My heart sunk as I realized there was no easy way to make the leap back inside. Everything was too wet. What if I slipped and fell?

I almost did when a figure appeared in my window.

"Here. Take my hand."

Tomé.

Relief flooded me before I could even wonder what he was doing in my room in the middle of the night.

"I can't," I protested, thinking he might throw out something else I could grab onto. Then it hit me.

"You're... not afraid?"

"I'm not afraid of anything anymore," he said, although the fierce declaration had behind it the tone of the defeated.

He reached his arm out further.

I looked around to make sure no one was watching, then back at his waiting hand. Lightening flashed, illuminating my cousin -- tall enough to reach the top of the window, blonde hair falling just to his shoulders, strong arm reaching out.

No smile like the sun. His lips made a flat line, his jaw

clenched. Something was very wrong to bring him to my chambers in the middle of the night.

But this I knew -

If there was *anyone* in this world I trusted, it was Tomé, above all others.

I clasped his strong hand and jumped.

Tomé caught me by my waist as I landed on the window's ledge. He helped me scoot safely inside, out of the rain and out of sight.

We separated and I fidgeted, wondering what to say about the two of us breaking Sacred Law.

In the quiet that followed I searched my soul, knowing I should feel shame. But, as with Kirwyn, I didn't really feel despoiled by Tomé's touch, and paradoxically, *that* made me feel ashamed.

What to do? If I didn't make a big deal of it, would Tomé know I'd already been touched? On the other hand, I was deeply indebted to him for taking the risk.

Tomé didn't seem concerned. Just angry.

Maybe I could avoid mentioning it at all, I thought wildly. Pretend it didn't happen. *Change the subject?*

"What are you doing in here?" I whispered. "How... how'd you get in here?"

"The same way as you," he replied, tersely.

He was definitely mad. Why was *he* mad? He had snuck into *my* chambers at night. Shouldn't I be mad?

Actually, I was.

"What are you doing sneaking out in the middle of the night?" I demanded.

"I could ask you the same thing."

I chewed my lip and didn't reply. I didn't want to reveal anything until I knew what was going on. We just *touched,* for crying out loud. *Aren't you going to say anything about it?*

Tomé snorted, softly. "I came here tonight, risking God-knows-what-punishment, to tell you before the announcement was made. I'm marrying Lida."

I hadn't heard him right. *Lida?*

"But... but..." I stammered. I seemed incapable of forming a sentence. "Why? You don't love her."

As soon as I said it, I was sure of it. Serious, snooty, social-climbing Lida, so different from her cousin Marcin, had nothing in common with Tomé. I'd never even seen them hang out together, let alone develop an attraction.

"She's pregnant. We're having a baby. Our wedding will take place two weeks after yours. I guess you can congratulate me, Zaria. I'm a father."

No, no, no. I shook my head vigorously. This was all wrong.

"Stop! Stop it!" I cried. I wished I could touch him again because I wanted to push Tomé, to make him break the stoic façade. But I didn't dare a second time.

"Tell me what's going on? Why are you marrying her? I know it's not your baby!"

Tomé let out a low chuckle. Without meeting my eyes, without touching, he strode past me. He swung himself onto the window's ledge.

"I guess we both have our secrets, don't we?" he said, looking over his shoulder.

Tomé jumped out the window and climbed down the tree, far easier than I had climbed up. When he reached the ground, he didn't look back. He stalked off into the pouring rain.

I was left even more confused than before, staring as he disappeared into the night.

CHAPTER 27

One hundred times I turned onto my left side and one hundred more onto my right, but I never found a deep sleep that night.

When I woke for the last time, I quickly tossed on my tunic, grabbed my sack, and ran out the back patio without remembering to get any food.

The storm had cleared the sky and only the faintest wisps of cloud could be seen on the horizon. Blazing sun had already begun to dry out the earth, but it was still mucky and puddled both in the orchard and in the thick forest. Mosquitos attacked relentlessly all the way to the cave.

"Tomé is marrying Lida," I blurted, as soon as I arrived, "and I know he doesn't love her."

My voice had a bitter edge, even to my own ears.

"Well good morning to you, too." Kirwyn replied. He was running his hands over his cheeks, and I could see from a nick he'd just finished scraping his stubble. He tossed the blade onto the table and came over. "Why is he marrying her?"

"Because she's pregnant."

"It's not his," he said.

My eyes rounded. "That's what I think! How do you know that?"

"Zaria... your cousin..." Kirwyn sat down on the rug, resting his elbows on his knees. He gave a half chuckle, half sigh.

"He doesn't like girls. Not romantically." Kirwyn's chuckle deepened. "Oh man. Your island... it's uh... religious here. But nature is nature, wherever you go."

Kirwyn stroked his chin and started again, "Not everyone is destined to marry the sea god... or whatever it is these Mystics are trying to dictate. Tomé would rather be with a guy. It's just that your island... it's probably some kind of religious taboo here, and I'm guessing he has to hide it. Probably from your Mystics... though who knows what they get to behind closed doors." Kirwyn made a noise at the back of his throat. "Hypocrites."

"That's..." I tried to wrap my head around it. "And how would you know?"

"I've seen it. Can't *you* tell when a man and a woman like each other?"

"Yes, but-"

"Well, it's the same. I've watched Tomé and I've seen it. He likes someone else, a boy."

"Wait, when have *you* seen it?" I asked, narrowing my eyes.

Kirwyn paused, then admitted, "The day after that old priest attacked you, the day you didn't come. I found you. I saw you, Tomé, and some boy on a beach."

My cheeks flushed. Kirwyn had been spying on me? How often? I pictured us poring over the book and panic shot through my chest. Had Kirwyn watched Tomé find it?

Kirwyn read the alarm on my face and soothed, "Don't worry, princess. I'm not a stalker. I just got worried when you didn't come that day. I saw you frolicking on the beach and I left."

I lifted my chin and crossed my arms. On the one hand, I understood he must have been concerned for me, not showing up that day. On the other, I didn't like being watched. My privacy violated. And I didn't need one more person lying to me.

Another mosquito landed on my arm; they were swarming the cave. I swatted too late, suffering another bite.

"Let's talk about it elsewhere. The hills by the ridge. On the way to Shady Beach. There'll be less pests there."

But we didn't talk about it, and we didn't discuss the Fire Maidens yet either. Because as we hiked toward the hills, wheels began to turn in my head.

"You think Tomé likes Marcin? Romantically? That's the other boy you saw on the beach," I explained. "Tomé is marrying Marcin's cousin."

"And she's pregnant..." Kirwyn added, nodding slightly to himself and then bobbing his head more certainly.

"I bet you a night's feast that baby isn't his. She's in trouble and Tomé is marrying her for Marcin's sake."

Kirwyn stopped walking and turned toward me, face full of scorn or disgust.

"He also probably doesn't have another option. It's not like your people will let him marry this Marcin guy. Or any other."

"Tomé loves Marcin..." I repeated.

Now that I thought about it, he did spend a lot of time with him and they were... affectionate to one another.

Kirwyn studied me. "How do you feel about that?"

I stopped walking and stared ahead, not seeing the trees but picturing my cousin instead. Probably the most intelligent member of the Braeni. As carefree and playful as a dolphin in the waves.

Until now.

"If it's true, well it's, I don't know..." I pictured Tomé and Marcin, together. The truth was, alone each boy radiated like the sun itself, together they were practically blinding. When they weren't being totally annoying, of course.

How could I begrudge Tomé his happiness? Hadn't I disobeyed all the rules of Keroe and done the same?

"I guess it doesn't really matter if that's what he wants... I just want my cousin to be happy," I said slowly. "But he's not. He's marrying Lida."

"Good," Kirwyn replied, tone clipped. "I know you've been raised on this sheltered island and I get the feeling your parents intentionally try to keep *you* naïve, but-"

"Well, but," I cut Kirwyn off, ignoring his insult.

"But what?" Kirwyn asked, narrowing his eyes.

"It's just..."

"What?" he repeated.

"Well, okay, Tomé loves Marcin. But, it's just, what I don't understand is..."

I bit my lip, embarrassed. Looked down at the dirt.

"Yes?" Kirwyn asked, impatient.

"Don't they ever want to have sex? How can they have sex?" I blurted.

Kirwyn laughed so loudly I jumped.

By the time we reached the hills, I received a thorough education in all kinds of coupling, according to Kirwyn.

My reddened cheeks flamed so hot they threatened to burn off.

Kirwyn didn't have such modesty.

In fact, he delighted in the details, seeing me squirm and unable to meet his eyes with every shocking new description. I suspected he embellished unnecessarily for the sardonic thrill of it.

I was breathing hard and my pulse was racing when we stopped. It wasn't from the hike.

I'd forgotten food that morning. Kirwyn was sick of fruit, and since he refused bugs, we decided to pick mushrooms on the hillside. Sunshine after the rain was the perfect weather to gather fungi, and a few different varieties grew nearby. I was a little bit worried about being exposed, but almost all the guards were busy protecting a replacement tribute to Keroe today.

I told Kirwyn we were looking for Oyster mushrooms, which grew on logs and didn't have anything to do with oysters of the sea, but he was already aware of that fact. As we searched, something bothered me, but I couldn't put my finger on it. I started to bristle at things Kirwyn said. After a few minutes, we found a cluster of creamy mushrooms growing on a stump and I was surprised when Kirwyn picked them all. Perhaps sustainability wasn't an issue where he came from.

"Rule of thirds," I said, with a frown. "You take a third for yourself, leave a third for wild animals, and a third to repopulate."

"Thanks," Kirwyn said, with an edge to his tone.

"What?" I asked.

He spread his hands. "I don't want to push, Zaria. But are we gonna talk sex and mushrooms all day, or do you want to discuss what happened last night? It's like you're in denial."

He didn't look at me, instead returning to gather fungi, moving on to a different cluster nearby. He stooped and filled his bag with handfuls of the thinner, longer mushrooms. We couldn't eat that type without becoming ill, but I was too distracted to mention it.

"I'm not in denial. Nothing conclusive happened." With Kirwyn's back turned, I raised my voice to reply.

"Nothing conclusive?" He roughly plucked one brown cap after another, shoving them into his sack. "The Fire Maidens all but told you about the world out there... You don't believe them, either, do you?"

"I- I don't know," I stammered. "What difference does it make?"

"What difference? What difference? You can leave! You can go there! You know everyone's been lying to you!" Kirwyn angrily tossed his sack on the ground.

"I don't know that," I shouted. "They spoke in riddles! And just because the Fire Maidens know something about you - think they know - doesn't mean everyone else is wrong. And it doesn't change things. I'm getting married, Kirwyn."

"You're getting married? And kissing me? And that's okay?"

Fury boiled in me and I spat out what was bothering me.

"And you're kissing god-knows-who! Those things you mentioned... all those... intimate things. Have you done those things?"

Kirwyn's shoulders fell as he sighed. "Some."

"And it's okay to keep that secret?" I asked.

"Secret? Zaria, I didn't even know you before. You can't be jealous of my past. I'm not jealous of your past-"

"I don't have a past!" I said. My foot, with a mind of its own, stomped in emphasis.

"Well you sure are making up for it with one hell of a future." Kirwyn grabbed the sack of mushrooms and stalked deeper into the trees.

"You want to talk secrets!" I yelled, following him. "What's this?"

Reaching into my sack, I withdrew the book I'd been carrying for days.

"Hey, that's my book!" Kirwyn smiled, surprised and delighted. He grabbed it from my hands and opened it, checking the name inside. "Where'd you get this?"

I folded my arms. "You tell me. Did you plant it? After all, you were there that day."

"There what day?" Kirwyn asked. "Zaria, where'd you get this?" He waved the book in the air. "I had it on the ship when the storm hit. Do you have my bag, too?"

I glowered, trying to tell if he was lying.

Kirwyn studied me in return, then decided something and threw the book on the ground.

"You want to talk secrets, Zaria? Why do you have a bomb?"

He removed something from his pants pocket and opened his hand.

It was my beautiful, egg-shaped box.

The one that belonged to the First Feet. The one I planned to open on my wedding day. The one I'd hidden in the back of the cave.

"That's mine," I growled. "You had no right to take it!"

"Oh?" Kirwyn gloated. "How's it feel? But more importantly, where did you get this weapon?"

"It's not a weapon," I explained. "It's a decorative box, for a braenese probably, and it's mine. If you must know, I found it. Half-buried in the palace orchard. I'm saving it to open on my wedding day, to find out what's inside."

Kirwyn's mouth fell. "Open it? Zaria, what do you mean?"

"Well, you see, you can open it here-" I reached forward to explain and Kirwyn yanked the treasure away, holding it above his head where I couldn't reach.

"Zaria. This. Is. A. Bomb." Seeing my blank stare, he continued, "Like a grenade. An Old World weapon that explodes. Jesus, Zaria," he raked his hand through his hair, "if you opened this, you'd explode. You'd die. Get it? Zaria go boom. My god, you're like a child."

His voice rose angrily by the end of his speech and his face looked as furious as I felt. I was so mad my hands shook and my arms tingled. He'd been spying on me, lying to me, *and* stealing from me. And he thought I would trust him? I didn't even want to look at him.

"And you're like a goat's ass." I turned on my heel and stalked off, back toward the tree where we'd first found the Oyster mushrooms. I couldn't believe my box was a weapon and how *dare* he speak to me like that?

Out of the corner of my eye, I saw Kirwyn throw himself down on a log. He opened his sack, brushed the dirt off the bad mushrooms with his stupid white shirt, and began eating them.

I turned back around. *Good. Let him.* What did I care if he picked the wrong kind? He thought he knew everything. Served him right.

I stared beyond the copse of trees, listening to the wind rustle the heavy, leafy branches. From here I could just make out a sliver of the sea, sparkling in the distance.

I refused to believe my decorative egg was a weapon. And even if it was, he didn't have to speak to me like that.

Unless...

Kirwyn did know a lot about Old World objects.

It couldn't be true.

But... if the silver box was some kind of weapon, or if Kirwyn actually believed it to be, then he had saved my life -- or at least *thought* he did.

I turned back around. Kirwyn was still popping mushrooms into his mouth.

"Stop!" I shouted, jumping to my feet and running to his side. Kirwyn looked up at me, one eyebrow cocked.

"You can't eat those," I commanded, swiping them out of his open hand and onto the ground.

"They're... poisonous?" Kirwyn asked, eyes wide, mouth half-full. He began to spit them out, panicked. "Am I going to die?"

I shook my head. "No. But you might wish you had."

Kirwyn, speechless, looked up at me, too shocked to move.

"Come on," I said. "We need to get you back to the cave. You'll want to be... comfortable."

KIRWYN FOLLOWED me on the long trek back through the forest, holding his stomach and complaining, even though the mushrooms couldn't have taken effect yet. I apologized profusely, but he refused to accept it. Fuming, he was, however, forced to accept my help.

Inside the cave, I set up a fresh pitcher of water and the clean cloth, the only thing I could do against the... gastronomic effects of the fungi.

"Do you want me to stay?" I asked gently.

"No!" Kirwyn shouted, holding his stomach and doubling over.

I didn't mean to, I really didn't mean to... but I laughed. Seeing Kirwyn -- always so superior, always so cocky -- leveled like this... it made me sort of smug. He did deserve it.

"I'm sorry," I said. "I really am. I didn't see..."

"You saw!" Kirwyn accused, then moaned.

"Okay, I saw. I should have stopped you sooner. But you shouldn't have yelled like that. I'm sorry. We can talk about it later. Are you sure you don't want me to stay? The pitcher of water-"

"Get out! Get out!" Kirwyn yelled, waving his arm.

"Okay. Well. I'll come back tomorrow? You'll be fine in a couple of hours. It's not a big deal. Really."

Kirwyn glared at me, his eyes threatening *wait 'till I get better.*

It sent a tingle down my spine that both frightened and thrilled me a little. I slipped out of the cave giggling, even as I anxiously wondered...

How would he retaliate?

CHAPTER 28

I wasn't used to having a lot of free time back at the palace. Whenever I was home, I had measurements taken, another dish to sample, another practice session for the ceremony. Having a few hours on my hands before night's feast, I decided to go back to the records in the Mystic's library, to see once more if I could find any mention of Elowa. For some reason, I felt like she was the key I needed to unlock all the mysteries around me. If only I could find her, talk to her – or her daughter - I could get real answers.

But hours poring over the same large tomes yielded nothing new. Whoever Elowa's daughter was, she seemed not to exist on land. At least not in any census.

Closing the latest record book and rolling out my stiff shoulders, my mind wandered back to Kirwyn and guilt crept up inside me, picturing – and trying not to picture – what he was going through at the moment.

The sun hung at a heavy angle as I headed back to the palace. When I reached my room, I saw Mazriah bent over, stripping the bed. She gave a slight bow as I entered but did not speak. I nodded in return and then went into my bathing room to clean up.

Midway through sponging the dirt off my arms, I had an idea and practically leapt off the stool to catch her before she left. I grabbed my tunic as a hasty cover for my body.

"Mazriah," I called out, stopping her just before she turned into the hallway. "Do you know who Elowa is?"

Her mouth parted, and the sheet she carried slipped in her hands. She looked behind her, down the hall, then turned back around and shook her head rapidly.

My heart raced.

She knew.

"Mazriah, are you sure..."

Still shaking her head, she gripped my linens to her chest, and, without meeting my eyes, hurried down the hall.

"Wait!" I called out, but I couldn't follow her in my half-dressed state.

MAZRIAH DIDN'T RETURN for night's feast. She had a sick niece to care for on the other side of the island – or so my mother said. Mazriah had never used any time off before, so it had been granted, even at the last minute.

Dejected, I ate little of the fish and rice and went to bed early, wondering when I could find Mazriah and ask her again. Surely she'd return in the morning with the other servants.

But the next morning a knock on my door surprised me.

"Yes?" I called out, sliding into my leather sandals.

"Darling, will you join us for breakfast?" asked my mother, from the other side of the door.

I stiffened at the unusual request. "O...kay."

"Wonderful. I'll see you downstairs."

I listened to the fading sound of her footsteps against the stone as she walked back down the hallway.

Breakfast meant I'd be delayed in checking on Kirwyn. I grabbed a chewstick and some paste and quickly cleaned my teeth. I ran my fingers through my hair and bolted out the door.

My mother had re-styled her hair -- it was smoothed into its elaborate updo and the silver crown rested upon her head. My father, dwarfing his stool as usual, sat to her side. Jona, affixed into a child's chair, sat on the other side. They were all looking at Gereth and laughing. A small, green lizard had wandered in from the patio and Gereth was wild with enthusiasm to hug the creature, who only wanted a speedy exit back outside. For a moment, I had an odd feeling. Like I didn't belong. Like an outsider, looking in on the picture of someone else's happy family.

My thoughts were interrupted by two young kitchen maids bringing out bowls of breadfruit in coconut milk, and trays of sliced passion fruits and sunberries. As I took a seat at the table, my stomach rumbled, and I was suddenly glad I had stopped to eat. With a shelled spoon, I heaped the breadfruit into my mouth, tasting the addition of vanilla and cinnamon spices. Then I dug into the tart passion fruit, scooping out a large portion of the black-seeded, jelly innards.

"How are you feeling?" my mother asked.

I blinked. "I'm okay. Why?"

Suddenly, I had a feeling I knew why she asked. Distracted by Kirwyn, I hadn't given much thought to it...

"You're... well?" my father asked. He stroked my mother's hand as he spoke.

"I'm good. Why?"

And then, my mother told me. What tomorrow's final pageant would entail.

Suddenly, I didn't feel so hungry anymore.

CHAPTER 29

I strained to hear above the drumbeat of rain against the broad, leafy trees. It was one of those magical thunderstorms where the rain fell and the sun shone at the same time, and the effect fragmented deep under the forest canopy. Raindrops pooled on branches, dripping down in clusters and the sun broke through boughs in scattered beams.

"Kirwyn?" I called into the rain. I swept my wet hair back off my face. He wasn't inside the cave, and I began to worry that the mushrooms hit him harder than I thought.

Or worse, what if he dragged himself to the grotto and one of the guards caught him?

"Kirwyn!" I shouted louder, spinning in circles and blinking against the rain that ran into my eyes.

The tackle came from the left. I didn't even hear him coming.

"Ah!" I screamed.

Kirwyn pounced, sweeping me off my feet and laying me – not entirely gently - onto wet earth, slick and slippery with soggy leaves. He pinned my arms above my head with one hand. With the other, he began tickling me all over.

"Stop!" I gasped, rain pelting my face. I was very, very ticklish.

"Say *mercy*," Kirwyn commanded, working on a spot at my belly. His hard body held me down; I could barely kick.

"Mercy!" I shouted, without hesitation.

"Say *'Kirwyn is telling the truth about everything,'*" he instructed, having moved on to a more sensitive spot on my neck.

"Kirwyn... is... tellingthetruthabouteverything." The words tumbled out my mouth between giggles.

"Say, *'I'm falling for you, Kirwyn,'*" he said, tickling in the worst area possible, the underside of my arm.

Laughing so hard I couldn't get a full breath, I repeated the words without any real feeling behind them.

"I'm falling for you, Kirwyn."

"Louder," Kirwyn said.

"I'm falling for you, Kirwyn!" I shouted, squirming and laughing and panting.

Fighting for air, I barely noticed he had stopped his assault. Kirwyn no longer laughed or tickled or even moved.

I looked up into his eyes.

Praise Keroe. His forest gaze could smolder like wildfire raged within.

"I'm falling for you too, Zaria," Kirwyn said in a low, husky voice.

That strange, pleasurable sensation shot up inside my chest again, like butterflies or lightning, running from my stomach to my heart.

Kirwyn leaned down and slid his tongue into my mouth

for a deep kiss, dizzying me. I closed my eyes, but somehow everything still spun in the dark.

"Wow," I smiled, opening my eyes and blinking against the rain. "If this is what happens when I let you eat stomach-upsetting mushrooms, perhaps I should poison you more often."

Kirwyn squeezed my side. "Ouch. Okay, okay."

"Say you'll leave with me," Kirwyn ordered. His soaked shirt pressed against his torso in a distracting manner. Raindrops slid from his dark hair onto my face, my neck.

"Let's get a boat and leave tonight. Say you'll come with me, Zaria. If you're leaving this place, your family anyway... let it be with me."

My smile fell. I turned my head to the wet trees.

"Zaria. You can't possibly..." Kirwyn picked himself up off me and backed away.

I sat up, but my shoulders fell, defeated.

"Kirwyn, I can't let my people down and dishonor my family, myself. You have to understand. I have a duty..." I took a deep breath. "My mother told me what my last pageant is, tomorrow. I have to touch the Goodnight Fish."

Kirwyn scowled. "The what?"

"It's a poisonous fish. I'll be fine, it's very rare that anything fatal happens. It'll just hurt a lot."

"Zaria, are you crazy? This is madness! You can't still want to go through with any of this! No. *No.* I won't let you!"

Kirwyn lunged at me and scooped me up. I screamed carelessly, and, worried someone might hear, abruptly stopped. Instead, I hit Kirwyn with my fists as he threw me over his shoulder. I kicked my legs and beat his back, but he carried me into the cave.

"Stop it, put me down!" I seethed.

He did -- tossing me, wet and muddy, onto the rug.

I crawled past him, stumbling to my feet as I made a break for the forest. Kirwyn grabbed my waist and yanked me back. I clawed at his slippery limbs and we tumbled as he threw me back on the rug. Kirwyn shot to his feet above me. He stood tensed, ready.

"You can't keep me here!" I shouted, hands balled into fists while I found my own feet.

Kirwyn's nostrils flared. His breath fell heavy, animalistic.

"Let me go," I ordered in a measured, controlled voice.

I could see the conflict in his eyes. He was debating what to do with me. *Would I end up tied to the rock, like the day he had awoken?*

"Kirwyn, let me go," I repeated, with calm I didn't feel. "You can't keep someone who doesn't want to stay."

A pang shot across my heart as I said it, but I didn't stop. "What are you going to do? Steal a boat yourself? Gag me? Sail us into the Blue Beyond? Think about it rationally. You can't ask this of me. You can't ask me to trust you, someone I just met, someone who doesn't make sense -- over my own people, my own family."

"Then don't," Kirwyn said, holding my gaze. "I'm not asking you to. *You* think about it, Zaria. *Trust yourself.*"

"I- I..." I stammered. Not allowing myself to consider his words, I declared, "I'm going."

Kirwyn's face changed. It hardened into a blank, stone wall. In response I tensed, waiting to see what he would do next. Rain continued to pound the ground outside.

"Fine. Go." He moved aside so that I could pass.

I swallowed. This wasn't what I wanted to happen. I didn't know what I wanted. But, *not this.* On the other hand, I didn't want him to change his mind. I quickly walked past him.

His arm shot out, his hard grip clasping my wrist.

I stopped, meeting Kirwyn's eyes. He was so close I could feel his breath on my forehead. I watched his chest rise and fall through his soaked shirt.

I flicked my eyes back up to his strange and beautiful face. So *impossibly* gorgeous. I was unable to turn away. My feet refused me.

Was I making a mistake? Should I stay?

Suddenly, with disgust, Kirwyn threw aside my arm. He rested his hands on his hips and turned to stare into the back of the cave. His face took on a faraway look, as if he gazed at some distant horizon.

I had the unsettling feeling that, even though he physically stood right there, I was alone in the cave.

That was what I wanted, right? To be left alone, to go?

I went.

CHAPTER 30

The wind picked up, just like the day before. Afternoon rains would pour down any minute. As ominous as the storm seemed, I hoped it would last.

At least they'll be able to keep me cool when the fever rages.

I had known *something* of this pageant all my life, the display of my spiritual faith, my belief in Keroe to carry me through the darkest of nights to the light of recovery. But now, I approached the trial with absolute dread in my stomach, due to more than just the fear of pain.

Had I lost my faith?

"Braenese Zaria!" the villagers called to me, whipped into a celebratory frenzy as I walked up the path to the grand courtyard. Many threw white petals at my feet.

But this time, their jubilance did not reach my heart.

Once again, they made a wide path. Only women lined the front, blocking males from accidentally spilling out and touching me.

As I neared the platform, the cheers died down, and a somber mood settled over everyone, respectful of the dangerous feat. I swallowed, *hard,* unsure what chilled me more -- the ridiculousness of the joyous cheers or the eerie quiet of the rapt crowd.

Nasero stood at the edge of the dais, ceremonial robes touching the ground. I wondered if the dark seashell necklace he wore was the same as the old High Mystic's, or if they fashioned a new one. It was a preposterous thought to have at that moment; perhaps my mind began to snap.

"Children of Keroe," Nasero bellowed, "today, on Braenese Zaria's final pageant, she will touch the Goodnight Fish with her fingertip. She will cross the dark night, carried by Keroe's arms into the light of his love. She will fall as his betrothed and arise as his bride."

Don't do it, I heard Kirwyn's voice shout in my head.

What choice do I have? I silently cried, echoing yesterday's argument.

There was no other way. I could touch the Goodnight Fish or I could leap into the unknown with Kirwyn.

Which scared me even more.

There were no other options. I *had* to touch it, I *had* to burn.

Would dying hurt? I wondered.

No. I was young and strong. I *wouldn't* die and I wouldn't let morbid pessimism consume me. I would *fight.* The strong developed fevers, but they passed.

But you might have a deadly reaction, a voice inside my head countered.

I'd seen men – tough, able-bodied men -- carried to a water's grave by the poison. No one knew what caused the rare allergic reaction, but sometimes... victims didn't survive.

There was no use in debating. I could not refuse and shame my family. I shook my head and swallowed again.

There was no other way, no path around the pain, only straight through it.

I could hear whispers from the crowd. Prayers for me from the lips of the elderly. Questions from children, bored and unable to understand what was happening or too young to care.

I longed to switch places with the beseeching old ladies, the restless children. I wanted to be *anyone* but myself right now.

If I die, he'll never forgive me.

I looked out into the sea of faces around me.

Was he here? Hiding in the crowd? Or could he not bear to witness?

I shifted my eyes to the dais as I climbed. The Mystics stood further back in their semi-circle, all wearing their long, ceremonial robes. Nasero alone stood in front.

On a wooden table before him sat a clear bowl of Old World glass, permitting the crowd to witness the touch.

Inside the bowl floated the insidious creature.

The container wasn't big enough for it to swim, it simply *hovered* with malicious energy.

If a person didn't know the fish was poisonous, it seemed harmless, stupid even; with its dull expression, its mouth opening and closing mindlessly. The undulating fins were almost pretty.

"I cannot hold your hand," my mother whispered in my ear. She carried a bowl of water that had been warmed by the fire, for after, to draw out the sting. "You must go alone. You *must* be brave. Make our family proud."

She pressed the side of her face to mine, turned toward me, and kissed my cheek. I inhaled her distinctive, floral perfume. "You *are* so brave, Zaria. So much braver than I ever was."

What did she mean? She was unflappable. I wished I had *her* strength for this.

I didn't have time to mull over her words because Nasero beckoned. I had to step forward, I had to put one foot in front of the other.

How badly will it hurt? I wondered.

Every victim's reaction differed. The pain could last for hours or torture the body for days. Maybe I'd be lucky and experience only a blistering agony in my hand. More likely, I'd have intense stomach pain and unrelenting nausea. Possibly I'd lose myself in delirium or temporary paralysis.

Though it was unlikely to expect the worst case, *death...* some victims experienced a breath-shock, reacting to the venom with an allergy closing off the lungs.

A very painful way to die.

Of course, no one believed Keroe would abandon me to death.

Fear, coursing cold through my belly, nearly doubled me over as I thought, *but no one knows what I have done.*

I stood beside Nasero, facing the silent crowd. The strong winds rustled the trees louder than the quiet breath of the entire village before me. Was it my imagination or did it carry the sweet scent of frangipani? I closed my eyes and inhaled, wondering if it would be the last time I'd smell its perfume.

Nasero intoned another of his long speeches, but now more than ever, I couldn't hear a word of it. An ocean roared in my ears, drowning out everything else.

It's only a touch, I told myself. *That's all you have to do. One touch and then, fight it, heal.*

I knew my face was the pale of death. I knew fear shone from my wild eyes. I wouldn't have been surprised if everyone could hear the thumping of my heart against my ribcage. I was beyond caring.

I didn't want to do this. I didn't understand why any longer.

It was time.

Nasero stepped aside, folding back into the crescent of Mystics.

I was alone.

I looked back at my mother, searching her face for some desperate exit or some secret store of courage to face what I was about to do. She stood quietly, back straight, face blank. But hidden from the crowd by my father's body, her right hand twitched -- the thumb running up and down her opposing fingers, wringing upon itself.

My father's face was firmly set. I don't know what I expected. A smile? A nod? What could they possibly do to make this easier for me? The task was mine alone.

My family disappeared as I turned back to the bowl. The village didn't exist. It was only me and the fat fish. Slimy, undulating fins. Moronic expression. Mouth opening and closing stupidly.

Landdammit, this pageant.

Why couldn't I spear one of these instead? Prove my prowess on the hunt? Why must I fall, like a maiden in a fable, awakened by the Sea God's love? Wouldn't it be more useful to show I could *kill* a Goodnight Fish, than to get myself poisoned like a silly schoolgirl? Didn't that make me a more worthy bride?

I didn't want to put my hand in the glass, I wanted to spear it. Fling it's bleeding, lifeless body onto the grass before the crowd.

But I had no spear. I had no way out.

The only way out, was through.

As I lifted my hand, I realized it trembled and I couldn't make it stop. Everything in my body screamed, *no, no, no,* even as I stepped forward. It was like I wasn't myself. I was out of my body, my limbs possessed. Someone else was moving my hand toward the evil creature before me. Tears leaked out the corners of my eyes.

Don't put your hand in there! my mind screamed. But my body kept moving toward the bowl.

It was all rather passive, really, compared to the other pageants. Just stick one finger inside, and the fish would do the rest.

My hand rose over the bowl, shaking. *Please let me get through this, please let me be strong.*

Like Kirwyn.

Why didn't I run away with him when I had the chance? It was too late now. If I ran, the guards would follow.

I'm sorry, Keroe, I thought. *I... don't want to marry you. I'm sorry. I'm not worthy to be your bride.*

At that moment, everything became clear. I wondered why I didn't see it before. *His* handsome face, *his* devil-may-care smile appeared in my mind.

I want to be with Kirwyn.

I no longer cared if he was a liar or a madman or if his burning world was real. It didn't matter if we set sail and fell off the great waterfall to the west, it didn't matter if we were doomed to die at sea. I would take the chance.

If I make it through this and you still want me, I will run away with you, I vowed.

I fought against the instinct to close my eyes.

Kirwyn, I whispered, as my finger broke the water's surface.

I didn't have to do more. The fish moved lightning fast

in its defense, striking my index finger with one of its venomous fins.

I jerked my hand back.

Oh Keroe, it should have ended there, that should have been the worst of it.

If only.

Panicked, I stumbled, and took the bowl down with me.

The fish seized upon my whole hand as it crashed beside me. I screamed ceaselessly as I threw myself backward, as if I could move away from the impending torture.

For a few seconds I didn't feel anything.

Then, *fire.*

It *burned* inside.

Oh Keroe, it burned inside my very muscles, my veins, the fire was *inside* me. My hand dripped blood, cut from the stinging spines or glass, I didn't know.

The pain, too intense, couldn't possibly be borne. I needed to escape my body and I couldn't. I thrashed on the floor, a spectacle for the entire island. My mother knelt beside me, grabbed my hand, and thrust it into a bowl of hot water to draw out the sting. With gloved hands she examined my own for any stuck spines to withdraw.

"Please," I moaned. "Help me - ow!" I yelped as she removed a spine.

The scenery around me blurred. Searing fire coursed through me. I couldn't bear it, I couldn't, I would die.

"Help..." I moaned, and air whooshed under me as healers lifted me onto a thin, flat bed. The women carried me toward the palace and my mother kept pace beside me. One of her hands held the bowl of hot water to ease the pain, the other used a blissfully cold cloth on my forehead, wiping away the sweat.

I didn't remember returning home. I only remembered

unbearable pain and my mother wiping my face, shoulders, and chest, as I soaked the stretcher with sweat.

Just once, I spared a thought for the fish, gasping its last breaths upon the dais. It was supposed to be ceremoniously killed with a spear after stinging me, a ritual to be performed by the High Mystic. There would be no need now.

In and out of consciousness, the next thing I registered was that we were in the sitting room that led out to the water table. There was nothing in my stomach and yet I gagged, bringing up bile.

"Zaria, you must keep this down," my mother said.

Confused, I looked up and saw that she was handing me a white tablet, formulated from an Old World medicine recipe, and a cup of water.

I shook my head, dizzier than ever. "Please make the pain go away."

"My darling, swallow this. It will help. Please, you must."

I opened my mouth and she dropped the medicine inside, but I gagged with a sip of water – no, not water, Tamarind tea - and it fell onto the floor in a puddle.

My mother, all business, wiped my head with more cold water and tried again. This time, I got it down.

"The tea, make sure you drink some tea."

I struggled to swallow two gulps.

"How long?" I begged. "How long will this last?"

"I don't know," she replied. "The pain should subside in a few hours, but it will get worse before it gets better. You did not go into the breath-shock, my darling, you survived, you're safe."

Wiping my body, she said, "You're to be Queen, Zaria. Keroe saved you. You're to be his Queen."

My eyes seemed incapable of focusing on the room around me. Delirium? The pull of sleep began, maybe from something in the medicine. I had no strength to fight it and no desire. I wanted to run to a place of not-feeling, to escape the fire in my bones.

The real world faded away, morphing into a delusion or a dreamscape. I was half in each world.

Beside me, I could see the edges of the sofa -- but slightly ahead a path appeared, lined with trees on either side and leading to a beach.

Kirwyn stood knee-deep in the waves and the sun was at that perfect angle where it threw a thousand silver sparkles off the water around him, shining and glinting like Old World diamonds.

"Kirwyn..." I called, not sure if I said his name in this world or the one ahead.

CHAPTER 31

Speechless, I surveyed the swooning, rapturous crowd before me.

Women tossed pink and white petals into the air. From the back, men linked arms over shoulders and broke out into the jubilant hymn *Glory be the Sea*.

My final tiara, inset with pearls and wrought from Old World gold, rested upon my head.

I was the Sea Queen.

A goddess.

And I no longer saw a way out.

How could I leave? Disgrace my family before all... *this?*

Two days ago, on this very dais, I writhed in pain.

Now I stood as Keroe's bride, worshipped by my people.

"All you alright?" my mother asked. She had to shout for me to hear her.

"It's a bit... overwhelming." I smiled weakly. "If there's time today, after lunch, I'd like to go for a swim."

My mother nodded. I wasn't sure she would agree but she seemed distracted by something. She wore her formal, embroidered tunic and her hair was twisted up into perfection, set with her silver crown. I could smell her strange, floral perfume.

My father shifted Jona, sleeping despite all the noise, from his right hip to his left, in order to stand closer to my mother. Gereth played by their feet.

"Let's retire," my mother said.

"Yes. I'd like a cup of tea," my father replied.

"I'LL BE BACK in a few hours," I called, slinging my sack over my shoulder as my stomach growled.

My mother had requested Chicken with a Baby again and I'd only picked at the edges. There was no sense in telling her that I no longer liked the dish. Whatever happened, I didn't have much time left.

Questions played in my mind as I ran under the cloudless sky, through the leafy Pawpaw orchards and the royal forest, straight for the cave.

Would Kirwyn forgive me?

How could I make him understand?

Had he spied on me again?

Did he even know I lived?

"Kirwyn?" I called, pushing aside the vines and bursting into the cave.

Empty.

Yet all my Old World objects remained in place... as if no one was ever there.

I tensed, expecting an attack from behind.

Nothing came.

"Kirwyn?" I called outside, careful not to shout too loudly.

Nothing moved among the trees except two orange

butterflies dancing in flight. I strained my ears, but there was no sound other than the low buzz of insects and the flutter of leaves in the breeze.

Had he gone?

My stomach tightened and I felt I might get sick.

Or had he been caught?

I couldn't breathe. The world seemed to close in on me and I thought I might faint.

Where was Kirwyn?

I plopped onto the ground and propped my back against a large rock, trying to quell the rising nausea.

At Kirwyn's sudden absence, the truth I did not know or did not want to know pierced my heart -- I literally clutched my heart, pained.

The truth was always there, really. Standing right next to me. While my gaze remained fixed on some far away horizon. All I had to do was turn and look.

At him. I should have been looking at him.

Closing my eyes, I folded my arms across my knees. I dropped my forehead to rest upon my hands.

But I was too late.

I knew too late.

He was gone. Kirwyn was gone. As mysteriously as he appeared; he disappeared.

Slowly, I opened my eyes to stare at the dirt below.

That's when I saw it.

The lumpy skin of a sugar apple. I reached down and grabbed it.

Sticky. Fresh.

He *wasn't* gone. Kirwyn was *here* this morning.

He might even be here now. Watching me.

At the thought, my head shot up, scanning the grassy

roof of the cave above. I jumped to my feet and spun in circles, searching the surrounding forest.

I wouldn't put it past him to be lurking.

No, he was most likely up to something. Perhaps seeking a boat to steal.

I needed to make amends.

I needed him to know... that I knew.

Withdrawing his book from my sack, I resolved several things. First, I would leave him a note. *But what to write with?*

I searched the ground for a stick, then took out the knife I'd been carrying in my tunic since the day Kirwyn had awoken and attacked me. Using the blade, I scraped one end of the wood into a sharp point.

I tapped my lips, trying to figure out a colorant to use for writing. If I had a fire, soot would work, but it was too risky to build one.

Berries, maybe? A fireberry would do.

I put everything back into my sack and trekked through the wood, searching for the bright pink flower adorning the fireberry tree. It took longer than I thought. I was so used to their presence in our gardens, I wasn't sure where the tree grew near the cave. Eventually, I found one, and plucked fistfuls of red berries ready to burst.

Single-mindedly, I ran back to the cave, smashed the fireberries with the back of a shelled spoon, and dipped the stick into the dye.

I opened the first page of Kirwyn's book and wrote.

I'm sorry.

Meet me tonight, outside the cave.

I want to take you somewhere.

CHAPTER 32

The moon, a winking sliver, glistened upon waters. Three days until it disappeared completely, three days until my wedding.

But not tonight.

Tonight, the moon is mine. It existed just for me. *For us.*

I felt like I could fly right up and touch it if I wanted.

But nothing I desired was there. *Everything I want is right here, with Kirwyn.* In fact, it seemed more like the Lady Moon, shrinking in the sky with envy, was jealous of *us.*

I laughed as I swam and Kirwyn laughed in return. With some persuading, he'd forgiven me. Kissed me. Followed me.

Now I was delirious, drunk on moonlight. I didn't even need the sea-wine we brought. Not that I wouldn't have some.

The swim in open water - out around the cliff - led to the enclosed beach of Lover's Cove.

I had tied a rope to Kirwyn's waist; the other end bobbed with a wooden basket containing our food and supplies, meant to stay dry. Being the better swimmer, I told Kirwyn I could carry it, but he'd insisted on doing it himself.

After slogging our way onto the beach, we each collapsed on the sand. He was heaving and breathless.

"Thought you said it's not a long swim?" Kirwyn gasped between gulps of air.

"I've been swimming since I was born," I shrugged.

"Man, that worked up an appetite. I'm so hungry I could eat a beetle," he teased.

I swiped my hand on the beach, tossing sand at him as he laughed.

Reaching over, I opened the wooden basket and laid out the contents.

First, a thin blanket, inside which we had wrapped a bottle of sea-wine. Next, a sharp knife, wooden utensils, two coconuts, and a leather skin with freshwater. Then I pulled out our meal.

To start, unleavened bread, topped with goat cheese and sea-grape jam. Next, a tri-green salad of cucumber, celery, and beans. Then I laid out roasted, spice-rubbed potatoes to accompany pots of tender goat meat, served over rice with pepper sauce. Lastly, for dessert, squared, little pink-and-white coconut crèmes.

It wasn't easy to sneak out this much food from the kitchens. I told the servants I was planning an early-morning picnic with Tomé to celebrate his engagement and my triumph, and that I wanted to have everything ready to go that night, as we'd be leaving before dawn. Tomé was spending so much time at Lida and Marcin's house, I didn't even worry that he'd show up at the palace and ruin my lie.

Then I snuck out my window by climbing down the tree again. The jump hadn't gotten any easier, but I had gotten bolder.

When I finished laying out the feast, I noticed Kirwyn staring at me with his intense green stare that threatened to make me swoon.

"I've never had such a meal," he said. "Thank you."

"What did you eat where you come from?" I asked.

"When we lived in the library we ate well. Fresh vegetables from the farm and game we hunted. I even grew herbs in the attic. Things weren't so bad then. But once we decided to try for the southland ship, food on the road was scarce. Sometimes we'd meet people and could barter. In the beginning, when we had more supplies, we'd trade. Pickled vegetables for bricks. We ate a lot of bricks on the journey."

I scowled. "I know what a brick is. We have them from the Old World. We can make our own, too, in a fashion."

"No, no," Kirwyn shook his head quickly. "I mean, yes, we have those bricks too. But bricks are what we call food the Blackjacks produce. Ah, I use the term *food* lightly. It's a sort of a dried, powdered concoction of the barest vitamins and minerals needed to keep you alive, formed into a brick shape. They use them to feed their slaves. It's not tasty, but it'll do the job."

While he spoke, Kirwyn had uncorked the sea-wine and he held it out to me. I took a deep swig and passed it back to Kirwyn, who drank a deep sip as well.

"That's good. A little sweet, but not as much as I expected. More fruity, really. Would do well if you traded it." He cocked a lopsided grin. "Wine is a big deal in the Northern Continent. Everyone wants to drink to forget, but the good stuff is hard to come by, so it's very valuable. Long ago, wildfires ravaged many of the vines beyond the Cold Mountains and what's left is controlled through guarded roads. There's a guy who has a monopoly on the western route."

"What?" I asked, having difficulty following.

Kirwyn let out a low whistle. "Mal-Yin. Can't be more than twenty-five. Runs his own clan, he staged some kind of coup. They don't make wine, but they bring it from the west because they control the trade routes there. Blackjacks pay gold for it. Mal-Yin... the world's on fire and he's roasting sausage in the flames. They've got some kind of Chinese symbol on their backs. It could stand for wine or grape, I guess," Kirwyn spreads his hands, "or maybe it stands for something else entirely. Who knows? I don't speak Chinese."

I frowned. "What is Chinese?"

Kirwyn exhaled slowly. "Right. I keep forgetting all you don't know...crazy. It's a... another land, a different language."

I blinked. "How do you expect me to believe you when your lies get bigger and bolder?"

"I swear I'm telling the truth," he protested. "Where I come from is just *one* place. There are other lands, other continents. People speak different languages and when they travel and move around, they bring the languages with them."

"Prove it." I crossed my arms. "Speak the different words, the Chinese ones."

"I can't," Kirwyn admitted. "I don't know any Mandarin."

"Convenient."

But... there could be some truth to his claim, I thought. After all, we had books in an Old World tongue no longer used.

"How many languages are there?" I asked, skeptically.

"Countless. Tens of thousands, hundreds of thousands maybe. For millions of people."

I couldn't picture that many people. Where did they all fit?

We passed the sea-wine back and forth a few times and started nibbling on the cheese and jam bread.

"Okay, so, can you speak anything else?" I asked. "Say something in another language."

"I know a little Gaelic from my uncle," Kirwyn said, and rolled a string of nonsense off his tongue he could have easily made up.

"And what's that supposed to mean?" I asked, narrowing my eyes.

"I'll make you a deal. I'll tell you when we get off this island."

I rolled my eyes and grabbed the coconuts.

"Here, I'll do that," Kirwyn offered, taking the knife from my hand.

He cut holes into the coconut flesh, for drinking. He liked the sweet water so much, I wished I could have brought more. There were no palm trees on this beach, no trees of any kind. Just sand, and, abutting that, sheer rock. Which also meant nowhere to hide. But who would come looking in the middle of the night?

We ate the crisp salad and then Kirwyn dug his wooden fork into the goat. Ravenous, as usual, he took a huge bite and swallowed.

Kirwyn's eyes bulged.

Cough.

"Oh my god!" he sputtered.

Cough, cough.

"Spicy..." he croaked. "What's in that?"

Exhaling heavily, as if to expel fire, he cried, "Need more water!"

Had I all the strength in the world, I wouldn't have been able to hold back my laughter.

The sea-wine probably didn't help.

Kirwyn shot to his feet and ran to ocean. He ducked his head under water and popped it back up, shooting seawater out his mouth like a fountain. He repeated the gesture over and over.

"*Don't-*" I gasped, holding my belly as I fell into a fit of laughter so wild, I may have snorted. "Don't swallow it, it'll make you sick."

Kirwyn sloshed back to our beach picnic, dripping.

"Whatever is in *that,*" he pointed with contempt, "needs to be killed. It's trying to kill me."

"I'm sorry. It's just a little blood pepper. Here. You can have my potatoes-" I handed him my portion, "-and if you just eat the rice, without the sauce, it's not so bad. I'll eat your goat."

Kirwyn grudgingly accepted and poked delicately around the rice for pieces without sauce.

By the time we finished our meal, the bottle of wine was three quarters empty, and it was as if it had poured liquid giddiness into me.

"I've never met anyone like you on the mainland," Kirwyn said, passing me the bottle. He smiled, genuine. Not a smirk in sight. "My princess who saved me."

I blushed. I wanted to kiss him.

And more.

I couldn't deny it. I knew why I brought us here.

Oh Keroe, this is crazy and I don't care.

Kirwyn leaned toward me. A school of minnows swam in frenzied circles in my stomach. I could smell the musk of him as he bent closer. My heart pounded so hard it shot out of my chest and soared into the sky.

Kirwyn's lips neared. Inches from mine and coming closer.

Up, up, my heart went, straight past the moon.

"Wait," Kirwyn blurted.

Wait?

He grinned ear-to-ear. "You haven't eaten any bugs today, have you? Hey!"

With all the force of my weight behind it I pushed him back onto the sand, straddled his body between mine, and brought my mouth down to the softness of his.

Kirwyn's tongue entwined with my own. I could taste the sea-wine on his lips. My heart re-commenced its shot into the sky and exploded, bursting into a thousand stars.

If I wasn't drunk on moonlight and sea-wine already, I'd be drunk on those lips. On Kirwyn's woodsy, masculine scent.

On his touch, tender but urgent, lifting my tunic as we kissed.

"Zaria..." He whispered my name in my ear and like the tide, it pulled me out into a blissful sea.

CHAPTER 33

The moon saw it all, but the moon has no tongue.

"Tell me more about your life in the other world," I whispered, stretching out beside Kirwyn, my heart still thumping in my chest.

In my bliss, I felt we forged an unbreakable connection and I wanted to know everything possible. I could listen to him talk for the rest of my life, truth or lies.

I drew lazy, undulating patterns on his flat torso. "You read and farmed all day?"

"I practiced fighting, too, and marksmanship," he said. "We kept two stallions in an abandoned barn outside of town. Years of practice in the mountains helped me become good at horseback riding."

"What's a horseback?" I asked.

"Oh. A horse. It's like a goat. But bigger. And quicker. You can ride them to get somewhere faster."

"You ride beasts in your world? Sounds magical. Do they fly?" I giggled and jumped on top of Kirwyn. He slipped his tongue into my mouth and we rolled, one over the other, kissing as the waves lapped at our feet.

"You're a beast," I whispered into his ear, *"and I fly riding you."*

I had tossed my head back and declared the last part to the cove, to anyone who could hear it. I didn't care that I said something silly, or lewd, or blasphemous, or that I was getting married someday, far away.

All I cared about, all that existed, was Kirwyn. This beach. Our moon.

KIRWYN PUT his arm under his head as he looked up at the fading stars. Morning wasn't far off. We hadn't much time. No amount of my wishing could stall the dawn. No Mystic spell; not even my mother and one hundred Steel Guards could command its halt.

"This reminds me of a poem," Kirwyn said.

I flipped onto my side and propped my head on my arm.

"It's called *The Love Song of J. Alfred Prufrock.*"

He recited,

"Shall I part my hair behind? Do I dare to eat a peach?
I shall wear white flannel trousers, and walk upon the beach.
I have heard the mermaids singing, each to each.
I do not think they will sing to me.
I have seen them riding seaward on the waves
Combing the white hair of the waves blown back
When the wind blows the water white and black.
We have lingered in the chambers of the sea
By sea-girls wreathed with seaweed red and brown
Till human voices wake us, and we drown."

"That's beautiful," I breathed. "Am I the mermaid? Or the human voice to drown you? Or wait," I smiled and pointed my finger. "You're the mermaid."

At the sadness in Kirwyn's eyes, my stomach tightened, even before he spoke.

"You're Alfred," he said, surprising me, "this place is the mermaid. And something's coming to wake you up and drown you."

"That's… no. Don't ruin tonight. Don't start. We don't have much time left. Please."

"I'm sorry," Kirwyn said, pulling me closer. He ran his hands down my side and I shivered. Would I ever get used to all this touching?

We lay like that for several minutes, saying nothing, just holding onto each other.

Then Kirwyn swept his gaze across the sky and spoke. "We better leave before it gets light. Look, there's Mars," he pointed at something above us. "Dawn's not far off."

"What's Mars?" I asked. "Is that one of your names for a star?"

"No, a planet," Kirwyn said.

I frowned.

"I keep forgetting all you don't know," Kirwyn marveled, taking on his teacher voice again.

"There are planets out there, like this one." He pointed to the earth below us. "All kinds of shapes and sizes, although none can support humans. We never found life on other planets when the space program was still running, but the odds are, it's out there. I've always been fascinated by the idea of aliens, of people living on different planets. It's a lost cause that we'll ever build back up to search for them, but I always hope they'll find us. Someday."

As Kirwyn spoke, I grew from curious, to shocked, to enraged.

My blood boiled by the time he was finished.

Nonsense. He spewed the outrageous lies of a madman.

It was one thing to cover up his own origins with colorful stories about land past the Blue Beyond, but it was something else to make up worlds levitating in the sky.

Kirwyn read the look on my face.

"Zaria..." he began, but I stopped him by holding up my hand, jaw clenched.

Unbelievable.

I didn't even want to talk about it.

Just like that, the connection broke. A wall of tension rebuilt between us. It was as if the coming dawn reinforced it, telling us our night together was over.

I sat up, turning away from both Kirwyn and the dawn, facing the dark sea. I began packing up the dirty plates.

"Let's go," I said. "We have to swim back."

CHAPTER 34

The sky remained blessedly dark as we swam, no orange-gray predawn threatening to poke out behind the promontory of the Fire Maidens.

Kirwyn had tied the basket, full of empty plates and containers, to his waist. He managed to keep up with the brutal pace I set.

Other worlds.

I gritted my teeth, pounding the water with my strokes.

Kirwyn relished making up unbelievable stories about different lands, now floating in thin air.

And what was wrong with this one? Who was Kirwyn to come in and tell me I should leave with him? Who did he think he was to tell me anything at all?

I'd worked myself into a nearly blind rage as we trampled through the moonlit forest. By the time we reached the cave, gray in the morning light, my head ached. I needed sleep.

"Zaria, please," Kirwyn pleaded, ten paces behind me. "I'm going to leave this island."

"As am I," I said, flipping my wet hair. I didn't turn back.

"No, I - *goddammit, Zaria!*"

I peeked behind me. Kirwyn kicked at the dirt.

"Come with me. I won't force you. Just...come."

"To the floating worlds in the sky? No thank you. I prefer the sea."

"Zaria," Kirwyn growled, grabbing my arm.

I raised my eyebrows.

He dropped it.

Kirwyn raked his hand through his hair and opened his mouth to speak again, but I held up my hand.

I didn't want to hear it. *More lies, more tales.* He *should* entertain children at the Story Gathering, I thought. He'd be a hit.

Who *wasn't* lying to me anymore?

Enough.

What was I thinking anyway? *I was marrying the Sea God, for crying out loud.*

My whole life, I'd prepared for this. My family, the entire *island* expected it of me. And here I was, throwing it all away for... what? One night with a compulsive liar?

"The celebration feast is tomorrow night," I said in my haughtiest voice. "The following evening I'll set out to sea, after my wedding ceremony."

Lifting my chin, I said, "I suggest that you not snoop on either event. The entire Steel Guard will be present."

"Stop," Kirwyn commanded, grabbing my arm again.

"Don't. Touch. Me." I spat. "It's forbidden."

Kirwyn's face looked as if I had just slapped him.

I yanked my arm free and left him staring as I stalked into the forest. Shades of green came out with the growing light and I picked up my pace.

Who did he think he was? Who did he think *I* was?

I was *Braenese Zaria.* Not some deceiver's conquest.

With each step I grew more enraged. I swatted at leaves. Mosquitos. Branches. I sent birds flying to the safety of the treetops.

I thought I couldn't get any angrier by the time I reached the orchard.

I was wrong.

"*My, my,* where has princess of purity been at this hour?"

Lida stood by the gate, deep brown eyes studying me carefully.

"Where have *you* been?" I demanded, directing my rage at her pinched face. "Or should I say, *with whom?* Because you and I both know that baby is not Tomé's."

"I know nothing of the sort," she replied curtly.

It took all my restraint not to grab her, to shake the truth out.

Enough of everyone lying.

"Tomé doesn't love you and he doesn't want to marry you. Ruin his life, why don't you? Just don't lie about it. No one believes for a second that you two are in love. Tell yourself whatever you want, Lida. But don't tell it to me."

I pushed past her.

"Did you ever think that what I was doing was good for him too?" Lida called out behind me.

I paused but did not relax my shoulders or unclench my fists.

"Everything's so easy for you, isn't it? The rest of us have to make difficult choices. Choices for ourselves, our families, difficult choices for *you.*"

I spun on my heel. She didn't know *anything* if she thought choices were easy for me.

"What are you talking about?" I grit out between clenched teeth.

Lida shook her head. "Nothing. Go marry your Sea God. None of this is your problem. It never was."

Lida turned and walked in the opposite direction.

"What are you talking about?" I shouted after her, but she kept walking.

I had to let her go, it was getting too light out.

That's it, I thought.

I'd had enough of being lied to. Of people speaking in riddles and half-truths.

I was getting married in two days.

I needed answers before my wedding.

And I knew where to find them.

SHE WRUNG HER HANDS, fidgeting on the wooden stool before me. From the moment I summoned her, she knew what I wanted.

"Mazriah. I need to know. Is there something out there, in the Blue Beyond? I mean, above the sea. I mean, land?"

She continued to look around, anywhere but at me.

"Because I'll find out soon enough. But I'd like to know beforehand. It's important that I know. Now."

She brought her hand to her mouth. I tried another tactic.

"The Sea God... is he really going to be my husband? Does he really exist?"

"Please don't speak such blasphemy," she whispered, eyes round. "Of course he exists."

Hearing her speak astonished me, but I quickly seized the opportunity.

"And in two night's time. My wedding. Is it real?"

Mazriah nodded and I was surprised to find a heavy weight settle into the pit of my stomach. Deep down... part of me hoped she would protest.

Eager to leave, Mazriah tried to stand. I held her shoulder, keeping her on the stool.

"Just one more question," I said.

Mazriah pursed her lips again.

"Who is Elowa?"

No answer.

"Mazriah. I know you know."

Silence.

"Who is Elowa? Who is her daughter? *Please.* Tell me."

Mazriah's eyes shifted left and right. She rose to her feet and I let her, dropping my hand. As she backed toward the door, she clutched her tunic.

But she didn't leave. She stood in the doorway, wringing the fabric of her tunic through her hands. Her eyes clouded, lost on some faraway point.

"Mazriah, who is Elowa? *Please,* I need to know."

Her mouth parted. Her gaze suddenly ripped from the distance and she looked at me squarely.

"Not who," she whispered. *"What."*

Mazriah slipped quickly out of my room, leaving me frowning.

She did not return the next morning.

CHAPTER 35

"I don't think I've ever seen such a cheerless bride," my mother sighed. "And that includes cousin Balryine, who married the retired guard twice her age and three times her size. What's wrong?"

"I'm just nervous." I smiled. Weak. Fake. *I should be thrilled, shouldn't I?* I was marrying the Sea God. There was no better fate.

Two days had passed. Painfully long and then, suddenly, moving too fast. Two agonizing days since I'd seen Kirwyn. Two days which I spent in my room, staring at the forest beyond the orchard, as if I'd see him appear under the trees. Two days in which I puzzled over Mazriah's reply. *How could a thing have a daughter?* Two days during which I grilled my mother about every detail of the wedding, trying to find some clue that made everything make sense.

I kept my word and never mentioned what the Fire Maidens had said, though I played out our meeting over and over in my mind. The riddles made no more sense now than they had at the time.

I also never betrayed Mazriah's confidence. I wanted to find her and demand she tell me more. But she had suddenly taken ill, catching whatever sickness her relatives had, and now it was her turn to be cared for. Or so I was told.

"This is all happening so fast," I protested. "Why can't I meet Keroe before we are married?"

My mother smoothed the loose hair behind my ear. "It's tradition. Besides, I don't believe the Sea God is in the habit of making village appearances and going on swim dates."

Her eyes softened. "Please don't worry, darling. You really are the most beautiful bride I've ever seen, and I'm sure Keroe will agree."

"Thank you," I said. I wore the purple dress from my betrothal, and my mother wove white frangipani into my hair, twisted up in the royal style.

But I closed my eyes against my image in her murky gazing glass. The flowers made me think of Kirwyn.

What if this were our *wedding feast?* came the unbidden thought.

My mother reached for her mask. The night before the ceremony, everyone wore masks of wood or leather to the village-wide feast -- or at least a painted face.

Traditionally, it was a game for the man to find his bride amongst the sea of hidden faces, although this didn't work very well any longer. Brides had begun wearing more elaborate garb – in my case the purple dress – and stood out against everyone else. It also wouldn't work for me in particular. As my mother said, Keroe wouldn't be descending upon the land to play the game. Still, the tradition held, and my mother secured her leather disguise - dyed red with berries and fruits - around her head.

I rubbed the soft leather of my own mask between my

fingers. Artists had stripped the color, faded and whitened it somehow, so that it would stand out as the palest amongst the many others -- most of which would be wood-wrought or weathered goat leather. I brought it to my nose, inhaling the distinctive, rich scent. I wondered, as I tied it around my head, what made me the *wrong* person, as the Fire Maidens said. This was my wedding feast. Was I the wrong person here, too?

"Your father is waiting at our table," my mother said, breaking my thoughts. She held out her hand. "Come."

MUSIC FLOATED on the air as a tall guard opened the door for us. Drums kept the beat while lutes and panflutes ran with a wild, joyful melody. Every so often a conch would blow, keeping tune.

As we walked, the first thing I saw were the fires, blazing in torches around the perimeter of the feast. To accommodate the entire village, it spilled out from the courtyard and into the gardens on either side.

Nearing, I inhaled, and the scent of thousands of flowers overpowered the leather from my mask. Every table, chair, and surface imaginable dripped with hibiscus, chrysanthemum, or cassia.

Where had all these flowers come from? I wondered.

Competing for space were endless platters and bowls of food – more food than I had ever seen in my lifetime. Plates of roasted almonds and dates. Bowls of custard apples. Powdered squares that looked to be hardened guava jelly. Towering kabobs of chicken and grasshopper.

I spotted my father, looking handsome in his embroi-dered tunic and black mask. He was drinking sea wine at our long table nestled by the dahlias, not far from the woods. Although several places were set, most people seemed to be dancing. Temporarily replacing Mazriah, one of the kitchen maids supervised Gereth and Jona, dining separately.

My father rose stiffly when he saw me. "You look beautiful," he said, echoing my mother. He poured sea wine into an empty goblet and handed it to me.

I gulped down large sips at once, then took my place in the center of the table, the position of honor. I picked at a bowl of candied flowers a servant placed before me.

After a few moments a new song played and my father rose, presenting me with the white ribbon. I forced a small smile. It was customary for the father and daughter to dance together. Since the chosen braenese couldn't be touched, a solution had been devised generations ago, whereby a ribbon would be held taut between them at all times.

I picked up the other end of the ribbon, about three feet in length, and wound it around my hand. My father and I wove our way to the dance area in the middle of the courtyard and joined in the village jig, keeping the ribbon stretched between us. I didn't know the steps, but its leaps and hops were not very formal and easy enough to follow with the up-tempo beat. The wide berth we were given expanded into a large circle while we danced. Everyone was curious to see the bride and her father -- and eager to ask for their turn next.

When the song ended my father bowed, and one of the faster members of the Steel Guard quickly took his place.

Despite the ribbon, I worried the dancing put me in danger of accidentally being touched -- both by my partner and by the other couples -- but I supposed that this was more of the rules relaxing as we neared my wedding. I danced once with a light-footed villager, once with a middle-aged Mystic, and lastly with an intimidating, scarred member of the guard I recalled as being one of my mother's most relied upon.

But there was an ache in my heart that throbbed with each turn. I realized I was scanning the trees, looking for Kirwyn with every spin.

I excused myself to return to my seat.

I drank some more wine and then, noticing I was becoming light-headed, beckoned the serving girl lingering shyly by our table. I took three oysters from her tray and ate them in rapid succession. Then I swallowed the rest of my wine, even though I was already tipsy.

As I watched the laughing couples, I thought of Kirwyn and the ache in my chest grew. I felt as if it expanded enough to swallow me whole, to envelop the entire feast and swallow every dancing villager into blackness.

The music seemed far away, as if I had to strain my ears to hear it. I couldn't see the dazzling array of colors before me any longer, they seemed to mute, to dull into gray.

Aided by the wine, I began to despair.

It didn't matter that the night was aglow with more burning torches than I had ever seen before. I was lost in the blackness. The *world* would never be light again. And in my mind, as I whirled madly to escape the dark nothing, there was only one person who was real. Solid. In full color before me. Only one person to lead me out, back into the light.

And it wasn't the Sea God.

It had never been the Sea God.

Not since Kirwyn arrived.

CHAPTER 36

I had made the mistake of my lifetime.

And now it was too late. Kirwyn would never forgive me. Not this time. *I was at my own wedding feast.*

The scrape of a chair beside me ripped my attention back to the table. My father had arisen. A new song played, slower, heavily featuring the lute. He extended his hand to my mother. She rose to her feet, slightly unsteady under the weight of her belly, and they were soon lost in the twirling crowd.

Once my cup was refilled, I swallowed another large sip of sea-wine. The seats beside me were pushed back, empty.

I was safe as long as I sat. No one approached a bride at her table to chat or ask for a dance.

Listening to the song, I watched the whirling couples. I had never heard the tune before, but I quickly fell under the spell of its melody. Was it mournful, a lover's lament? Or was it a song about falling under love's enchantment? Or both? Perhaps it was about forbidden love. I closed my eyes, inhaling and exhaling deeply. A wedding feast shouldn't be this... lonely. I picked apart a purple, candied violet until it crumbled.

A bold young man approached my table. His tunic was slightly misfitting, like a village hand-me-down, but his dark hair was longer and unkempt, like an artist. His arms bore black marks of soot in a design so intricate they covered most of the skin. He wore a wooden mask with dark eyebrows and a painted grin. There were two holes for the eyes, one for the mouth. I peered into the eyeholes.

My heart *stopped.*

My breath caught, disbelieving.

Kirwyn.

I would know those forest greens anywhere.

"May I have this dance, princess?" he asked, picking up one end of the white ribbon.

My heart threatened to burst out of my chest.

Suddenly, everything changed, everything would be right in the world.

Without hesitation, I leapt to my feet and grasped the other end. As Kirwyn led me to the dance area, my mind wondered if this was really happening or if I'd gone mad. Holding the ribbon high, he swept me into a wide arc and then brought me around to face him. He wound the ribbon around his fist a few times, shortening it, and the distance between us.

"You may have this dance, you may have this night, you may have this *whole life,*" I whispered, when he came close. Closer than we should be, but not close enough to touch.

Kirwyn pulled back. I could see his eyes study me with a question behind his mask.

I wouldn't mess it up this time.

Never again.

"Yes," I swore, smiling. "Yes. I will run away with you."

I wished I could see his face, I wished we could touch. Instead, Kirwyn spun me on the floor and the world spun with us, colors melding into one another, shadows dancing beside us.

"Tonight," I whispered. "After the feast."

"After the feast," Kirwyn agreed, voice sultry.

"I'm so sorry for... everything," I said. "I thought I'd lost you. I thought I was going to have to marry Keroe."

Behind the wooden mask, his deep green eyes held mine.

"No god can keep me from you, Zaria."

I would have swooned if a hundred curious eyes weren't forcing me erect. The most delightful pleasure shot up inside my chest; part rapture, part bliss. We weren't even touching, but it didn't matter. Kirwyn created an intimate bubble with his words, heated with his eyes.

I couldn't find the right words to explain the part of me Kirwyn touched. Perhaps it existed in one of those other languages he spoke of.

Soul, yes, but even that was insufficient. My soul was a bottomless lake -- still, eternal.

Spirit, yes, that too -- but my spirit was like a stream -- sometimes playfully dancing in the sun, sometimes powerfully churning forth, carving out a path of its own choosing, shaping the very rock below.

It was as if Kirwyn touched the very wellspring of my being, the joinder of both soul and spirit, as well as their secret source.

"Not Keroe, nor any other god, can have my heart. I'm irreversibly in love with you."

I breathed into my declaration all the passion I had to restrain by not reaching out and holding him.

"Let any god be damned," Kirwyn swore. "You have mine too. I love you, Zaria."

I grinned and whispered, "Just remember that I said it first."

"What?" he blurted. "I think that showing up here, declaring war against any *god* for you, is more than saying it."

I feigned being unimpressed, frowning and shrugging.

"Really?" he said a bit too loudly. "I'm the one who - you're the one who - Ugh! If we weren't on this dance floor right now I would stop your ridiculous talk with a kiss... *and more.*"

Kirwyn whispered the last part as close as he could get to my ear -- a low, hot promise that bordered on threat. My body shuddered involuntarily.

"It's easy to make threats from behind a mask," I chided.

"Just wait until it's off, princess," he said, then added, "or maybe I'll keep it on."

I gasped and blushed as Kirwyn laughed.

The feast couldn't end quickly enough. One more hour and I could claim fatigue and return to my room.

My heart raced with excitement. I couldn't believe I was doing this. I'd leave a note for my mother and father, of course. In time, they'd forgive me. I mentally started making a short list of items to bring in my sack: some fruit, two skins of water, a spare tunic. My heart skipped a beat.

What was out there in the God Sea? Was Kirwyn really taking me to different lands?

"Excuse me, Braenese Zaria," came an unwelcome interruption behind me.

Turning, I saw the long-nosed Steel Guard who usually

manned our front door. "Your mother would like your friend to join you for the next course."

I involuntarily gulped as cold water ran down my spine.

"Of course," I replied, trying to sound relaxed.

I looked at Kirwyn, but he was already wearing a mask *under* the mask. He was so cool, so much better at this than me. I heard my breath quicken and tried unsuccessfully to slow it down. I wished that I could reach out and hold Kirwyn's hand, share his strength.

I led the way to the table, conceiving and rejecting ideas of what to say to my mother, but my anxiety eased slightly as we approached. She looked pleasantly curious, not suspicious or upset.

"Mother, may I present Corlis, son of Grester, from the village."

Kirwyn removed his mask and bowed low. My breath came in quick gasps. He had tanned since we met but his face still didn't look like right, didn't look like anyone else's.

As he straightened, I exhaled in relief. Kirwyn had painted his face with soot as well, under the mask.

"Thank you for regaling my daughter," my mother said. "It seems you've helped Zaria forget her apprehension for her nuptials tomorrow, for a time."

She smiled, but her careful words carried a weight and my panic rose once more. *What did she suspect? That I had met a village boy and let him touch me?*

I sat, and a servant quickly produced an extra chair for Kirwyn to sit across from me. The next course was being served.

"How are you finding the feast?" my mother asked. "Do you think we went too far with the frangipani?"

Kirwyn shook his head and did his best to cover his accent, but it wasn't quite right. "They perfume the air, intoxicating your guests on the scent. If you had no musicians, no wine, no lights and no dancing, the feast would be success on air alone."

Kirwyn seemed to sniff at the air as he spoke, but I couldn't tell for sure under the mask.

My mother gave a high laugh, the tinkling one.

So smooth. He was always so smooth.

I felt as if each piece of me - my blank face, my innocent hand, my unremarkable posture - screamed my guilt.

I glanced at the bowl the shy serving girl set before me.

Oh no.

Oh no. Not now. Not this course.

Beetles.

Carcasses floating in a broth of beetle soup.

I flashed my eyes to Kirwyn.

His mouth tugged on one side as he fought a grimace. I could practically see his brain scanning the situation to find a way out, rejecting possible escapes. There was no way without raising suspicion.

Figuring it best to get it over with, he spooned a small bug and some salty broth. Slowly, mouth set in that tight grimace, he brought his spoon to lips he practically had to pry open.

I wished I could make him relax and enjoy the nutty-apple taste, but his serious face told me he was disgusted underneath the surface.

It would have been funny if I wasn't terrified. I might have laughed.

I hoped this was something we could look back on and laugh about someday. If we got away and had a life together, I promised never to serve bugs at the feasting table.

Quickly now, he dumped the contents of the spoon -

beetle and all - into his mouth. He swallowed without chewing.

"How do you like the soup?" my mother asked.

"Best I've ever had," Kirwyn replied.

As he looked down at his bowl I could practically read his mind. *One spoonful down, twenty to go.*

The next five minutes must have been excruciating for Kirwyn. He ate quickly to get it over with, maybe too quickly, for he looked ill by the time the spoon hit the bottom of the empty bowl.

"Excuse me," Kirwyn said, as the dishes were cleared. "I think I've had too much sea-wine."

He did look green as he scurried into the woods. But if he got sick, I knew the real reason.

My father returned, taking his seat beside my mother. Finishing the last of his wine, my father called for a cup of soursop tea.

I turned back, searching the dark forest for signs of Kirwyn returning. After a few minutes, I forced myself to stop turning around, afraid of looking too anxious. For something to do, I watched the servants scurry about the tables, cleaning plates and refilling glasses.

"Your friend is charming," my mother said, breaking the silence.

"He's no friend of the crown," came a sudden whisper by my ear.

I gasped and whipped my head around.

Nasero appeared beside me, something hard behind his once-warm eyes.

"P-ardon?" I asked.

"My Queen," the High Mystic said, more loudly. "Would you mind if I borrowed the bride for a moment? I have a gift I'd like to show her, back at the palace."

My stomach twisted and my pulse quickened.

Where was Kirwyn?

"Now?" my mother asked, holding Nasero's eyes. "In the middle of the feast?"

"My gift is of a timely nature. Please. A moment of her time. Will you allow your daughter to follow me back to the palace?"

My mother looked to my father, who shrugged his approval.

She turned her gaze back to Nasero.

"So be it," she conceded.

Where was Kirwyn?

My eyes darted between Nasero, my mother, and the forest.

"Well then." Nasero looked at me expectantly.

Shakily, I rose to my feet.

Please. We're less than an hour away from escaping. Please don't let us get caught. Please tell me Kirwyn's okay.

My legs didn't want to move, but I forced them to follow the High Mystic. The further we walked, the more my stomach knotted...

...Into the palace, where two guards stood at the doorway...

Down the stairs, to the barely-used cellar...

I heard my uneven breathing. Too loud. Nasero could surely hear it too...

Through the dark, cement hall, splitting off into outdated and vacant Old World prison cells.

No.

We walked to the large room at the end. The largest cell, in back.

Please no.

Where two Steel Guards held Kirwyn between them.

CHAPTER 37

His soot was gone, revealing Kirwyn's unobstructed face.

Like a beacon, it dominated the room, demanding attention. It was as if I saw it again for the first time, saw its strangeness through everyone else's eyes.

"Kirwyn!" I shouted, without thinking.

I ran, but Nasero grabbed my tunic and yanked me back. Somewhere in my mind I registered astonishment at nearly being touched, but all I could think about was Kirwyn. I struggled as Nasero beckoned two Steel Guards to assist in restraining me.

They hesitated.

Old habits died hard.

"You won't be punished," Nasero vowed, exasperated. "Unless you *don't* hold her, right now."

They didn't move.

"I said now," Nasero demanded, low and strong.

Reluctantly, the two Steel Guards shuffled forward and grabbed my arms, touching the least amount of skin possible. When I struggled, they were forced to tighten their grip.

Nasero crossed the distance to stand between us.

"We know who he is," he waved his hand, dismissively. "We know you've been sneaking off to see him. We've known everything, right from the day you dragged him out of the sea."

My mouth fell. My mind raced back to the beginning.

That explained why there was never a Steel Guard on the cliff when I pulled Kirwyn off the beach.

And the footprints we saw in the sand... I bet those were from someone spying on us.

And that day by the cave - when we thought we heard someone - had they been there?

Coquina clams ran up my spine at this revelation. Did they know about our night at Lover's Cove?

Then why didn't the High Mystic stop us before?

"I don't know what you think you are going to do – run off with him?" Nasero asked. All that kindness I thought I'd once seen in his eyes evaporated. "But those plans are going to change. Tomorrow night, you will marry Keroe."

So there *was* somewhere to run to.

Hope sprang in my chest, despite being held between the Steel Guards.

Were the worlds Kirwyn described real? With mountains so tall they kissed the clouds?

"I won't," I growled, surprised at my own ferocity. I had waited my whole life for my wedding. Now, any future that did not involve Kirwyn sickened me, abandoned me to that creeping blackness.

Nasero raised his eyebrows and the expression on his face chilled me.

Stretched helplessly between two Steel Guards, Kirwyn

had nowhere to go when the High Mystic swung. Kirwyn turned his head, and the intended punch hit the side of his face. Nasero swung again quickly, pummeling him with two hard punches to the gut.

"Stop!" I cried, "No, please!" I tore at the men holding me, but my arms might as well have been stuck in the concrete walls.

"I can do this all night," Nasero said, patiently.

"Go ahead," Kirwyn taunted, slowly lifting his head. "Don't do it, Zaria. I can take a beating by this wind bag. I've taken worse."

"You know, boy, you might be right," Nasero agreed. *"But can she?"*

For a confused moment, I thought he meant me, and from the panic on Kirwyn's face I could tell he did too.

But then, with the flick of two fingers, Nasero beckoned something from the shadows of the passage behind us.

Once again, chills ran through me. Warning bells tolled in my head.

No.

I yanked, twisting my arms to no avail.

An ugly guard – the same one I'd just danced with - his neck marred by one long scar, coaxed my mother forward, gagged, pointing a sword at her throat.

"Mother!" I cried.

Her wide, watery eyes shifted from me to Kirwyn.

"You might have taken worse," Nasero said to Kirwyn, then turned his attention to me. "But has she?"

Nasero crossed the room and swung, smacking my mother's face as I screamed.

My mother crumpled to the floor. Half of her hair had fallen out of its hold, covering the side of her face. Blood dripped from her lip onto the tile. The traitorous guard stood closely above her, the tip of his sword poised by her neck.

"Stop, no, please don't hurt her!" I pleaded, hysterical.

"I'll tell you how it's going to be, Zaria," Nasero began. "You're going to marry the Sea God tomorrow night. You're going to do everything I say from now on."

"No!" I shouted, thrashing.

"You're going to put on your wedding dress, you're going to be happy at your wedding. And you're going to get on that landdammit boat after." He kicked my mother's legs, avoiding her pregnant belly, but dangerously close to its swell.

If it weren't for the guards holding me, I would have collapsed on the floor. My mother curled into a ball to protect herself and her unborn child.

"Stop it, please, stop!"

I screamed as he struck a second time, and a third. Every sickening kick felt as if I had taken the blow directly to my heart. The weight of witnessing the beating pressed down onto my lungs, my windpipe. I couldn't speak, I couldn't even get in air to say the words, to consent to everything he wanted. I gasped, hiccupping, choking

Kirwyn spoke a word softly, but it didn't make sense. The bizarre utterance had no meaning.

He said it again, at a normal volume, but I still couldn't hear him.

He repeated it a third time, his face contorted in a snarl, *"Lavender!"*

"Lavender, lavender, lavender!" Kirwyn yelled the nonsense word.

CHAPTER 38

Confused by his outburst, everyone stopped and stared at the deranged boy.

I looked around the room, searching faces for comprehension. Nasero and the guards did the same. No one understood the meaning of the outburst. One of Kirwyn's captors still held the grip on his arm but backed away slightly.

Kirwyn, delirious, jerked that arm free and pointed at my mother.

He uttered in a low, accusatory voice, "Lavender."

"What?" I whispered, breaking the silence. "Kirwyn, what are you saying?"

"The flower," he cried. "It's a flower. It doesn't naturally grow here."

I blinked. Confounded by the gibberish, still no one spoke.

Kirwyn had lost his grip on reality.

Okay... I thought, parsing out the meaning. *He's saying there's a flower called lavender that grows somewhere else. So what?*

Kirwyn straightened his back, jutting his chest out as he spoke. "I couldn't figure it out at first. There are so many exotic smells here, I couldn't place it. But I should have known. I've hated it ever since I was a child. And she-" Kirwyn crooked his arm and threw it back out, pointing once more, "it's in *her* perfume."

I stared at the boy I loved, heart sinking. He wasn't making any sense.

Kirwyn shook his head at all of us. "Don't you see? She's wearing perfume! *With lavender.* It doesn't naturally grow in this climate. I couldn't figure out if she was in on it. Not at first. But I bet she knows, I bet she's working with some-one, trading... for *perfume,* for god's sake! She knows what's going on. She's even benefitting from it."

What? No.

His words sank into my muddled brain, and I began to understand he was accusing my mother of betrayal.

The realization came easier to everyone else.

I looked back and forth between Kirwyn -- chest heav-ing, pointing; and my mother, crumpled on the floor.

Everyone else looked at me.

"Enough!" Nasero roared, snapping me to attention.

From within his robes he withdrew a silver, L-shaped, object -- some kind of Old World artifact. He pointed it at my head. Then he pulled a lever and it made a clicking sound.

"You know what this is, don't you, boy?" Nasero asked.

Kirwyn stiffened, and the fear in his eyes sent cold water through my veins.

What was it?

I stiffened, too. I could see Kirwyn's mind working by the expression on his face. His eyes widened, then narrowed, then relaxed.

"You need her," he replied coolly. "You're not going to kill her."

Nasero turned and pointed the silver object at Kirwyn.

"You're right again. But I don't need you."

I didn't understand what device Nasero held, but I knew from Kirwyn's reaction that it could hurt him. Panic bubbled inside my chest, ready to pour out into my open mouth. I drew a breath to speak. I would say or do whatever it took to save him...

"Stop!" an authoritative voice commanded. It was my mother's.

The gag hung loosely around her neck.

She stood, wobbling to her feet, wiping the blood from her chin. The guard stepped back and bowed, lowering his sword.

"This is getting out of hand. He's more useful alive." She finished cleaning her mouth and ripped the gag from her neck. "For now."

Dumbfounded, I stared. And then, with dawning comprehension came a searing pain, like the blade of the steel sword piercing my heart.

Was everything Kirwyn had predicted true? My marriage -- a ritual sacrifice? And my mother -- in on the plot to kill me?

The idea felt like someone squeezed my heart with the intent to crush it.

Everyone stared at me.

My mother betrayed me? She wanted me dead?

I was free from restraint, I felt that now. The guards had let go of my arms. And yet I had no will to move.

I gaped at my mother looking for a protest in her face -- something, *anything* to tell me that this was a misunderstanding, *anything* to explain.

Why? My mind repeated the question, over and over, until I was forced to say it aloud.

"Why?" I asked, voice cracking.

To anyone else, my mother seemed poised as she regarded me without replying, but I could read tension in the stiff way she held her neck.

My own mother wanted me dead.

I turned back to Kirwyn. The silver object must not have been assurance enough, because he'd been restrained again. Huffing through his nose, he struggled against the two men holding him, despite the Old World metal pressed to his temple.

Don't. I read the plea in his eyes.

I knew what he was asking.

And he knew what I would do.

I would die for him. I was dead already.

My eyelids fluttered as I breathed my reply, as if they wanted to stay closed against what I was about to say.

"I will go with you. I will cooperate," I whispered. "On two conditions."

I held my mother's gaze and tried not to allow my voice to crack, or worse, to fall into blubbering. "First, you tell us the truth. About everything."

Then I turned to face Nasero, "Second, you let Kirwyn go. You help him return to his home."

"Accepted," Nasero agreed, but he didn't lower the silver object.

I turned back to my mother.

She nodded, once.

"No deals!" Kirwyn cried. "They're going to kill you, Zaria. Tomorrow, they will toss you off that boat and leave you to drown."

I made a sound between a gasp and a gulp. I didn't want to die. But I couldn't allow Kirwyn to die for me.

"Kill her?" Nasero asked, disbelieving. "You think we want to kill her? She is Pama's daughter. She is like a-" The High Mystic stopped suddenly, then asked. "Why would we waste a perfectly good braenese on drowning?"

"To sacrifice to your sea god, you religious freaks," Kirwyn spat, but there was doubt in his voice.

"You and I both know there is no sea god," Nasero replied. My mouth fell.

"But... no," I whispered. Despite *everything,* I couldn't accept his dismissal.

Our prayers. The marriage. My *life.* I couldn't believe him, I *would not.* Even if he had been led astray, even if my marriage wasn't real, it didn't mean that Keroe didn't *exist.*

"There is no sea god and you're not going to be his queen," the High Mystic said, sounding resigned. "That's the trouble with braenese. Each one thinks she's a queen-to-be. She's a pawn, even *the* queen-to-be."

Nasero smiled sadly. His gaze flicked toward my mother. "Just like the rest of us."

"That's enough, Nasero," my mother silenced him. She reached for me and I stumbled back, out of her range.

"I wanted to protect you from the truth, Zaria," she said, voice full of either pity or self-pity, I couldn't tell. "I wanted you to have a family you could trust."

Involuntarily, I gave a strangled chuckle.

My mother tried again. "There are other islands," she confessed, head high. Despite the pummeling she'd been given, despite the bruises and her haphazard hair, she was every bit the High Braenese as she doled out information only she'd been privy to for so long.

"Some so big they are called continents, where you can walk for many moon cycles and never reach the other side." She lifted her hand toward Kirwyn. "Your friend is from one of those... but that is not where you will be going."

Stop, I pleaded, searching her eyes. But she continued.

"Elowa, our paradise here, comes at a price. We are spared the ravages of war through protection."

Her voice took on a formal tone, like we sat an official dinner at the water table.

"We hold a treaty with another island, northward. Much bigger in size than our own, and more equipped at defense. It's a beautiful place, the Island of Lights. This is where we send the God tribute. Offerings meant for Keroe are shipped there, for our safety, our peace."

She caressed her Old World diamond as she continued. "The other condition is... once a generation, a braenese, a *Daughter of Elowa,* gives her hand in marriage to a nobleman of their court. I'm sorry my darling, but, that's you, Zaria. No one can take your place in this role. But, it's not all bad. The island is beautiful place."

Her eyes shone as she continued, "And there were some... complications a few years ago. You will not be marrying a nobleman of the king's choosing, you will instead be married to his *son,* the *crown prince.* He will become their High Braenar, and you get to maintain your title, you will be queen. You get to protect Elowa, your people *here,* and rule *there.* Everyone remains safe, happy."

"Everyone but me," I whispered.

My life was a lie.

Everything I'd known crumbled around me. It was as if the palace collapsed, and though I tried to shield myself, heavy beams of wood and jagged chunks of concrete hit me as they fell. Each truth a blow, injuring me further and further, until I was unable to do anything more than lay down and accept each, buried under the rubble.

"What do you have here? There's nothing. This is nothing. There you will be queen of a great island." My mother spoke the words almost reverently.

"I don't want to be queen. I don't want to marry this prince."

My mother regarded me, then said slowly, "We all pay a price."

"Why the pageants?" Kirwyn demanded. If he was relieved to know I wasn't being sent to my death, it didn't show. If anything, he was angrier at learning the truth. "Why all the pomp and circumstance if you already knew she was going to marry this prince? Why endanger her with poison?"

My mother smoothed the loose strands of her hair back. "Elowa's daughter is sought for her unique beauty, but the... limited breeding pool hasn't always produced the healthiest brides. Over many generations, there have been in our family some feebleminded Braeni, or Braeni of ill-health, who've died shortly after marriage. During such occurrences, no doubt the bridegroom felt he'd been cheated. To ensure a robust specimen, they've instituted these basic tests to confirm she is neither weak, nor dim-witted, nor sickly."

I flinched at her depiction of me: a specimen, potentially inept. Possible damaged goods to be inspected before trading. I wasn't a braenese. I was property.

But then...

"Solan was trying to protect me by declaring me unworthy, wasn't he? So why did he want to kill me?" I asked, puzzled.

Nasero shook his head. "Protect you? He was doing

nothing of the sort. He didn't care for you one way or the other. Some of the older Mystics want to change the way things are done. They want to start a war. Solan thought denying your hand was the quickest way to provocation. Through disapproval or death, it mattered not. We knew what he was planning before the pageant, but we needed to dispose of him publicly. He was given a poison, meant to kill. I'll admit we cut the timing a bit close... as well as administered an inaccurate dosage. He later awoke, escaped, and tried to kill you during your second pageant."

Wheels turned in my mind as I listened. It was like someone had thrown open the curtains and the light nearly blinded me.

I heard Danaire's voice in my head, *"It was better than killing her..."*

"And the goats," I whispered. "The Fire Maidens. Some of them want the same thing? War? I know someone amongst them poisoned the goats, set fire to the God tribute. It was preferable to killing me."

Nasero met my mother's eyes once more. I was beginning to feel they silently communicated in a way I hadn't noticed before.

"Some want change, not necessarily war," Nasero said. "But they have dealt with the one causing the disturbance. It will not occur again."

My mind raced further. Is this what the Arch Priestess meant when she spoke riddles about people arriving at the same destination, but not walking my same path? And of those who want what I want not necessarily being my friend?

Conspiracies and counter-conspiracies. It reached further than I understood. My family, Mystics, and the Fire

Maidens all having a stake in everything from my wedding to the God tribute. Another thought flashed in my mind.

"The shark? It wasn't a coincidence, was it? How did Solan get it there on my pageant day?"

Both my mother and Nasero paused.

"We don't believe it was a coincidence, no," my mother said, slowly. "But we don't know who was behind it."

Silence fell upon the room, almost respectful. I heard a slight rustle as one of Kirwyn's guards shifted his weight. My mother seemed pitying. Kirwyn looked pleading, Nasero expectant...

I realized everyone was looking at me. Waiting for *me*, to continue.

I struggled to picture years of my life, stretching ahead on some other land, married to an unknown man.

A stranger. Not Kirwyn.

Kirwyn, with the smirk I sometimes wanted to smack right off his face. Kirwyn, with the hot kisses that melted my resolve. Kirwyn, with the muscular arms I ached to encircle me, even now.

Kirwyn with the courage to be brave when facing the unknown. Courage I wished I had.

I held my head in my hands, trying to process everything.

But it didn't matter, whatever happened to me.

All that mattered was that I kept Kirwyn safe.

"I have your word he will remain unharmed?" I whispered.

"Zaria, no!" Kirwyn cried.

My mother nodded.

"And you'll return him to his mainland?"

"You have my word."

My voice cracked as I consented, and the walls of the room seemed to spin around me.

"I will marry this prince from the other island."

CHAPTER 39

My mother paused on her way out of the cell, passing Nasero.

"Are you alright?" he whispered, and the tenderness in his voice surprised me.

"You were quite adept throughout your performance," she replied, evenly.

Nasero held her eyes, held himself stiffly. When he next spoke, his hard tone matched my mother's.

"I live to serve, your grace."

Despite my vow, the High Mystic and the two guards led me to a cell down yet another flight of stairs. I wouldn't have been surprised to have been the first occupant since the First Feet. Unlawfulness had been a common problem back then, but with peace that came from Braeni rule, I couldn't recall anyone ever held captive here.

I heard a groan of protest and then, a heavy clang behind me as the cell door swung shut. Metal bars, cold as I wrapped my hands around them, made up one wall of the little prison. The other three walls were thick, Old World concrete. One wooden slab – a bench – stuck out from the wall to my left. Under it, a metal chamber pot.

The guards departed, and Nasero stood alone, separated from me by the thick, metal bars. He seemed to be debating something.

"What?" I croaked. "I said I would go with you and you've locked me up anyway."

"Keeping you in ignorance may not have been the wisest course of action all these years, but there was never a perfect time to tell you. When you were old enough to be trusted, but young enough to-"

"Be brainwashed into accepting it?" I offered.

Nasero smiled, sadly. Gone was the man who'd punched Kirwyn, who kicked my mother. If I didn't know the monster underneath, I might at that moment have mistaken him for kind, even weary. The façade made him all the more chilling.

"You should know," Nasero began, "the reason men cannot touch you. It wasn't to protect you from them. It was to protect *them* from *you*. You can thank your mother for allowing this dalliance with your friend, for permitting it to continue. It was she who wanted you to have, ah, something, before."

I tightened my grip on the bars, fuming at my mother for secretly allowing me to see Kirwyn and then taking it away with a snap of her fingers.

"Before she forced me to marry someone else?" I spat. My blood boiled – she didn't even have the courage to face me now.

"And what choice does she have, hm?" Nasero said, rubbing his chin. "Keep you here and start a war? Sacrifice her people, our island? When you'd likely be taken anyway, in the end?"

"I don't know! But not *this*. She should have found a way, she should have fought. I would never do this. Sacrifice my own daughter."

"Zaria, you're not the only one to give up her choices for Elowa, the only one with deep regret. When your mother was young, she was required to make great sacrifices."

"I don't care what she sacrificed!" I cried. "Good! I'm *glad*. This whole time... she was on your side this whole time."

"There are no sides. No one is against you, certainly not your mother. Everyone is doing the best they can for the people... I would take your place if I could." Nasero shrugged. "But I can only play my part. You must play yours."

I licked my lips and asked, "The people on this island... do they look like Kirwyn, or us?"

I hated being at Nasero's mercy, but I desperately wanted to know.

"Elowa's people are unique, especially the Braeni," he replied. "Which is part of the allure."

"Why?"

"That, I'm afraid, is a story for another time," he said.

Nasero bowed – an act I found *ridiculous* after what he'd just done. Then he turned and left, footsteps echoing down the empty corridor. A door slammed behind him.

Alone, I shouted Kirwyn's name, stopping only to strain my ears for a reply.

None came.

Kirwyn must have been taken somewhere else.

Please, Keroe, I prayed, even though I wasn't sure if he even existed. He was the only God I knew. *Please, I don't want to get married.*

I sat down on the bench and refused to sob.

I sobbed anyway.

~

"Well, I never thought I'd see Braenese Zaria in prison."

I snapped up my head.

Lida.

Her smug face looked down at me and I now noticed the slight belly bump through her best tunic. Her hair was braided and twisted into a bun, decorated with an orange seashell comb.

How much time had passed? Twenty minutes? Thirty? I'd been staring at the cracks in the floor, wondering how my absence was excused at my own wedding feast. Never, in all my life, had I imagined I'd spend the night of my feast in an Old World dungeon.

"Did you come here to gloat?" I asked. "Or are you in league with my mother?"

"Neither," she replied, curtly.

"What do you want?" I wished she would just leave me alone.

"I want to unlock this door and set you free."

I snorted. "And why would you want to do that?"

"Because I owe Tomé."

Lida produced a key from within her tunic, dangling it in front of her. My eyes widened, and I jumped to my feet.

"You're serious? You're going to set me free? What about Kirwyn, my... friend? Do you have a key for his cell, too?"

Lida nodded, smiling. "Go up the stairs at the end of the hall and through the door. Turn right, and in the second cell you'll find your lover boy."

"But... why?" I asked, bewildered. "You hate me."

I didn't add, *and I don't like you, either.*

"I told you," she said, "I'm not doing this for you. I'm doing it for Tomé. I owe him. We both do."

"I know," I said, cringing at the loud *click* of the key in lock, metal grating metal. "Please tell him I'm sorry for the way I acted that night."

Lida shook her head. "No. Not you." She placed one hand on her belly. *"We* owe him."

I nodded and slipped out of the cell, heart racing.

"Thank you," I whispered.

I took my first step and then abruptly stopped.

"Lida?" I asked, quickly, quietly. "Where did you get that key?"

She paused before answering, still holding her belly.

"From his father."

When no further explanation came, I nodded and took off, following the instructions she provided.

"Kirwyn!" I whisper-shouted as I came to his cell. He was on his feet, reaching around the bars and trying to pick the lock, unsuccessfully, with a thin piece of metal. Fumbling, I worked the key into the lock, cringing again as the door squeaked and swung open.

"Zaria!" He kissed me quickly and I grabbed his hand. "Come on!"

I led the way upstairs, cautiously, but it seemed, unnecessarily. There was no guard... either because we'd been safely locked away or because Lida had somehow disposed of them. Carefully, Kirwyn and I crept toward the back of the palace, heading for the rear parlor.

I skidded to a halt as we neared the patio. Blocking the exit, I saw the broad back of my father, encircling my mother in the cradle of his arms.

If they turned, they would see us.

I swallowed, twisted around, and signaled to Kirwyn to back up.

In the shadowy parlor, our eyes met, and he nodded.

Silently, praying nothing would squeak or creak, we backtracked to the front entrance. The door remained blessedly clear. Either all of the guards wanted to join in the wedding feast or Lida had worked some trick to get rid of them. We opened the door and slipped into the night.

Oblivious to my absence, the feast roared on. The torch-lights still blazed, the music rang out, the dancers leapt and whirled.

"Come on!" I shouted, yanking Kirwyn toward the revelry. I had an idea. We would astound the crowd with Kirwyn by my side, and then, having everyone's attention, we'd reveal the truth about everything. The other islands, Keroe, my wedding.

"Get them!" I heard a cry from behind us and whipped my head around to see the Steel Guard running.

"Zaria!" came another cry and I turned back in its direction.

Tomé. Marcin.

"Tomé!" I shouted. "You were right about the goats, and more. I have so much to tell you, but not now. We need your help."

He nodded, but neither he nor Marcin took their eyes off Kirwyn.

"We know," he began, "Lida sent-"

"Ahead!" the guards cried behind us.

"*Please.* We need a distraction. Anything! Can you help?"

Tomé looked over my shoulder to the Steel Guards racing down the hill. They were close enough now to make out five figures.

I wasn't sure *what* Tomé and Marcin knew. Maybe they believed we were nothing more than illicit lovers caught by the guards.

Marcin grinned at Tomé. "I can help. Give me your tunic."

"What?" Tomé asked.

Marcin didn't wait for a reply. He yanked my cousin's shift up to his elbows.

"Trust me." Marcin met Tomé's eyes and Tomé smiled widely in return. He raised his arms and after a quick pull, stood stark naked on the path.

I looked away, respectfully.

"Go!" Tomé whispered.

Then he shouted as loudly as possible, turning heads in the crowd.

"Give me back my tunic!"

"Woo!" Marcin yelled, waving it in circles in the air above his head.

Tomé, bare as the day he was born, jumped to retrieve it while people nearby started laughing and pointing.

Marcin danced ahead, forcing Tomé, in all his naked glory, to run and jump after him. The crowd swelled and I started in that direction, intending to run through it and come out safely on the other side. With the press of bodies between us and the guards, we could use the time to command everyone's attention and start telling the truth.

"No!" Kirwyn grabbed my arm and pulled me toward the trees. It was as if he read my mind. "They'll never believe you and that's exactly what they're expecting us to do."

"This way," he urged.

CHAPTER 40

With the moon barely a sliver, it was difficult to see more than a few feet ahead. I felt as if we'd been swallowed by a great beast and stumbled in the darkness of his belly.

Behind us, a scream tore through the night, piercing my heart.

Tomé?

I instinctively stopped and pulled against Kirwyn to return to the gardens. But he grabbed me by the waist and held me back.

"Come on, we have to go!" he cried.

"What happened?"

"I don't know. But whatever it was, Tomé wouldn't want for it to have been in vain. Zaria, we have to keep running."

A guttural sob tore from my throat as I reluctantly followed Kirwyn, sprinting in the darkness. We stumbled often, sharp branches tearing at our arms and legs. After a few minutes, I realized we might be headed to the cave.

"It's not safe in the cave!" I shouted. "If they've been spying on us, they know. We'll be trapped."

"We won't," Kirwyn said. "There's a way out."

I didn't understand him, but I kept running. I'd figure it out once we got there, once I could slow my heart so it wouldn't burst.

We passed the grotto. I could see its murky surface ripple in the darkness. Moments later, Kirwyn pushed back the cave's vines and we fell onto the crimson rug – about the only thing we could make out in the black hole of the cavern at night.

I shuddered, never realizing how scary it could be without the sunlight.

Kirwyn crawled on his hands and knees, feeling in front of him as he headed to the back of the cave.

"What are you doing?" I whispered, straining my ears to keep track of him in the darkness.

"The tunnel... I need to find the boulder... here!"

I shivered again. *Was Kirwyn planning for us to hide in there?* I couldn't...

I heard the deep scrape of rock on rock as he pushed the boulder aside and the hairs on my arms stood on end.

"Kirwyn. What are you doing back there?"

"I've hidden supplies back here," he said, as he withdrew items from the darkness. "Lanterns, rope, food. I've been trading with the Fire Maidens. Mostly at night, when you returned for night's feast."

Suddenly, my cavern filled with light. Kirwyn had lit some kind of oil lantern I'd never seen in person before. I squinted at the curious device with its Old World metal.

"Is that from the Fire Maidens?" I asked.

Kirwyn nodded. "They have tools, books, history. But no contact with the outside world – I mean, my world.

Since, well, hundreds of years I guess. I tried to exchange information for information, but they refused. Instead, I bartered supplies, things I thought we might need. I can catch you up later, we have to go."

You've come to the right place, but you're the wrong person.

The words of the Arch Priestess echoed in my mind. They had information but weren't willing to share it with *me* in particular. Another realization dawned. So *that's* where Kirwyn had been the day I couldn't find him at the cave...

"But they did tell me one thing," he said. "Mostly because I think they want to get rid of me. There are boats. From my world. Modern ones, with engines. That's, well, it means they have machinery, they go very fast. Elite members of the Steel Guard hide them in one of their training huts by the water."

Kirwyn shook his head as he spoke. "We can't go there now. They'll expect it. But maybe we can watch, can spy on *them*. We'll hide in here. There's a tunnel, it leads to an underground river. Well, more like a deep stream. That's what's back here. That's where this freshwater comes from." He waved his hand to indicate the drip I used to fill the water jug.

"We can follow the river until we reach the end. It empties into the sea not far from the boat house. At least, I think it's the boat house. You can't see the tunnel's entrance from the ocean. I don't think anyone else knows of its existence."

My mouth fell in disbelief. I knew the island better than anyone. *Didn't I?* I could swim a circle around it. I was one of the few who could freely walk the royal side. And I'd never heard of an underground river.

Then again, I'd had access all this time, and never wanted to explore that passageway.

No.

I didn't clearly hear what Kirwyn said next, I only understood that he wanted me to go -- in the darkness, inside the tunnel.

I shook my head vigorously.

"I can't... Kirwyn, no. It's too tight. What if I get stuck? What if it collapses?" I continued to shake my head.

"Zaria, we have to. I can fit through there. You can too. It will be okay. I'll be right there with you." He held up the lantern. "We have light."

I scooted back on the carpet and held onto the edge as if that would keep me anchored to the cave, keep the dark tunnel from sucking me in. I pictured the tight walls tightening even further as I crawled, trapping me forever. Until I died.

"I won't let anything happen to you. I promise. It's only a short crawl, maybe ten minutes, and then it widens. It's downhill, and at the bottom there's a small river. It will push us and we can swim-"

"Why didn't you tell me before?" I asked, aware that I channeled my fear toward anger.

Kirwyn licked his lips and sighed. "Two reasons. The first is, if we got caught, I figured the less you knew, the better... The second is, I wasn't sure I could trust you in the first place. No matter what happened, it seemed you were always bounding back to your sea god the next day."

His words stung, even though I knew he was right. And I had to admit, I'd never stopped carrying the knife, had I?

"No more secrets," I growled.

Kirwyn nodded. "No more secrets."

Then, he added, "And full trust?"

I took a deep breath and whispered, "Full trust."

Kirwyn leaned forward and kissed me, holding my face between his hands, even after he broke our kiss.

"Then you have to trust me here, Zaria. I won't let anything happen to you. Our best chance of escape," he nodded to the black hole, "is through that tunnel."

Still, I couldn't do it. I shook my head. We'd be captured here. But it was better than dying in darkness.

A bang rang out in the air, not far off, maybe minutes from the cave. The guard was near.

"Now, Zaria, we have to go!" Kirwyn pulled at my arms. I let him drag me, but my lip quivered. I *couldn't* go in there. I would do anything not to go into that black oblivion. I'd rather touch the Goodnight Fish again.

"I'll go first. You can follow me. Here." He shoved one of the lanterns into my hand. "Carry this in front of you as you crawl. We won't be able to cover the tunnel behind us, it's too tight to turn around. But maybe they won't know where we've gone and they're too big. It will take a while until they find someone who can fit inside and follow us."

"Okay, okay," I whispered, already breathing so hard I felt dizzy and light-headed. "I'll do it. Okay."

"It will be okay, Zaria. I promise. As long as you keep moving, it will be okay. I've done it more than once. Just follow me."

I looked around the cave. There was no point in hiding my Old World objects. The Mystics, the guard... they already knew.

Kirwyn lifted his lantern in front of him, lowered himself to his belly, and inched his way through the entrance of the tunnel until I saw nothing but his feet.

Feeling like every part of my body screamed in protest, I forced myself to do the same. The lantern shook in my hand. I laid on my belly and slid forward, letting the small mouth of the tunnel swallow me.

As soon as I was fully inside, unable to stand or turn, barely able to lift my head or move my arms for anything other than a slow, difficult crawl along the rocky hole, I panicked. I heard my breath come sharp, shallow, and so rapidly that I knew I needed to calm myself somehow. I needed to do something to prevent paralysis, or worse, fainting.

"Kirwyn, help!" I cried.

But what could he do, stuck in front of me, unable to turn around?

"Zaria, just listen to me. Listen to my voice. Ten, fifteen minutes and we'll be clear. Hey, did I ever tell you about snow?"

"What's snow?" I asked.

"Listen to my voice, Zaria. Keep crawling and I'll tell you." Having paused, he now resumed his worm-like burrow into the darkness.

"Snow is what happens to rain when it's very cold. It falls from the sky in a different form. It's not yet ice-"

"Like the ice wall?" I asked.

"Yeah," he said.

I dragged myself forward, inch by inch, focusing on his words.

"Snow is white and fluffy -- although sometimes it's hard, packed on the ground. In the winter months the clouds block out the sun and snowflakes fall from the sky. It can be soft and magical, or harsh, relentless."

I felt jagged rocks scrape against my legs and knew that Kirwyn must certainly be suffering the same. I couldn't stop from imagining my light would illuminate a Black Titan crawling ahead of me any second, and I pictured the sharp, venomous bite sinking repeatedly into the tender flesh of my unprotected cheek.

"Listen to me, Zaria," Kirwyn repeated. "If it's warm, the snow may melt in a day. If it's very cold and the snowfall heavy, it can last for weeks. Further north, it lasts for months. Until spring."

I tried to picture cold, fluffy water, but it was difficult.

"Very little can grow during the winter snows. We harvest in the fall when the leaves change color. Zaria, it's beautiful. Maybe my favorite season. You can't imagine the colors. Red, orange, yellow. You know, most people don't know this, but that's actually the tree's true colors. There's a chemical, called chlorophyll, that gives the leaf its green shade. That breaks down in the autumn and reveals just a... a splendor of hues, hidden throughout the rest of the year. Imagine all the green you see in your forest, but red, orange, and yellow instead."

That, I had the tools to picture, but it still seemed too magical. Our leaves changed slightly, but not into different colors entirely.

"Will you take me there?" I asked. "To the forest of colors? Can we ride a horseback through it?"

"I will," Kirwyn promised. "Listen to my voice Zaria, just a little bit further.... once we get the boat, we can't be more than a few days' travel from the mainland. Fall will be here in a few weeks. We'll find my uncle and make our way north, back to the library, where you'll be safe."

Suddenly, something occurred to me that I'd missed before. I was so worried about the guards, so scared of the tunnel, that I didn't realize it.

"Kirwyn, you said you knew about the machine boat a few days ago..."

"Yeah," he replied.

"But you didn't leave. Why didn't you take it?"

"I was waiting for you," he said. "I was hoping you'd change your mind and come with me."

If we don't make it, I thought, *I will be the reason he got caught.*

I would never forgive myself.

Guilt at my fickle behavior washed over me, but my heart pounded.

Impossibly gorgeous, clever, stubborn Kirwyn -- *wouldn't leave without me.*

For the first time since we'd been caught, I felt a smile, albeit a sad one, spread across my face.

Ahead, Kirwyn shuffled forward and scooted from the tunnel into another, wider opening. I heard water slosh as he put down his feet. The new tunnel was almost tall enough for him to stand erect.

Behind him, I reached the end as well and Kirwyn helped me climb down from the smaller tunnel, setting me into a shallow stream.

The cold water attacked my feet like little daggers, but I was too overjoyed at being able to stand to care.

I heard the rush of the river ahead, echoing off the empty chamber. I shined my light around me to get a better view, gaping. I couldn't *believe* all this was down here.

Still, even if I'd known, I wouldn't go through that tunnel again to get there.

"Be careful," Kirwyn warned. "It's very slippery and the ground is uneven, full of holes. Test your step before you put your weight on it. Here-" he pointed about twenty feet ahead, "it deepens. We can flow with the current to the sea."

Kirwyn lifted his lantern back to the small tunnel we

came through and exhaled deeply. "No one seems to be following us."

Carefully, I trudged forward through the stream, one hand in front of me to steady myself or catch myself if I fell, the other holding the lantern. It was difficult keeping my leather sandals on my feet, and once I reached the deeper river, I removed them and placed them inside my tunic. Barefoot and shivering, I waded into the cold depths after Kirwyn.

The current carried us forward - we didn't even need to swim - but it was tricky to hold our lanterns above our heads and out of the stream. My teeth chattered loudly and my arm began to ache at its awkward angle. Only the fear of being plunged into total darkness kept it up.

"Not much further," Kirwyn shouted back to me, his voice bouncing off the cavern walls.

At that moment, my foot hit a hard rock jutting out of the bottom of the stream and as I yelped, I dropped my lantern into the river -- which eagerly gobbled it up and swept it downstream. The fierce current had forced my foot to hit the rock hard.

"Kirwyn!" I shouted, fumbling in the total blackness. My panicked voice bounced off the echoing chamber.

"Zaria!" Kirwyn called, and I saw his light bob in the air as he fought against the stream to swim back.

Blindly, I felt next to me for a hold and pulled myself onto a rocky, narrow bank at the river's edge. I waited in darkness, focused on Kirwyn's light ahead.

"I'm coming!" he called, and I could hear in his voice the struggle to swim upstream.

Trying to mitigate the pain in my foot, I held my ankle tightly and leaned against the wall behind me.

To my utter shock, my back fell directly through it and

my shoulders slammed onto the ground with a painful *thump.*

I blinked in the dark, as if that would help clear my sight. Feeling around the edges of the wall beside me, I wondered if I had fallen through some kind of door.

Where was I?

"Zaria!" Kirwyn called again.

"I'm here!" I cried. *But where was here?*

Finally, Kirwyn made it back and hauled himself onto the bank with his free hand. Crouching, he crept closer, shining the light at me. As it illuminated more and more of the cave around us, I turned around to see where I was.

It wasn't a cave at all.

It was a corridor.

Smooth, polished walls.

Old World concrete. Man-made.

And at the end of the short hallway, three burly guards, muscles tensed, looked back at us.

The one closest cocked a smile.

CHAPTER 41

Kirwyn immediately jumped backwards, throwing himself into the river and reaching his hands up for me.

I scrambled to my feet and sprang toward the stream's bank.

As I lunged for Kirwyn, arms outstretched, our fingertips nearly grazed.

Two rough arms grabbed my waist and yanked me back into the concrete corridor.

"Zaria!" Kirwyn shouted, dragging himself back up onto the rocky bank.

"Kirwyn! Kirwyn!" I called, as a guard half-dragged, half-carried me away, all edicts against touching long forgotten.

I struggled and kicked to no avail. The guard must have been three times my size. He barely flinched when I scraped my fingernails against his hairy arms, drawing blood.

The other two guards blocked my view as they advanced on Kirwyn. Unable to see what was happening, I screamed. Then I heard a sickening thud and Kirwyn's body slumped to the floor.

I screamed again, then gasped as something sharp pierced me between my neck and my shoulders.

Within seconds, the corridor began to swim around me. I had difficulty seeing. Difficulty hearing. Difficulty... *being*.

I am dying, I thought, feeling myself lose consciousness.

I wondered if Kirwyn would be waiting on the other side.

CHAPTER 42

I awoke in my mother's chamber and the feeling was so jarring I wasn't sure if it was real or a dream. Hot, bright sunlight beat into the window. I felt a light sheen of sweat all over my skin.

Why was I here? Where was Kirwyn?

Then, slowly, snippets of memories came back in waves, like seashells carried in by the surf.

The corridor. The guards.

Kirwyn captured.

We were never going to escape. It had all been false hope.

I shot up in bed.

Two guards stood in the center of the bedroom. They were tall and muscular, of course, but not as broad-chested as those from the tunnel. They had sharp blue eyes so similar I always thought they could be brothers.

My mother stood beside them.

"It's alright," she said, with a dismissive wave of her hand.

"We'll be just outside the door," the guard on the right

replied, firmly. Then they departed, closing the heavy wooden door behind them.

"Where is Kirwyn?" I asked. "Let me go."

"Zaria..."

"I hate you," I spat.

Closing her eyes, my mother wiped a hand across her brow. She walked two steps toward the bed and I instinctively scooted back. She stopped. In her condition, I could overpower her. But I wouldn't get past the guards.

"Please try to understand," my mother said. "I wanted to protect you, for as long as I could."

"You didn't tell me because you wanted to protect *yourself*. Where is Kirywn?"

My mother toyed with the Old World diamond at her throat. "I know you're hurting, but it's not so black and white, Zaria," she said gently. "Maybe this is my fault, for raising you like this, shielding you. But I wanted to give you what I never had. You can't know the sacrifices I've made..." she trailed off, wanting to say more, but stopping herself. "And I pray to Keroe you never will."

I nearly laughed out loud. How could the Sea God answer prayers when she said he didn't even exist?

"Where is Kirwyn?" I demanded a third time.

"He's back in a cell," my mother replied. "Unharmed."

"Where were we? What was that place?"

"There's a network of tunnels. Some Old World. Some we've expanded upon. They run underground for much of the island. They're used in case defense becomes necessary."

I was a fool.

Beneath me lay a network of secrets all my life and I never even knew it.

A memory came to mind – the day that Kirwyn and I

thought we heard someone in the forest - and I realized we'd likely been right. Perhaps a guard was watching and we couldn't track him because he'd ducked down into one of the tunnels.

I wondered just how much I thought had been private, wasn't.

My throat closed as I tried to ask the other question that burned in my mind.

"Where's Tomé?"

My mother paused. "He's fine."

Relief washed over me, despite her tone. Whatever happened, at least he was alive.

"But..." I whispered, "Is he hurt? Is Marcin okay?"

My mother sat on the bed and reached for me, but I jumped off the other side, standing. My legs shook and I steadied myself by holding the wall.

She flinched and deep down, some old instinct in me almost felt sorry for her. Then I remembered what she had done to me. *What she continued to do.*

"There was an accident. One of the Steel Guards drew a knife and Marcin was badly wounded. He's with the healers, but...." she trailed off.

I heard her, and yet I didn't. The words came out of her mouth, and yet they were not-words. I wasn't really there, being told this news. I was somewhere else. I was asleep and this was a dream, not reality.

"If he doesn't pull through... there will be a sea-funeral..." my mother said.

I clapped my hands over my ears. It wasn't true.

"Liar!" I said. "You're nothing but a liar!"

My mother shook her head. "In this case, I wish I were."

A lump formed in my throat the size of my fist. I wouldn't cry. I wouldn't cry because it wasn't true.

I covered my face, but other faces floated by in my mind.

The young boy they thought touched me. Solan. Marcin, too? Three deaths, all my fault.

Tomé... I thought, hiccupping a sob.

"In case of the worst, we are making preparations for the funeral tomorrow. As much as we want to weep, we must proceed with your wedding, the treaty depends on it. I'm sorry, my darling, but it must be so." Her voice hardened. "And though you broke your word, we are prepared to honor ours. If you cooperate, if you go through the ceremony tonight as a happy bride, then we will return Kirwyn, unharmed, to his home."

"And why should I believe you?" I scoffed.

"Because I'm your mother. And I've given you my word of honor."

I snorted, but it sounded more like a strangled cry. "I see how much your honor is worth. What does your honor mean to me? To Marcin?"

My mother flinched and I was glad. "What choice do you have, Zaria? If you want to save Kirwyn, you will get on that boat tonight. Once I have word that you've safely arrived at the Isle of Lights, we'll let Kirwyn go."

"So now he's not free until I'm there?"

My mother said nothing.

I walked over to her window and looked toward the forest, toward the cave.

Why didn't I leave with you when I had the chance?

Kirwyn and I would be free. Marcin would still be alive. I had choices then. Myriad choices. Now I had none.

"You let me fall in love with Kirwyn, then you take it away and tell yourself it's a kindness you gave me."

My mother paused. Sighing she said, "I allowed it to

continue so that you could have an... experience... before you married. But this is childishness to believe you're in love with someone you just met, Zaria. Love takes time, years to build. Love is what your father and I have. You're confusing love with lust."

She and father? The way he always sought her out but she barely returned the affection? No, that wasn't love. I turned back to face her.

"You're confusing love with dependency."

It was a bit of a stab in the dark but could tell I struck a nerve by the way she held her mouth.

Gloating, I felt bolder and pressed on with another blind stab. I wasn't even sure where the question came from as it tumbled from my lips.

"What does Nasero want? More power?" I narrowed my eyes. "You? Both?"

I swore her hand flinched around her belly -- but my mother was my mother, smooth in her reply.

"What do all men desire? Whatever they cannot have."

I chewed on her words. Didn't it depend on the man?

"Not all men," I argued.

"All but a rare few," my mother allowed. "Remembering that will serve you well in your rule, Zaria."

"I will tell them I've been despoiled. Will this prince want me then? I'll let him know I've been *very* well-touched."

"And lead them on a hunt for Kirwyn?" my mother asked.

"I – I wouldn't endanger his life... I'd say a village boy did it."

"So you'd kill an innocent?" she countered.

"No! I'd say... say he'd already been punished. Died accidentally or something."

My mother scoffed, "Zaria. You're not that skilled a liar."

"Then I'll be an awful bride he won't want!" I exclaimed.

"That won't set you free and you'll just make life harder on yourself. I may have shielded you, may have kept you naïve, but I didn't raise a fool."

Landdammit. I hated my choices.

There wasn't a choice even, not really. I was just deluding myself. There was only one thing I could do.

Kirwyn must live. I had to go along with the wedding, for his sake.

"Marcin's family," I said slowly, turning to face the window. "If he... they can never be compensated for the loss, but you will do whatever can be done."

"It's already in place," my mother replied.

"And Tomé," I added.

"Of course."

I closed my eyes as I spoke.

"I will marry this crown prince. But I won't smile. And I never want to see your face again after today. In fact, it will be my request to this prince, as a wedding gift. Unless I can have him erase you from land completely."

My mother said nothing, but I could feel her eyes boring into my back. I refused to turn around.

Finally, I heard her stand and leave the room, closing the door behind her.

The moment she was gone, I threw myself onto the bed and sobbed with abandon. I let the hot tears soak my cheeks and fill my mouth, hoping I'd drown in them.

CHAPTER 43

Two young serving girls bathed me in my own chambers. They scrubbed me with pumices and scented polishes until I shed at least two layers of skin. If I thought that painful, I was in for a surprise next, when, instead of scraping my leg hair, another process entirely was performed.

Under my mother's supervision, the servants poured a warm, sticky liquid on my legs and pressed white strips of cloth to them. With a sudden, shocking rip, they pulled away the cloth, taking with it the soft, downy hair on my legs. The process was repeated under my arms. I never got used to the torture and yelped with each pull.

It was the only sound I made as I refused to acknowledge my mother's presence. I kept my gaze forward and my chin high, suffering each attention while pretending no one else was in the room with me.

I thought only of Kirwyn.

The servant girls brushed out my hair, oiled it, and styled it half-up and around the gold-and-pearl tiara, securing it tightly to my head.

But the strangest of all my wedding preparations was when, once again under my mother's direction, they painted my face. Not like a design with soot, or polish from berries, but with Old World tools I'd never seen before. The servants hadn't either, because it took a lot of correcting from my mother -- *"No, line the eye, closer, here,"* and *"Sweep the pink powder upwards on the cheek,"* she'd instruct, to get it right.

When my mother brought her gazing glass to show me the effect, my eyes widened at my own appearance. It was me but *enhanced.* Like the prettiest me I'd ever been. My lips were shiny, tantalizing. My cheeks had been kissed by dewy flowers. My eyes seemed sultry and beckoning.

"Careful not to get any face paint on the dress," my mother said, carrying a long white gown into the room.

Despite myself, I gaped. This dress had to be the most beautiful Old World gown... *no, New World,* I corrected myself. I had to remember that all of these things were being made today. Somewhere far away.

Somewhere I am going.

Pearls and clear gemstones, like the diamond on my mother's necklace, decorated the fitted bodice. Thin straps came across both shoulders, but I didn't think it needed the extra hold, as the top looked tight enough to stay up on its own. The skirt gathered loosely around the waist, then plunged in a grand sweep of layers to the floor. If I hadn't known better, I would have thought the dress belonged to a goddess.

I allowed myself to be draped in the gown, and then my mother produced sandals. They were not unlike my everyday thongs, but they were white, and fastened securely around my ankles.

Once again my mother held up the gazing glass and my pouty, pink mouth fell into a soft "o" shape.

Who was this person before me? How could this be me?

My hair shone in ripples down my back. My skin glowed with its flower-dew-kisses. My eyes seemed to hint at some mystery, a secret to unlock.

I shook my head. This beauty was a goddess. But she wasn't me.

"You may leave us," my mother dismissed the servants.

She paused after they cleared the room, then said, "Have some tamarind tea, darling."

She raised a clay cup from a tray one of the servants set while I dressed. I automatically stretched my hand to accept it, knowing it would soothe me... then suddenly recoiled, covering my mouth as the realization hit me.

I quickly lashed out my arm, smacking the cup from her hand so that it shattered on the floor, tea pooling around our feet.

"You've been putting something in the tea," I cried. "Herbs or Old World medicines that make me weak. Not myself."

I *knew* it was true. Something was in there, perhaps something like what the guard had pricked me with, diluted.

"How many lies? How many lies!" I shouted, not expecting an answer.

My mother said nothing. But at least she didn't insult me by denying it.

"Zaria," she began, but I ignored her. I looked away from my reflection and to the bedroom wall opposite where she stood.

"I did not wish to speak in front of servants, to add gossip to their tables," my mother said. "But I have news that will cheer you. Marcin is doing much better. He will recover."

"Is that true?" I demanded, scared to hope.

"You can see for yourself if you like. Or ask his family."

I exhaled and silently thanked whatever God still listened. At least he and Tomé might have a chance at happiness. Somehow.

"Where is Tomé?" I asked.

"He won't leave Marcin's side."

I was glad to hear it. I didn't want him to witness my sham of a wedding. But I also wasn't sure how much of that was true, and how much was my mother keeping him far away from the ceremony.

"You won't be alone," my mother said. "Your Aunt Alette will be waiting for you. She's so happy in her life there and I know you will be too. Zaria, you don't understand yet. But I do."

From the corner of my eye, I glimpsed something glittering in the gazing glass.

"I haven't taken off this necklace since my wedding day. I kept it as a reminder of… many things."

My mother stood behind me. I turned my head forward but that only brought me to our reflection together.

"Here, I want you to have it," she said, sweeping my hair to one side and encircling me with her arms as she fastened the Old World jewel to my neck.

I wanted to reach up and rip it off, to watch the little conch pearls fall and scatter about the floor. But the necklace was too beautiful, I couldn't do it.

Instead, I turned away from the stranger in my reflection. I walked to the bedroom door with heavy steps, as if I was marching to my own funeral.

Wasn't I?

~

WE JOINED my father by the palace gardens. Like my mother, he donned his best embroidered tunic, cleaned from the night before. Both my parents wore silver crowns encircling golden heads. I held my chin high as they walked me down the long path. It had been lit with hundreds of torches on either side, blazing in the early twilight.

I kept my face blank and my back straight as I marched to my doom, thinking only of Kirwyn.

Would he be okay? Would he, could he, *find me on this Isle of Lights, once they set him free?*

My mother and father walked behind me, but I did not look back.

I would never look back.

The path closed off in a bright semi-circle on the beach, the same inlet where I'd been ceremoniously dunked at my betrothal. Once again, we held the ceremony there so that the stilt-dwellers could also bear witness.

Now, however, instead of a chair, a wooden boat bobbed in the surf. White flowers hung from the edges. I noticed the hull remained empty and figured no one had time to gather the God tribute with everything that had happened.

The wind picked up and the torches flickered. *Was it going to rain?* The air held that certain tingle it did before a bad storm. I suppressed a laugh. How holy would the ceremony be if a gale poured down?

Every villager, healer, artist, Mystic, even many of the Fire Maidens had descended from their mount and lined the pathway to the beach. Quiet, but for a few fidgeting children and the occasional whispers about my gown, whose hem dragged on the grass as I walked.

Unbridled revelry was for the wedding feast the night before. Tonight's ceremony would be a reverent affair.

Nasero stood in his long, ceremonial robes in the center of the torches. The Mystics lined the sides of the semi-circle. We bowed to one another and then my parents stepped out of the ring, leaving me alone with the High Mystic.

I should be here with a groom by my side.

I should be here with Kirwyn by my side.

My lip quivered. I couldn't cry.

If I break my promise, they might not let him go.

I knelt, I rose.

I knelt, I rose.

I ignored the long sermons and stared out at the darkening sea. The wind picked up again, several torches blew out, and soon the guard lost the battle to stay ahead of re-lighting them. After the opening ceremony, I felt the temperature drop, and gullflesh broke out on my arms and shoulders, kissed by the chilly wind.

I repeated hymns. I uttered vows I had no intention of keeping to a deity that didn't exist. It meant nothing.

To me.

Behind me, there didn't seem to be a dry eye in the crowd and frequent sobs and sniffles broke the air.

The first cool raindrops caressed my bare arms by the time Nasero declared, "I give you Queen Zaria, Goddess of the Sea!"

Earsplitting cheers erupted.

Whether in haste due to what was now clearly a coming storm, or because they feared I'd change my mind, I was quickly ushered onto the bobbing boat.

My mother said goodbye to me, wiping tears I'd never seen before escape her eyes. I didn't know if they were for me or herself, and I didn't care. In a rare moment of emotion, even my father looked forlorn.

I clamped my lips shut as the entire island cheered in farewell. But inside, I was *screaming*. I turned my back on everyone I ever knew and faced the blackening sea.

Nasero climbed into the boat with me and took the oars, paddling us forward. We rode by the solemn stilt-dwellers, faces worshipful for the one they believed their new goddess.

If they only knew. Their lives, all our lives, dedicated to a lie.

I guess we had something in common after all.

Soon, Nasero and I floated out into the open sea. I faced forward, refusing to acknowledge him.

And then, a great boom sounded from the island, behind us.

CHAPTER 44

I whipped around to see an explosion like I'd never seen before -- big and bright, illuminating one spot on the royal side of the island. There was just enough light from the boom to make out black smoke pluming into the air.

It came from the direction of the palace.

Kirwyn?

Was he okay? Had he gotten free?

Hope bloomed in my chest, warm against the wind.

I leaned over the edge of the boat, straining to see more. But we were too far out.

Was that... my silver egg?

Nasero withdrew a lantern from a sack that, in my distress, I hadn't noticed he carried. The lantern was of the same strange making as the one Kirwyn gave me for the tunnel. Metal and oil. He lit it, creating a small ring of light against the darkening sky. Then he took up the oars once more and paddled faster.

I had to fight the urge to jump into the sea, to swim

back and see what happened. I had to be smart, bide my time.

It was Kirwyn, I just *knew* it was.

Nasero kept paddling. The sky continued to blacken and a light rain pelted us. Wind whipped my dress in a frenzy, blowing the soft white folds up into the air around me.

"Zaria," Nasero said, gently.

Reluctantly, I looked at him. The High Mystic struggled to paddle, balance the lantern between his knees, and keep it dry from the sea and rain. He became that kind, open-faced man again; his imposing command during the ceremony shed like a dead skin.

The startling way he could don a façade reminded me a lot of my mother.

"I am truly sorry that you are fated to be the one to uphold the treaty. If there were any other way..." he trailed off. "I know this must sound strange to you, but the Mystics are not allowed families, as you know, and, I've always looked on you as a daughter."

I stared at him, unable to believe this speech from the man who kicked my mother, threatened Kirwyn's life, and locked me up in a cell. *Some father he would have made.* My own may have failed to notice my existence most of the time, but at least he never struck me or anyone I loved.

And yet, the sincerity in Nasero's voice told me that he truly believed this, in his own twisted way.

"Then let me go," I begged. I briefly contemplated attacking him, but I didn't have the strength to overpower him physically and I didn't think I had the stomach to try to push him overboard and kill him.

Nasero shook his head. "I cannot. Zaria, I'm sorry, but I must-"

Nasero was cut off as he crouched low to keep his

balance against the rolling waves. The lantern dropped, but remained lit. He picked up the rope from the bottom of the boat. My heart skipped a beat.

Had he read my thoughts on my face?

Of course he did. I was a terrible liar.

"What do you think I'm going to do out here, alone?" I asked.

"I must insist," he said.

"I thought I was like a daughter to you."

"There are more important things than my feelings, or yours."

I snorted, shaking my head. *What did it matter?* I was a prisoner either way, headed for a marriage I did not want.

I turned around and Nasero tied my arms behind my back. Then he motioned for me to sit and secured my legs as well.

I heard a crackle of thunder as he finished. The skies finally opened and rain came pouring down.

Crouched low in the bottom of the boat, I found it difficult to stay inside with my arms tied and the waves rolling higher. A flicker of fear shot across my stomach. If I fell into the water, I couldn't swim to protect myself.

Cold and sopping wet, I listened to the rain strike the boat, *ping, bang, crack, crack.*

If Keroe was down there in the God Sea, his anger at tonight's turn of events manifested in growing swells.

Where are we going?

Nasero rowed, fighting against the wrathful sea, but it was a fruitless effort. Our little boat climbed waves like a hiker climbed hills, cresting at the top and plunging down into a watery valley once more. My hair, once elegantly wound, stuck in wet clumps to my neck and my arms. The sopping dress imprisoned my legs as much as the rope. We stopped our pitiful course forward and I turned around. Nasero checked some device he'd hidden within his robes.

"We wait here," he shouted above the rain.

And we waited. But the storm did not. The meager flame in the lantern flickered wildly, struggled, and then went out, plunging us into darkness.

"We should go back!" I cried as we rolled. We hadn't even made it to the Blue Beyond. The island wasn't far behind us.

"We cannot," Nasero said.

I hunkered down into the bottom of the boat, now coated with an inch or two of water, pressing myself against one side so as not to fall into the sea. The beautiful wedding dress, soiled with seawater and grime, clung to me. I couldn't imagine I'd make a pleasing bride now, and the thought pleased *me*. Maybe I'd be sent back.

If I lived that long.

Up and down the sea tossed our little boat without mercy. If I wasn't so frightened, I would have laughed as a wave knocked Nasero off his feet and onto his backside. I rolled, helplessly, to the other side of the boat.

All that time Kirwyn worried that I was going to be ritually sacrificed, and all that time it was never the plan. But it might come to pass anyway.

No.

The thought came so sudden and sharp, almost as if it came from somewhere or someone else.

No, that will not happen.

A feeling hardened within me, as abrupt as if I'd been struck by lightning above. Surely something momentous or magical must have happened to instill the will that rapidly began to grow, solid as wood, within my breast. But I couldn't pinpoint anything extraordinary that occurred at that moment as I was filthy, rolling around in the bottom of a dirty boat.

I'd just had *enough.*

I would survive. *I must.*

Whatever awaited beyond the God Sea, whatever I faced with a stranger-prince, I would endure. And then I would *fight.*

At that moment, restrained, pelted with rain and terrified of not living to see another day, I made a vow.

The angry sea could toss me about, could hold my life in its grasp, but no longer would I be a pawn for others. I would play the game too, until I played it *better.* Whatever plotting, or bribing, or threatening had to be done to escape, to find Kirwyn, I would do it.

It was time to seize power over my life. And if I had to seize power over others who wanted to interfere, so be it.

I had been a fool before. But that ended this night.

First, I needed to live through it.

"Help me get my legs under," I shouted to Nasero, and he jumped to help me tuck myself under the board that served as a seat, in order to keep from falling out. Then he leapt back and clung to the sides. I began to wonder if this might be a Black Squall forming. Nasero lost his grip on one of the oars and it fell into the sea. I scooted further under, so that the board rested across my hips, forcing my weight onto my arms behind me.

"You need to untie my arms," I shouted. "Or at least re-tie them in front. I can't hold on."

"They should be here any minute," Nasero cried over the wind, shaking his head. My heart sped at his declaration.

Who, exactly, were "they?"

A rogue wave crashed over us and knocked the boat

sideways, nearly turning her over completely. My heart stopped beating as we rose into the air, my weight pressed against the wooden board -- the only thing holding me in. My legs, tied together, dangled in mid-air. It was only one or two seconds, but it seemed to last much longer.

I heard Nasero shout while I swallowed sea water, choking and sputtering as we righted.

I blinked against the rain and gasped.

Nasero was gone.

The boat was empty.

"Zaria!" came the cry from the ocean.

I pried myself from under the board that kept me secure and scrambled to my knees. I couldn't stand with my legs tied and the long dress tangling me. It wasn't safe anyway.

"Nasero!" I cried, helpless. He was far, already so far away from the boat. And the waves were carrying him further.

"Nasero!" I cried again, blinking against the rain. His head, a small dot on the sea, bobbed once and then rolled with the next wave out of my sight.

"Nasero..." I whispered. A sob broke from my mouth.

He was gone.

Through my shock, I realized that if I didn't get myself back under the board, I'd fall in too. *Survive, Zaria,* I told myself, crouching and scooting back.

Suddenly alone in the storm, fear spread through my veins like a venom I fought to keep from reaching my heart, from stopping its beating.

Live to fight. Live to find Kirwyn. Live to find freedom.

I repeated the words like a mantra. I whispered last rites into the sea for Nasero, feeling numb to his death.

Then I squeezed my eyes shut and prayed to Keroe to help me stay alive.

Over and over.

I wasn't sure if it worked but minutes passed... and the storm lessened.

Not a Black Squall then.

A thunderstorm, now abating.

The rain still fell and waves still rolled, but I managed to sit up.

Yet the feeling of my impending doom seized my gut. Like Nasero, I began scanning in all directions, searching for another boat headed this way. I struggled against my ropes, but the High Mystic had tied them too tightly.

I hated the feeling of helplessness as I looked toward the dark horizon. I focused on the rain caressing my face, dripping down my arms. I watched the lightning illuminate the sky, the vast ocean for a moment, before plunging everything back into blackness.

I bolted upright.

A light shined in the distance.

Kirwyn?

I couldn't pinpoint the direction of land and the sky was too cloudy to read. But something deep, something in my bones told me it was him.

He was coming.

"Kirwyn!" I shouted into the rain. He couldn't hear me, but I kept shouting, praying the wind would carry my voice.

The light moved, turned in the opposite direction. Where was he going?

He can't see me, I realized. *He can't hear me.*

I tore at the ropes behind me, slick with rain and blood, but I couldn't get one hand loose. I threw myself onto the floor and bent my knees to my chest. Wiggling, straining so hard I thought I'd rip my shoulders, I slid my bottom between my arms and yanked my hands over my legs and through the tangle of my sopping wedding dress.

There! At least my hands were in front of me now.

"Kirwyn!" I screamed. But it was useless. He was there, *right there,* but my boat had no magic light like his.

The conch.

Where was it? Every boat had one, wedged safely in front. *There!* It hadn't fallen out. Hands and legs tied, I stumbled forward in the rain, trying not to fall overboard. I grabbed the conch, put it to my lips, and blew.

Nothing happened, only a whisper and my spit ran through the shell.

I blew again and again.

Please, please, make a sound.

Nothing.

I took a few breaths and tried again.

Nothing.

Diaphragm, I thought, remembering what I'd been taught. *Pull from your diaphragm.*

Nothing.

Again! I told myself.

Bmmm...

A low horn-sound blew from the shell.

It worked!

Mimicking what I had just done, I blew again, louder this time, and a deeper sound resonated.

Bmmm...

Was I seeing correctly? Did the boat turn?

With all the air in my lungs and with all the hope I could muster, I drew a deep breath and blew the conch again.

Bmmmmm...

Yes, the light was coming this way!

I heard a sick buzz behind me and whipped my head around.

Another, larger boat was coming toward me. It was farther away than Kirwyn. But faster.

Please let him reach me in time. Please let that be Kirwyn.

I raised my hands as high as I could and smashed the conch against the side of the boat once, twice. My fingers bled, throbbed. Panting, I smashed the conch a third time and it shattered, breaking into several shards. I grabbed the sharpest and, using it as a slippery knife, worked it back and forth against the ropes, though it was a difficult angle with my hands tied.

I looked up.

Kirwyn! It was him! I could make out his sharp features focusing on my boat and my heart leapt. Then the waves bobbed his machine-boat and the light blinded me from his face.

The strange, large boat behind me *roared* as it neared.

Frantically, I filed the makeshift conch-knife and the rope splintered. I quickly threw off the binds and untied my legs.

"Kirwyn!" I shouted.

"Zaria!" he called.

I tried to judge the distance between the other boat and mine.

Should I swim? I couldn't just stand *here.*

But I didn't want Kirwyn to lose sight of me in the waves.

I looked over my shoulder at the roaring boat behind me. They were too late. Kirwyn was going to make it. But could we outrun them?

Every inch of my body was soaked, just as slick and slippery as if I had jumped in the sea, and I struggled to hold onto the side of the boat.

"Kirwyn!" I cried. I reached out one hand, leaning over, ready to leap when he neared.

"Zaria!" he screamed into the rain.

Almost here...

I stretched as far as I could go, fingertips aching to touch him. I could see him clearly now, brow tense in concentration, slick, dark hair framing his beautiful face. His eyes never left mine.

My Kirwyn.

A boom like the crack of thunder exploded behind me. Kirwyn dove or fell into the ocean, I couldn't tell which.

"Kirwyn!" I screamed. "Kirwyn where are you? Answer me, Kirwyn, please, answer me!"

My eyes scanned the water, but his head didn't resurface. I didn't even realize I was diving until I was under the chilly waves.

"Kirwyn!" I screamed. I didn't know if I could find him. All I knew was, if he had gone into the sea to die, I wanted to be there too.

The angry swells tossed me about like loose parchment. The wedding dress tangled around my legs, pinning them together.

"Kirwyn!" I cried, coughing up sea water as the waves washed over my head.

My arms and legs became clumsy, like I'd forgotten how to use them.

Please don't be dead. Please, please, please.

My mind refused to function. I'd forgotten how to swim. I'd even forgotten how to float.

Dimly, I wondered how much it would hurt when I drowned. I wondered if I'd see Kirwyn in the next life -- be it above, like the stories he told of his world, or below, like the sea kingdom, in mine.

As if part of me was out of my own body, I felt myself sink, yet at the same time I looked on like a disinterested observer. The peace of the sea washed over my head.

No more fighting, no more lies.

I floated downward.

And then, a rough hand grabbed my dress from behind and yanked me to the surface.

I didn't know how I knew, but I *knew.*

It wasn't Kirwyn's.

The End

**Beyond the God Sea continues in Book II,
Bound by Dark Waters: Wed**

ALSO BY ELORA MORGAN

<u>Beyond the God Sea Series</u>

Beyond the God Sea (Betrothed)

Bound by Dark Waters (Wed)

Borne to Salt and Sin (Fated)

Crowned in Shattered Stars